D0434797

The Education of Nevada Duncan:

A Family Business Novel

The Education of Nevada Duncan:

A Family Business Novel

WITHDRAWN

Carl Weber

with

C.N. Phillips

URBAN BOOKS

www.urbanbooks.net

Urban Books, LLC
300 Farmingdale Road, NY-Route 109
Farmingdale, NY 11735

The Education of Nevada Duncan: A Family Business Novel
Copyright © 2021 Carl Weber with C.N. Phillips

All rights reserved. No part of this book may be reproduced in any form or by any means without prior consent of the Publisher, except brief quotes used in reviews.

ISBN 13: 978-1-64556-216-0
ISBN 10: 1-64556-216-6

First Hardcover Printing September 2021
Printed in the United States of America

10 9 8 7 6 5 4 3 2 1

This is a work of fiction. Any references or similarities to actual events, real people, living or dead, or to real locales are intended to give the novel a sense of reality. Any similarity in other names, characters, places, and incidents is entirely coincidental.

Distributed by Kensington Publishing Corp.
Submit orders to:
Customer Service
400 Hahn Road
Westminster, MD 21157-4627
Phone: 1-800-733-3000
Fax: 1-800-659-2436

Prologue

"Oh my God! Don't stop! That's it! Right there! Right there!" I could feel a wave of pleasure take over my body. I pressed my hands against his chest as I leaned over to kiss him. I wanted him to know that I wasn't faking it, and that this was for real. Only I wasn't quite sure if I was trying to convince him or myself.

"That feels so good," I murmured, tasting his lips.

I'd said those words a thousand times to hundreds of tricks over the past five years, but not one time was it true until now. My job had always been to deliver the fantasy, and I was very good at it, but this wasn't a fantasy. This was real life, and I was actually in the midst of the most tremendous orgasm I'd ever had. Maybe it was the romantic in me, or perhaps the skeptic, but I'd always believed that sex and making love were two entirely different things. Now, as my eyes filled up with tears of joy, I knew my theory was right. I looked down at my boyfriend, Nevada, who was looking up at me with concern.

"Kia, you okay?" he whispered. "I'm not hurting you, am I?"

"No," I whispered back, nodding my head emotionally. "I'm okay. I'm just happy."

I kissed him, continuing to rock my hips. He'd been trying so hard to hold back. I could see the struggle on his face. He needed release, and now it was time for him to have his.

"Let it go, baby. Let it go," I whispered, and he did just that, arching his back and tightening his grip on my hips.

"Aaahhhgggh!" He let out the sweetest moan, pulling me in closer.

I studied the satisfied pleasure-pain expression on his handsome, half-Black, half-Mexican face as he released himself in me. I never wanted to forget that expression or this moment.

"Happy birthday, Nevada Duncan," I said, gently kissing him. "How do you feel?"

"Amazing. I can't even describe it," Nevada replied, seeming almost at loss for words. "How about you? Did you really have an orgasm?"

"I did. I had a fantastic orgasm," I replied, smiling emotionally. I didn't want to get into how special it was for me. This was his day. Not only was it his birthday, but three hours ago, I had taken his virginity. It was something I would carry pridefully with me the rest of my life.

"Good." He looked relieved. "Technically, a man should last longer after each—"

"Sshhhh, Mr. Harvard." I laughed playfully, placing a finger over his lips. "I don't need the technical rundown." Nevada was one of the most intelligent people I'd ever met. He'd graduated a year early and was going to attend Harvard University.

"Okay, Ms. Worcester College."

My smile widened. Thanks to his tutelage, I'd passed my GED and was going to Massachusetts myself. Worcester College was only a junior college, but to me it was just as good as Harvard or Yale or any of those big-name colleges chasing after Nevada, because it was validation that I wasn't just a whore and that I could be someone. No one had forced me to continue being a prostitute once I escaped my pimp and made my way to the Hellfire Club, but college would be a new beginning and a real chance to better myself. I would have options I'd never dreamed I could have.

"Come on. Let's get up and take a shower. Your father doesn't have any food in this place, and I want to eat before I go back," I insisted. "You promised me waffles."

"Okay, I know a great dinner on Queens Boulevard," Nevada said, reluctantly sitting up.

After an amazing breakfast, it was a little after 5:00 a.m. when Nevada pulled up in front of the Riverside Drive mansion they called the Hellfire Club. If you didn't know, you'd think the majestic old building was just another snooty old money Manhattan cigar club instead of one of New York City's premiere brothels. I'd been working there for the past four years, thanks to Marie, the madam of the Hellfire Club. She had taken me off the streets and away from a pimp and lifestyle that probably would have killed me by now. She'd given me a consistent roof over my head and a home I never had. Sure, I was still turning tricks, but Marie was good to me, and the Hellfire Club had given me the opportunity to save enough money for school and a better life.

"You're going to miss it, aren't you?" Nevada asked as he watched me stare at the building that had been my home the past five years.

I hadn't really given it any thought until then, but it was a good question. The Hellfire Club had been my refuge, and the idea of leaving it for college, romance, or anything else was both scary and exciting.

"Yeah, I guess part of me will," I replied with trepidation. I glanced up at my bedroom window that overlooked the park and shook my head. "I'm not going to miss seeing the johns or turning tricks. I'll never miss that, but I am going to miss the girls, especially Marie. Believe it or not, this place is more like a sorority house than anything else."

"Yeah, I can see that," he said. "You just have to be willing to turn tricks to pledge."

I stared at him and slapped his arm playfully. "That was a poor attempt at humor. This was the first place I ever had friends, felt safe and protected, if that makes any sense."

"It does," he replied sincerely. "And I'm sorry. I wasn't trying to make fun of you or anyone else, but now it's my job to protect you." I could feel Nevada's concern through his silence, which prompted me to take his hand.

A slight smile came to my face. "I know that. You've been protecting me since the day we met. You're not just my boyfriend. You're my best friend."

"And you're mine," he said, opening his door and stepping out. I waited until he opened my door like he always insisted. He'd learned that from his father and grandfather, both very classy men.

He took my hand, and we walked to the front door, stopping to kiss every ten or fifteen steps. I loved kissing him, and when we reached the door, I placed both my hands in his back pockets so he couldn't get away. I kissed him even more passionately.

"I love you," he said abruptly when we broke our kiss. "I love you more than anything in the world."

It took me a moment to respond because he'd never said he loved me before. He always said, "You know how I feel," or "Same," and stuff like that, and he wasn't wrong, I did know how he felt. He'd proven his love more than once when he helped me find and rescue my sister, who was being trafficked and held prisoner by a crazy racist tyrant. But to hear him say "I love you" was special, like someone putting together all my favorite holidays and handing them to me for safe keeping.

"Awwwww, baby, I love you too." I pulled him in close to kiss him again. We stood in front of that door and kissed until the darkness turned to light. I finally said, "You should go. I'll see you tonight." I removed my hands from his pockets and tried to step back, but he would not allow it.

"Do you have to go back? Can't you just go out to the Hamptons and spend the next two weeks with me until we have to leave for school? After tonight, I don't want you to be in this place." The sadness and jealousy in his eyes was real, and also why I loved him.

"I know, but I promised I'd come back and hang out with the girls one last night. After today, I'll be all yours, fighting off those Harvard girls."

"I understand. Go spend time with your friends," he said, kissing me again. "I'll see you tonight. I love you."

"I'll be packed and ready. Oh, and baby, you can never love me as much as I love you."

I watched Nevada reluctantly walk away and get in his car. He waited until I pushed the code, waved goodbye, and stepped inside before he pulled off.

I exhaled loudly as I locked the door behind me. God, I loved that man, and for a brief moment, I contemplated saying "fuck it" and running back out after him; but I'd given Marie my word, and I knew the girls were planning some type of sendoff for me.

As I turned to walk to my room, I was surprised the main parlor lights were still on. Marie always made sure the last customer was out by 4:00 a.m., and she always turned the lights off when she did her final rounds for the night. I grinned, assuming she and a few of the girls were waiting up for me, which was good, because I couldn't wait to tell them about my night.

"Marie?" I entered the parlor, and the smile on my face disappeared in an instant as my brain tried to grasp what my eyes were seeing. "Oh, shit!" I murmured.

It took everything in me not to regurgitate my breakfast when I began to comprehend the grotesque carnage that was spewed throughout the room. All twelve of the girls were lying across the floor, dead or near death, their throats cut from ear to ear. The only person alive was Marie, and she was being held by some sadistic-looking redheaded man with a twelve-inch knife to her throat. I could see the fear in her eyes, which no doubt mirrored my own.

"Run, Kia! Run!" Marie shouted.

"Shut up, you whoring wench!" The man holding her slammed his free hand into her chest.

I bolted for the door, but I didn't get far before someone grabbed me by the hair, pulling me back. Within seconds, I felt the rotten stink of his breath on my neck. When I glanced at Marie, she was still being held by the redhead. A second man had snatched me.

"I'm sorry!" Marie cried.

"I told you to shut up!" The maniac hit her in the chest again, then laughed like a madman. "You're going to watch her die just like the rest."

If I wasn't scared to death already, his words took me there. I tried to struggle and get free, but the dragon-breath man holding me was too strong. I could barely move. That's when I saw the large knife he was holding come toward my throat.

The only words I could think of were, "I love you, Nevada."

Nevada

1

Two months later

I was awakened out of a horrific dream by the slight jolt
of my family's Learjet landing. I opened my eyes to see my
grandmother seated across from me. She hadn't been there
when I dozed off, and unfortunately, the look she gave me
was the same look of pity she'd been giving me since we found
out that Kia and the rest of the girls at the Hellfire Club had
been killed. The only one who survived the massacre—if you
can call it survival—was Ms. Marie. They'd made her watch
as they killed each of the girls. Needless to say, in her present
state of mind, she had been no help in finding the culprits.

"You all right, baby?" my grandma asked.

"I'm fine, Grandma," I replied.

"You sure?"

I sighed, glancing over at my grandfather, who was in a
seat to my left, looking through a copy of *Car and Driver*
magazine. He must have gotten my vibe, because he quickly
shut my grandmother down before I could reply.

"Charlotte, leave the boy alone. He just woke up. Let him
breathe. I don't understand why you're always smothering
him," Grandpa said firmly. "I knew I should have left you
behind."

"Don't play with me, LC. I'm just making sure he's okay,"
Grandma snapped back at him.

"He's fine." Grandpa replied, making me feel bad for her.
I knew she was just trying to protect me, but that was just

it—after Kia's death, I didn't want to be protected. I wanted to be the hunter. I wanted twenty minutes with those bastards in a room by myself so I could carve them up like they had done to Kia. That was the reason we had just landed in Paris.

We taxied for about five minutes then stopped. A few minutes later, Rob, one of my grandpa's trusted security people who flew the plane, stepped out of the cockpit. "Welcome to Paris," he said.

"Happy to be here." My grandmother stood up to retrieve her things. "One of my favorite cities."

My grandfather, on the other hand, turned to me with an all-business expression. He didn't say anything. He didn't have to. LC Duncan had this way of speaking without words.

"I know you have plans for me, and I don't want to disappoint you, but I have to do this, Grandpa," I tried to explain.

"I understand your motivation, son." He sighed, standing. "And I can't begin to imagine how you're feeling, but Harvard's a pretty big deal. A life-changing—"

"So is Chi's Finishing School," I snapped, cutting him off before he could finish his sentence in a rare moment of disrespect. "Harvard's not going anywhere, Grandpa. I'm just taking a gap year, no different from Sasha, Aunt Paris, Uncle Orlando, Junior, and my dad."

"I know, but I never wanted you in the muscle side of the business," he said sincerely.

"I don't plan to be, but you can't order men into battle if you're not willing to do it yourself. They have to respect you." I forced myself to lift my head and look him in the eyes. "Your words, not mine, Grandpa."

"Yes, I know," he replied with a chuckle. "Kind of wish I could take them back at a time like this."

"But you can't, because they're true." Even if they weren't the real reason I was there.

"Tell me something, son. Your father and uncles came here because I thought they needed training. Paris came because she was out of control and needed discipline. Sasha because she looked up to Paris and wanted to get away from your Aunt Donna. But what exactly do you expect to get out of this?"

I answered him in one word. "Perspective."

He remained silent, waiting for me to elaborate.

"The only reason I'm not being checked into a mental hospital like Ms. Marie is because I'm going to Chi's to train. To learn how to protect the ones I love so something like this never happens again. Not on my watch. So, I'm here to get perspective, and hopefully some peace of mind."

He took a long, breath buttoning his suit jacket. "All right then, son. Let's go get you some perspective."

Vegas

2

"Don't leave me here. Please, Vegas!" Marie pleaded with tears in her eyes, ripping her arm away from the two orderlies escorting her. She ran desperately down the corridor toward me, but before she could close the thirty-foot gap, a beefy female orderly grabbed her from behind. "Don't do this, Vegas! Please don't do this. They are going to come for me again. You're the only one who can keep me safe. Please, baby! Please!"

I'd gone up against all kinds of killers and gangsters in my life, but none of them could have broken me down the way Marie's tears were doing.

"I'm sorry, babe, but you need help. Help I can't give you. These people are going to help you get better." I tried my best to explain, but my words were falling on deaf ears. She did not want to hear it.

"No, they're not! They're going to get killed. Just like my girls," Marie shouted. She continued to struggle against the orderlies, kicking and screaming, "I thought you loved me!"

"I do love you," I told her as they literally carried her down the hall. "That's why I brought you here."

"Bullshit! You're going to get me killed," she cried as she disappeared down the corridor. "You're going to get me killed!"

"Everything all right, bro?" I turned to see my brother Junior and his wife, Sonya, standing beside me. Sonya was a nurse, and she had recommended The Clayborn Institute for Mental Health as one of the best hospitals of its kind in the country.

"Ain't shit gonna be all right until we catch these mother-fuckers," I snapped back at Junior.

They'd been in the lobby, and I was sure they'd heard Marie screaming at the top of her lungs.

"Yeah, I know, but what happened? She seemed fine when you went back," Junior said.

"I don't know. One second she's docile as a lamb, and the next second she's screaming and fighting like a lunatic. I don't get it," I replied sadly.

"Nothing to get. You said it best—she needs help. Anyone would after what she's been through. You did the right thing bringing her here," Sonya said, placing a hand on my back to comfort me. It was no comfort. Nothing other than killing the people who did this would help.

"Then why the hell do I feel like shit?" I could still hear Marie screaming my name in the distance.

"Because you love her, that's why," Sonya replied.

"Yeah, I guess I do. That's the problem." From my pocket, I pulled out a thick envelope filled with crisp hundred-dollar bills and handed it to Sonya. "I need you to keep an eye on her, Sonya. Spread this money around the employees on her floor. Nobody outside of our family is to know she's here."

"What about her brother?" Junior asked.

"Especially not her brother. I'm not saying he did it, but that weaselly bastard's a suspect until I say he's not. And get the twins down here. I want her to have twenty-four hour security," I demanded.

"You think whoever did this will come back?" Sonya asked timidly. It was pretty obvious the thought of whoever killed those girls returning was troubling to her.

"I doubt it. They coulda killed her along with the girls if they wanted her dead," I said angrily. "Those bastards wanted her to remember this for the rest of her life. They knew how much those girls meant to her and how much their deaths would haunt her." She may have been their madam, but Marie had practically raised most of those girls. They were the only family she had other than her no-account brother.

"Makes me want to put a bullet in them," Sonya snapped.

"A bullet's too kind," Junior replied, looking down at his phone.

"By the way, that was Pop. They landed in Paris."

I nodded my head. At least something was going right. Nevada being in Paris was a good thing, despite the argument it had caused with his mother. Consuela wanted him to go to college, but Chi's was the best place for him, especially since his girlfriend had been one of Marie's girls. Death was the worst kind of heartbreak. Finishing shool was the kind of distraction he needed while I figured out who was behind this.

"So, what now?" Junior asked.

"Now we dive even deeper into this shit. And in order to do that, we have to go back to where it started."

"The Hellfire Club?" Junior asked.

"Exactly. Get Bryant on the phone and tell him I want to see him," I demanded. "And let's get down to the Hellfire Club. I wanna see if I can find Marie's little black book. See if she owed anyone money."

Nevada

3

The ride to Chi's Finishing School was about an hour and a half long from the Paris-Orly Airport, and it was beautiful. I'd never been to Europe, but I liked it already. It had a totally different vibe than anywhere I'd ever been in the States or Mexico, and I looked forward to exploring it. All I could think of was how much Kia would have loved it.

When we reached our destination, I was kind of astonished.

"Is that it?" I asked. I'm sure my jaw was hanging down as I stared at the huge medieval walls, stone gates, and the actual moat that surround the huge castle we were stopped in front of. There was even a boy sitting on the bank, fishing. "Is that Chi's Finishing School?"

"Yep, kind of amazing, isn't it?" my grandmother replied.

"Pictures do it no justice," Grandpa added as we drove over the drawbridge.

From the outside, you would never know it, but inside the castle walls was more like a college campus than anything else. I watched dozens of groups, dressed in different colors, practicing martial arts, archery, hand to hand combat, and countless other physical activities on the grounds of the campus.

"What building are you in?" Grandma asked. I rummaged through my backpack to find my first day of school instructions.

"Paris Hall," I replied.

Rob, now driving the SUV we were in, followed the signs to Paris Hall, and eventually we pulled in front of a large stone building. There were several people coming and going from the building, all dressed in navy blue uniforms. One guy in particular, a tall lanky white guy, stood out more than anyone, mainly because he was staring at us like a groupie. He walked up to the car as we were getting out.

"You must be Nevada Duncan," he said in a thick accent that sounded Irish.

"Yeah, I'm Nevada. Who are you?" I asked. He wasn't threatening, but it was kinda creepy that he knew who I was, and we'd never met.

"Name's Clem McCloud. I believe we're roommates. Pleased to meet you." He held out his hand. "It's going to be a fun year."

I hesitated to take his hand at first, but when I saw the smile on his face was genuine, I gave in. "Yeah, it is. Pleased to meet you too, Clem. These are my grandparents, LC and—"

"Oh, I know who they are. It's a real pleasure to meet you, Mr. and Mrs. Duncan." Clem shook my grandpa's hand then hugged my grandma like he had known her his entire life. Once again, very creepy. "Are you still making those peanut butter cookies, Mrs. Duncan?"

Grandma smiled, looking flattered. "Yes, I am. How do you know about my cookies?"

"My brother Kevin went to school with your sons Junior and Vegas," he said. "They still talk about the care packages you used to send."

Grandpa raised an eyebrow. "Did you say your name is McCloud? Are you one of Patrick McCloud's sons?"

"Yes, sir, I am," he said with pride.

"Geez, how many kids does Patrick have?" Grandpa questioned.

"Thirteen boys and six girls. That we know of. My father has been a very busy man over the years," Clem replied as if it was no big deal.

"Apparently." My grandpa chuckled. "Please, give him my best."

"I sure will." He lifted one of my suitcases. "Why don't I give you a hand with your suitcase? We're not allowed to have visitors in the building except on weekends."

My grandmother looked disappointed, but what could she do? If it weren't for my grandpa pulling some strings, I might have not been admitted at all.

"Bye, Grandma." I walked over and hugged her tight, then my grandpa. I gave Rob a nod. "Take care of them."

"For sure." Rob nodded back.

Clem and I grabbed my bags and headed inside. I could feel my grandparents' eyes on me as I made my way through the doors. I wanted to look back, give them a reassuring wave, but I didn't want to take a chance on looking soft to Clem, so I kept my head straight. My plan from day one was to stay under everyone's radar, not draw any attention to myself, and just learn as much as I possibly could over the next twelve months.

Once inside the common area, I quickly found out that staying under the radar was going to be damn near impossible. It felt as if I was being watched, not by one person, but by everyone in the room.

"Um, Clem?"

"Yeah?" He turned to me.

"Why is everyone staring at us?"

He looked around and chuckled. "They're not staring at me. I can assure you of that, mate."

"Then why are they staring at me?"

"Most of them haven't seen royalty before," he replied. "I mean, we do have some genuine, honest-to-god princes and princesses on campus, but nobody like you."

"I don't understand. What do you mean nobody like me?"

"You don't get it, do you? You're Nevada Duncan, the son of Vegas Duncan, the nephew of Paris and cousin of Sasha. Hell, this building wasn't named after the city of Paris. It was named after your aunt. And the dining hall is named after your dad."

"What? Are you serious?"

"Look for yourself." He pointed to a picture above the huge fireplace. I took a few steps toward it and stared. Hanging over the mantel was a full-sized portrait of Aunt Paris.

"This is the elite dorm, the cream of the crop. Your aunt is a god around here, and so is your dad. Being your roommate is the best thing that's ever happened to me. You're going to get laid every night, and so am I as your wing man." He wrapped his arm around my shoulder and smiled. "You're our new leader."

"Shit," I murmured to myself. "I think I've bitten off a little more than I can chew."

I knew my family members had been high achieving students at the school, but I had no idea I was walking into this. So much for staying under the radar.

"Yeah, you got some pretty big shoes to fill."

Vegas

4

Junior and I entered the Hellfire Club through the back entrance and made our way toward Marie's office. Yellow crime scene tape was still everywhere, despite it being months since the killings. As we walked inside the blood-stained parlor, I could almost smell the stench of death, and from the look on Junior's face, so could he. Now, we'd seen our fair share of death. Hell, we'd even taken a few deserving souls over the years, but the senseless killing that had taken place here was chilling. I wasn't exactly a religious man, but I said a quick prayer before Junior and I continued on to Marie's office.

"Shit, looks like the cops beat us to it." Junior sighed angrily when we cautiously slid open the door to Marie's office. The place had been trashed, and it wasn't random vandalism. Somebody had been looking for something.

I shook my head adamantly. "Cops didn't do this."

"All right, then who?" Junior gave me an inquisitive look. "This place wasn't like this when they found the girls. Bryant let me inspect it."

"Most likely one of Marie's competitors, or maybe a client. That client book she kept was worth millions and could take a lot of people down," I explained, moving my flashlight from left to right across the trashed office. "A lot of people would love to get their hands on it."

"From the looks of this place, whoever was here may have already found it." Junior's face was full of concern.

"I don't know, but I hope not," I said, "because that book might be the best lead to who's behind all this. Come on. We're not gonna find it standing here."

Junior nodded his agreement and we stepped into the room, overturning the mess to search for Marie's books. Unfortunately, whoever had been there before us had beaten us to every hiding place imaginable, including the safe that Marie had hidden behind a picture of me. One thing was for sure: whoever opened that safe knew what they were doing. It was evident from the fifty thousand in cash and jewelry that was left behind that this was no simple robbery.

"I think they got it, Vegas," Junior said. The defeat was evident in his tone.

"Yeah, unfortunately, I think you're ri—"

I was interrupted by a huge crash outside the room. Junior looked over at me, and I placed my finger over my lips to silence him. We withdrew our guns from holsters, him from inside his jacket and me from the small of my back. I also carried a .38 in an ankle holster. After what had happened to Marie, a brother couldn't be too safe. Using hand signals we'd learned at Chi's Finishing School to communicate, we left the office to investigate the noise.

We made our way through the club and followed the sound of someone fumbling around in the parlor. Finding what looked to be a lone person lurking in the shadows by the bar, Junior and I split up. As we crept closer, it was Junior's job to distract whoever the hell it was, which he did by tossing a glass in the middle of the parlor. The damn thing broke into a million pieces.

"Freeze!" the shadowy figure shouted, reaching in his suit jacket for what I could only assume was a gun—which brought me to my job, which was to ease up behind him fast. It would be only a matter of seconds before he realized where that broken glass had come from and took aim at my brother, who, at six foot five and 350 pounds, was one big-ass target.

"I said freeze!" he shouted.

His gun was now pointed at Junior, and he was tensing to fire. Lucky for Junior, my gun was pointed at the back of this guy's head.

"If I were you, I'd drop that gun and keep your hands where I can see them," I growled.

He raised his hands and laughed. "You planning on shooting a NYPD detective? 'Cause that might not work well for either of us."

I recognized the sarcastic voice of Detective James Bryant right away. "Bryant, you fucking ass. Announce yourself!" I shouted, holstering my weapon. "Why the hell are you fumbling around in the dark behind the bar like that? I almost shot your ass."

"I was looking for the light," Bryant replied, holstering his gun.

Bryant was one of the NYPD detectives my family had on our payroll. He was an arrogant prick as far as I was concerned, which was why he usually worked with my brother-in-law Harris, but when the incident happened here at the Hellfire Club, my pops asked him to get involved. Bryant pulled some strings right away to get himself assigned to the case. It's amazing how money can motivate a person. He'd been reporting to Pop and Junior while I took care of Marie, but now it was time we met face to face.

"Looking for a light almost got you killed," Junior snapped at him, reaching behind the bar and flipping on the switch. The room became illuminated.

"So, what do you got? It's been two months and I haven't heard shit. You fucking cops any closer to finding out what the fuck happened here?" I asked.

Bryant took a breath and exhaled. "Honestly, we ain't got dick, but the folks down at One Police Plaza want us to act like we do. Twelve women murdered in an election year doesn't make for good politics, and the pressure your father is putting on his political contacts isn't helping. The Commissioner's trying to keep his job. I wouldn't be surprised if this doesn't get pinned on some career criminal or a sex offender we've been trying to nail for a while. They just want someone to pin it on."

"I don't give a shit what they want. I wanna know who did this. Am I making myself clear? We don't pay you ten grand a month to hold your dick, drink coffee, and eat donuts. We pay you for fucking results. So, you better tell me something."

Bryant didn't like the dressing down I was giving him, so he turned to Junior, hoping for a sympathetic ear. "You know I've been busting my ass on this case the past two months, Junior, telling you everything we find, and this is the thanks I get? What the fuck?" He looked like he was about to walk.

"Bryant, chill out. We all know you're doing the best you can," Junior replied, though he was mostly talking to me. "His girlfriend is Marie Hernandez. He's been taking care of the only survivor."

"Oh, shit. Sorry." Bryant's entire demeanor changed. "How is she?"

"She's fucked up. She's afraid of her own damn shadow. Only thing that's going to give her peace is us finding these bastards. We had to put her in a mental facility this morning."

"Yeah, I get it," Bryant replied sincerely. "You think we could talk to her? Might help the case."

"Not gonna happen," I replied adamantly. "You got questions, you give them to me or Junior. We'll see if we can get you some answers. Now, what the fuck do you got?"

"You ever heard of The Pulse?"

"Yeah, I've heard of it. It's a strip club over on the Lower East Side. What about it?" Junior asked.

"You might wanna pay them a visit." It didn't sound like a simple suggestion.

"Why?" I asked.

"Because from what vice is telling me, they seem to be the only ones benefiting from your girl Marie's demise."

Nevada

5

I'd managed to make it through the first night at Chi's without incident and make a few new friends with the help of Clem. He'd introduced me to quite a few people in the dorm, and to be honest, most of them were pretty cool, especially Raheem, our other roommate. He was a brother from Washington, D.C., who'd spent most of his life in boarding schools in Europe.

Clem was right about the girls. I'd been slipped at least four phone numbers from some pretty hot girls, and one dude named Richard who, despite his British accent and blue eyes, reminded me a lot of my Uncle Rio. I tried my best to be polite to him and the girls, but I had no intention of hooking up with anyone. I could never do something like that to Kia. I loved her too much for that. Besides, I wasn't there to meet women. I was there to learn how to find Kia's killer.

"Good morning," our second period teacher, a thin, very intense, sixty-something-year-old Asian woman said. I was in a class with Raheem and about fifteen other elite students from our dorm. "My name is Professor Susan Chin. I am your Criminal Science professor. I trust everyone had a sufficient amount of time to freshen up after your first class?"

Our first class had been PE, which consisted of calisthenics and a five-mile run with a profoundly serious drill-sergeant type of Muslim named Brother Elijah.

"No, I can smell most of them from here. Especially the one in front of me."

Professor Chin cut her eyes at someone sitting in the back, and when I turned my head to look, I was met with glaring eyes. They belonged to a kid who looked big enough to be a lineman in the NFL. Even though he was sitting, I could tell that he was well over six feet tall. He had dirty blonde hair and a light dusting of freckles across his nose that seemed to blend as he scowled at me.

"What the fuck are you looking at?" he growled.

I immediately turned around, but that didn't stop him from talking. "You think you're better than me. I know who the fuck you are, Duncan."

"I don't even know you. How can I think I'm better than you?" I asked without turning around to face him again.

"You're just like the rest. Looking for a beating, aren't you?" I could hear him slam his fist into his hand.

I wasn't trying to start any trouble, but my mother had taught me at a young age not to back down to anyone. I made a move to turn around, but Professor Chin spoke up to try to end this.

"Ivan Drovich, behave yourself. It's not anybody else's fault that you're frustrated about repeating another year here. Maybe this time you'll actually pay attention in class and your father won't have to come up and give *you* another beating."

The other students burst out in laughter. Professor Chin turned her attention back to the rest of us, but somehow, I knew her comment wasn't going to be good for me. I could hear Ivan grumbling behind me.

"Now, I'm sure you all think that just because this is the first day of elite classes that you won't be doing any work today. Well, let me reassure you that you are terribly wrong. Now, please take out your tablets and turn to page twelve of the Interpol training manual."

The entire class groaned at her words—except for me. This was the reason why I was there.

Professor Chin took class all the way up until the bell rang. I liked her. She was a good teacher, and even though it was the first day, I looked forward to being in her class the next day. Raheem, on the other hand, looked exasperated. He jumped up to leave the second the bell rang.

As I bent over to pick up my backpack from the floor, I felt someone's presence hovering over me. I didn't even want to look up because I was sure it was Ivan.

Thankfully, I was wrong.

"Hello. My name is Natasha Roman."

Hearing the sexy but slightly robotic Eastern European female voice, I looked up to see a stunning, six-foot-tall girl with long, auburn hair halfway down her back. She was wearing the same navy-blue blazer and skirt as the other elite girls, but none of them were wearing it quite like she was. She was a woman amongst girls, a genuine sex kitten.

"Do you have a girlfriend?"

I was kind of surprised by the question but began to answer her truthfully. "No, not anymore but—"

"Good," she said, cutting me off in that robotic voice. "I am your new girlfriend. You will come to my dorm, pick me up for date on Saturday. You will buy me expensive dinner, take me to a movie, and we will have great sex afterwards. Bring condoms." She gave me a quick peck on the cheek before walking out of the classroom, leaving me dumbfounded.

Huh? She did not say what I think she said, did she?

It took me a good five minutes to truly comprehend what had just happened, but I finally shook it off and left the classroom to find Raheem. I found him talking to Clem in the hallway near our next class.

"What a hard-ass," Raheem said when I caught up to him in the hallway.

"Who?" I asked, not sure if he knew about Natasha.

"Professor Chin," Raheem replied.

"She seemed all right to me." I shrugged. "I can tell we're going to have a lot of work, though."

"That's an understatement. Who gives twenty pages of reading on the first day as homework?" he snapped.

"That's nothing. We used to have fifty page of reading each night in my AP classes back home," I told him.

"Stop making excuses for her, Nevada. The woman has a god complex." Raheem gave me a strange look as if he knew I was only half paying attention to him. "Where the hell you been anyway?"

"Talking to a girl."

Clem laughed. "Is that why you're sweating? I told you you were going to get laid every night. So, who is she? Is she hot?"

"Ah, yeah," I said as nonchalantly as possible. "She's pretty hot."

Clem smirked. "Cool. Who is she? What's her name?"

"I think she said her name was Natasha. Natasha Roman? Everything happened so fast."

"Natasha Roman?" Raheem asked in an elevated voice. He glanced over at Clem. "The Amazon?"

"I wouldn't call her an Amazon, but yeah, she's pretty tall," I said. "You know her?"

"Hell yeah. We went to the same prep school in London, although she didn't know I existed." Raheem took a deep breath, looking over at Clem again. "Dude, Natasha Roman is like the woman of my dreams. She is so friggin' hot!" It took him a moment to snap out of whatever fantasy was going on inside his head before he asked, "What did you talk about?"

"You're not going to believe this, but she told me in no uncertain terms that I was her new boyfriend and that we were going out Friday for dinner and sex. Oh, and a movie," I added.

Raheem just kind of looked at me with a blank expression for a moment. I hoped he wasn't pissed with her being the girl of his dreams and all. I should have kept my mouth shut. Then again, he probably didn't believe me anyway.

"Dude! Are you fucking kidding me?" he shouted, grabbing me in a bear hug and lifting me off the ground and spinning me. "I wanna be you when I grow up!"

"Damn, will you hush and put me down?" I snapped.

Half the people in the hallway had turned in our direction. I looked around, embarrassed, pulling Raheem and Clem down the hallway and outside.

"I can't fucking believe it. My roommate's about to screw the hottest girl in the entire school. You guys are going to be the new power couple around here." Raheem was so excited, you would have thought it was him Natasha had approached.

This was all a lot to take in. It was times like this I wished I had my real best friend, my dad, to talk to.

Vegas

6

I walked through the doors of my condo illuminated only by the light in my eight-foot-long fish tank. I fed the four 13-inch Oscars Nevada and I had raised from minions, then took off my jacket and removed my gun from the holster. I glanced over at the bottle of tequila sitting on the counter but dismissed it, heading down the hall to my room. What I needed was a hot shower and some sleep, not a drink.

In truth, I was relieved to be alone once Junior and I went our separate ways for the night. He'd tried to talk me into coming back to my parents' house, but I wasn't in the mood to be around anyone. I didn't want to say the wrong thing to my Mom, who would hound me about Marie and the investigation. Don't get me wrong; I loved my family, but I could only deal with her nagging and my sister Paris and brother Rio's opinionated questions but so much.

It wasn't just the emotions swirling through my mind. It was the out-of-control anger and frustration on top of them. I was worried about Marie, I missed my son, and although Junior and I planned on talking to the people at Pulse in the morning, I had the overwhelming urge to go over there and bust some heads now. I was adamant about killing whoever was the cause of the agony felt by both my son and Marie.

I hadn't even reached my room before my phone rang. The caller ID flashed The Clayborn Institute.

I answered nervously, praying that everything was all right. "Vegas? Baby, please come get me." Marie's desperate voice caught me off guard. I hadn't expected it to be her on the phone. She was supposed to under non-communicational observation the first twenty-four hours, which was just a fancy word for lockdown.

"Marie? Is everything okay?" I felt my heart pounding in my chest.

"No! It's not. They're going to kill me. Please come get me!" She continued to cry.

"I know you're upset, honey, but they're trying to help you, not kill you," I tried to explain calmly. This was getting so frustrating. No way should she just be calling me out of the blue, unsupervised. I was beginning to wonder if Sonya was wrong to recommend this facility.

"No, you don't understand. They're here," she said, and her words hit me like a lightning bolt.

"Here, like in the hospital?" I asked.

"Yes!" she snapped.

"Shit!" I turned back around toward the door. "Marie, I need you to hide until I get there."

"Oh God. Hold on a minute."

There was a long pause. I listened carefully to try to understand what was going on, but Marie was so quiet I would have thought the call was disconnected if I hadn't heard voices in the background.

Finally, she spoke again. "They're gone."

"Okay, baby, it's going to be all right. I'm coming to get you. Where are you now?" I asked as I reached the kitchen and my gun.

"I'm under a desk, hiding. Vegas, they're after me. Shit, why did you bring me here? They're going to kill everyone." Her voice was trembling so bad I could hear the phone vibrating against something.

Fuck, she was right. Why had I brought her there?

"Okay, stay calm and don't hang up. I'm on my way." I snatched my keys from the kitchen table.

"Yes, baby, but hurry."

My phone beeped. I looked at the caller ID, hoping it was Junior. I needed him to meet me at the hospital. But it wasn't Junior's number that flashed on my phone. Once again it read: The Clayborn Institute.

What the fuck?

"Marie, hold on one minute." I clicked over to find out what the hell was going on.

"Mr. Duncan, my name's James Fester. I'm the head of security at the Clayborn Institute. I'm here with Dr. Jacobs, Marie Hernandez's psychiatrist. We have you on speaker phone."

"Hello, Mr. Duncan," Dr. Jacobs said.

"Is everything all right over there? Why are you calling me?" I wasn't giving up any information until I was sure I knew what the hell was going on.

"Not exactly, Mr. Duncan. We have a bit of a situation," the doctor replied.

"What kind of situation?"

He hesitated for a minute before he admitted, "Ms. Hernandez is missing."

"What do you mean? I'm not following you." I was confused as hell.

"We can't find her. She hit an orderly over the head with a dinner tray and locked her in a closet. We're sure she's on the premises, but we can't seem to locate her."

Given the fact that she was on the other line with a call from the Clayborn Institute, I knew they were right about her being inside the building, but shit, she hadn't even been there a full night and they'd already lost track of her? I wanted to laugh to keep myself from crying. I exhaled loudly. "Really, have you looked under any desks?"

"Um, under desks?" Fester asked, sounding stupid.

"She's on the other line. She says she's hiding under a desk," I snapped.

I heard Fester order someone and then heard some movement.

"What kind of fucking place are you running there?" I yelled before switching the call back over to Marie.

"Marie, are you there, baby?"

"Yes, but I think they're coming back. Oh God, Vegas, they are coming back! Oh, shit! They're going to kill me."

"No, they are not. They're coming to help you."

I heard her scream. As much as I wanted to console her, I couldn't. I felt for her, but the reality of the situation was that she needed help. Serious medical help. I needed her to understand that, but I knew she wouldn't. I clicked the call back again.

"We have her, Mr. Duncan. Thank you." Fester sounded relieved.

I didn't even respond. I just hung up, reaching for the bottle of tequila I'd bypassed earlier. I poured myself two quick shots, trying to enjoy the burn. I was about to pour a third when I heard a noise.

I wrapped my hand around my gun and removed it from my waist, cocked the pistol, and inched out into the hallway toward my bedroom. This was truly one of those days for the record books. Nobody knew about my condo other than my family. It was a place for me and me only, outside of the family business. So somebody knowing where I was, let alone being able to get inside, was alarming.

The sound of movement grew louder the closer I got. Someone was definitely in there with me. When finally I reached the end of the hall, I rounded the corner and prepared to let out as many bullets as I had. And then I saw who it was. I released the trigger quickly and breathed deeply.

"God dammit, Consuela. I almost killed you!" I looked at my baby momma. "How the hell did you even get in here?" I placed my gun on top of the dresser.

She was sitting casually on my bed, drinking a glass of wine like she belonged there, dressed as if she was ready for bed. Her long hair hung loosely around her shoulders as she cocked her head slightly at me. She tapped the wine glass repeatedly with her long fingernail and gave me a smirk.

"I used Nevada's key. He left it at my place before he went to Paris."

"Okay, well then *why* are you here?" I did not like the idea that she was in my house. She was my son's mother, so I had to deal with her to a certain extent, but we weren't cool like that.

"With Nevada gone, I was lonely. I guess I just *missed you.*" She patted the bed next to her. I didn't take her up on it.

"Where have you been?" she asked.

"You know where I've been. I've been taking care of Marie."

She frowned. "Yes, how is Marie?" The tone in her voice made it clear she couldn't care less how Marie was doing.

"Not well. She's having a hard time of things." When I saw Consuela trying to conceal a grin at that news, I added, "But she'll recover. My girl is strong."

She shook her head. "You and your charity cases. Instead of sniffing after her, you should have been dropping off our son at school. Instead, you're playing save-a-ho and passing your responsibility off on your parents."

"Don't go there, Consuela. You weren't exactly on that plane when it landed either," I snarled at her. What was it about baby mommas knowing how to get under your skin?

"Don't play stupid. Nevada knows why I wasn't there, and so do you, but that didn't mean I didn't want him to have his father's support."

"Don't act like you had some great excuse. You're just pissed off because he wouldn't listen to you and go straight to Harvard. Way to be supportive, Consuela." I folded my arms across my chest. "He's suffering too, you know. And he wants to be trained properly."

"He doesn't have to go to some fancy finishing school to learn how to kill someone, Vegas. Trust me, he's quite capable of doing what needs to be done," she huffed.

"I'm trying raise a man with genuine feelings, not some psychotic killer. He's still going to Harvard, but he'll be a better man when he gets there. Trust me."

She waved her hand at me dismissively. "I didn't come here to argue. I came here to make love. It's been almost four months since we made love. Don't you miss it? I do."

"The last thing on my mind right now is having sex."

"No, you'd rather be running around chasing after some crazy whore!" Consuela jumped up and grabbed me by the collar. "What about me? What about us? You promised we would try to make this work between us. We have a son—a son that's going through something real right now, and you're busy running around after a bitch? *Idiota!*"

"Yeah, maybe I am an idiot—but she needs me. Do you have any idea what that woman has been through?"

Her eyes began to well up with crocodile tears. "So, is that it? Do I have to be crazy to get you to love me?" she cried.

"Consuela, I'm just trying to do the right thing."

"So have I, Vegas. Do you have any idea what I have been through, loving a man who doesn't love me? I should have known you wouldn't have anything for me but lies and empty promises once Nevada was gone. I'm going to make you regret this. Tell our son I love him." She snatched my gun off the dresser and pointed it at her own head.

"What the fuck are you doing?" Consuela could be a manipulative drama queen when she wanted to be, but I couldn't tell if it was an act this time.

"What does it look like?" Real tears were now flowing from her eyes. "I'm going to shoot myself."

I reached for the gun, and she pulled back the hammer. I froze. One wrong move and I'd be picking her brains up off the floor. Last thing I wanted was to have to explain something like that to my son.

"Don't do this. Please don't do this."

"Why not? I don't have anything to live for." She pressed the gun against her temple. "I'm tired, Vegas. I'm tired of all this back-and-forth bullshit. All I came here for was to make love to you. Why did you have to throw her in my face?"

I'd misjudged Consuela's jealousy in the past. She was the type of woman who would use any means necessary to be with me, and that included using Nevada as a pawn. Two years ago, she'd given me an ultimatum to either stay away from Marie and be with her or forfeit my relationship with our son. I refused to lose the bond I had with Nevada, so I placated her for almost a year and a half with the help of Marie and Nevada, playing the happy, faithful baby daddy until my son graduated back in June. I thought she'd gotten the memo when I spurned her advances on graduation night, but evidently I was wrong.

"Okay, I'm sorry. You're right. Let's go back to when I first walked in. Let's make love," I replied desperately as I began to unbutton my shirt.

She stared at me with confusion.

"Come on. Get undressed, Consuela."

"You're lying. You don't want to make love. You're trying to trick me." She still held the gun against her temple.

"No, I'm not. You have access to all kinds of weapons. But if making love to you will make you put that gun down, then I will make love to you like never before." I let my shirt fall to the floor and began unbuckling my pants. I knew there was a good chance I was being played and she had no intention of harming herself, but at that moment, I wasn't going to take the chance. I was willing to do whatever was necessary to make her put that gun down. If she truly wanted to do it tomorrow or a week from now, it would be some else's problem; but I refused to explain to my son that his mother was dead because I wouldn't screw her.

"So, what's it going to be, Consuela?" I dropped my pants to floor. "You wanna make love or what?"

Nevada

7

I was sitting alone at a table in the dining hall, waiting for Raheem and Clem when Richard, the British guy who reminded me of my uncle Rio, and a dark-skinned girl with a shaved head and a real pretty smile approached me, carrying dinner trays.

"Do you mind if we take these seats?" she asked in a British accent.

"Sure." I gestured for them to sit. "I'm Nevada."

"Yes, I know," she said, sitting directly across from me.

I could feel my face growing hot. I hated the fact that everyone knew who I was, yet I barely knew anyone. It felt like everyone was looking at me all the time like I was some kind of freak. They probably thought I used my family name to get ahead. With that kind of speculation came jealousy, and with jealousy came altercations, both of which I could do without.

"My name's Arielle, and this is Richard."

"Girl, please. We've already met. Isn't that right, Nevada?" Richard tucked his napkin into the collar of his shirt. "Although I am disappointed that you've spurned my advances for the super model."

"What super model? Have you hooked up with someone already?" Arielle looked a little disappointed.

"Girl, where have you been? He's Natasha's man," Richard blurted out, sitting back in his chair as if he had spoken the gospel. "That Hungarian wench has hooked her claws into him that fast. Not that I can blame him. Those long-ass legs are enough to make me go straight—almost."

My cheeks were burning with embarrassment as Arielle turned to me, expressionless. I felt weirdly guilty, as if I'd somehow cheated on this girl I just met five minutes ago.

"I'm not her boyfriend," I replied weakly.

"Then why would she say that?" Richard asked. "Don't get me wrong. You're cute, and the legacy thing is kinda sexy, but she's . . ."

"The hottest girl in the school." Arielle finished his sentence. "She can have anyone she wants, including some of the professors. Why would she lie about dating you?"

"I wouldn't say she lied. It's more like a miscommunication," I tried to explain myself, but I was coming off like a real dick, which only made me feel like I needed to explain myself further.

I was halfway into my next attempt at explaining when I noticed their eyes were on someone behind me. My stomach did a flip because I was sure it was Natasha behind me, and she'd heard every word. I hadn't exactly said anything wrong or even insulting to her, but I hated the idea of hurting anyone's feelings.

I slowly turned around, half expecting to get a slap in the face, but then I saw Ivan, the huge kid from Professor Chin's class. Not that his presence was much of a relief. He wore the same hateful glare he'd had in class.

"Can I help you?" I asked with a tone somewhere between polite and annoyed.

He placed a heavy hand on my shoulder. "Are you ready for your beating, Duncan?"

"Look, I don't know what your problem is, but I'm not looking for any trouble," I said, glancing at his hand on my shoulder. I had no idea why he hated me so much. "Now, can you take your hand off me?"

He applied more pressure, digging his thumb into the flesh just under my collarbone until I felt the pain and involuntarily flinched ever so slightly. He lowered his face near mine. "And if I don't. What you gonna do?"

By then, a small crowd of students had formed around us, and of course, none of them offered to help in any way. Probably all they wanted was to see a fight. Clem and Raheem were nowhere to be found, so apparently, I was on my own.

I was not a fighter by nature, but I wasn't a punk, either. Duncan blood ran through my veins. My mom's words crossed my mind: Better to go down fighting than to look weak.

"How about this?" I grabbed Ivan's hand with my left and peeled it off my shoulder, twisting it counterclockwise until I was in total control. "Or this. Or what about this?" I kept twisting.

With my right palm, I delivered a hard blow to his chest, knocking him back and away from me. It all happened so fast that a surprised expression was frozen on Ivan 's face. Five years of karate and working out with Uncle Junior had finally paid off.

"Look, I don't want to fight you," I said, looking him square in his eyes. "Let's just go our separate ways. Pretend this didn't happen."

I should have waited until he walked off, but I turned my attention back to Richard and Arielle, and that proved to be a big mistake.

"Nevada, look out!" I heard Arielle shout, but it was too late.

Ivan struck me from behind with a one-two punch, causing me to stumble. I'd barely recovered from the first blows when he followed up with a gut punch, knocking the wind out of me. I'd been holding back, trying not to inflict too much damage, but it was obvious that he meant to hurt me. Now he'd caught me off guard, and I needed to recover from his blows before I could even retaliate. I grabbed my stomach with one hand and lifted the other hand to protect my face as I prepared for him to hit me again.

The blow never came.

"No!" I heard a woman shout.

I was still fuzzy, and it took me a moment to focus, but when I looked up, Ivan was being held from behind in a sleeper hold, and he was fading fast. For a second I thought maybe Clem or Raheem had shown up and jumped into the fray, or maybe even a teacher, but it turned out to be Natasha who'd neutralized Ivan.

"Are you okay, my darling?" she asked, dropping him to the ground. "This filth will not bother you anymore."

"Yeah, I'm okay." I was still holding my stomach, which hurt like hell.

"Good. I made you strudel. My grandmothers' recipe." She shoved it into my hands, kissing me on the cheek before walking away.

"Isn't that sweet, Arielle? Not only did she save his ass, but she made him strudel," he joked sarcastically. He wasn't the only one laughing.

Arielle looked at me and shook her head. Her words didn't say it, but her expression screamed *liar!*

Vegas

8

"That was Detective Bryant," Junior said, snapping me out of an involuntary nap. I didn't bother to look over at him, but I could feel his stare. "He thinks we should look into a Mafia guy by the name of Bobby Two Fingers. He's been doing a lot of talking on a Fed wire, and Marie's name has come up several times."

"Come up how?"

"He didn't say, but he was adamant about us checking him out."

"Bobby Two Fingers." I repeated his name. "Jeez, I'd almost forgot about him. I can't believe that reckless bastard's still alive."

"You know this guy?" Junior's interest perked up.

"He's a capo for Don Fredricko. We did time together up in Attica. He started off as a bag man, worked his way up to security, then a hitman. Last I heard, he'd taken over a lot of Sal Dash's territory. We're going to have to play him a little different."

I yawned, and Junior noticed. I hadn't told him about Marie hiding under the desk or my forced night of seduction with Consuela last night.

"You all right? You need to get some sleep, bro. You can't just keep going twenty-four seven."

"I'll sleep when we catch these motherfuckers." I cracked my neck, glancing over at my brother as I stretched my arms and shoulders. His face was full of concern. "Don't worry, man. I'm all right. I was just resting my eyes, thinking about Nevada. He's only been gone a couple of days, but I miss him."

"Yeah, me too. We should give him a call on our way home."

"Nah, I'm not trying to be the parent that calls every five minutes and smothers him. He's got a mother for that," I said, stepping out of the car. "Kid's been through a lot. He'll call when he wants to talk."

Junior made his way around the front of the car to stand next to me. We both took in the entrance of the seven-story building with a huge PULSE sign above the door.

"Doesn't look like much compared to the Hellfire Club," Junior commented.

"Looks can be deceiving. This isn't just a shake-your-tail-feathers type of strip club." I pointed at the six floors above the club. "From what Harris says, they sell more pussy here in any given night than anywhere in New York, including the Hellfire Club."

"No way." Junior shook his head, looking around the parking lot and the surrounding buildings. "This place is a dump in a shit part of town."

"What they lack in high-end appeal, they make up for in volume." I brought his attention to the entrance to the club, which was being manned by two big, burly bouncers. "I mean, it's nine a.m. and they have bouncers standing outside the door. Something must be going on in there."

"I guess I should say less." He laughed, patting me on the back. "So, what's the plan?"

"Sign on the door says members only. You a member?"

Junior shook his head, "Nope."

"Me either." We headed toward the bouncers anyway. "Guess we're going to have to gain entry the old-fashioned way. You strapped?"

"Always." Junior tapped his jacket.

"Good, then cover my ass."

"Damn, I was afraid you were gonna say that," Junior groaned.

Before Junior could reach for his gun, I had charged one of the bouncers, knocking him out with one punch. Then I used a roundhouse kick and knocked the other one out. It was that simple.

"Come on, Junior. Keep up."

With nobody to stop us, we walked right through the front door of the club. The sickly-sweet mixture of sweat and perfume invaded my nostrils. The entrance was dimly lit. In the distance, we could see a few women working the stage, while others were leading men into the many back rooms. By the entrance on the right, there was a winding staircase that led to more rooms upstairs.

I looked at Junior, signaling for him to pull his gun out again, and the two of us headed up the stairs. When we reached the upper level, I was on a mission and probably not thinking as clearly as I should have. There was a room at the end of the short hall, and I didn't think. I just opened it.

There was some kind of meeting going on when Junior and I barged in, and the dudes who turned around looked every bit as dangerous as you would expect a room full of mobsters to look. It didn't matter, though. We'd gotten the drop on them.

"Which one of you motherfuckas is the boss?" I growled.

"That would be me." A tall man wearing a tailored suit stepped forward until he was directly in front of me. Stupid move on his part. "You must either be lost or crazy as hell to barge in here like this. But I'll do you a favor and give you five seconds to walk your black ass the fuck up out of h—"

He wasn't able to finish his sentence because by then he had a mouthful of my knuckles. Before his goons could make a move, I had an arm around his neck and my gun to his temple.

"Jimmy!" One of his men tried to do the noble thing by drawing his own weapon. Junior quickly showed him why that was a mistake. His pistol barked one time and caught the man in his leg. The pain dropped him instantly. He lay writhing on the ground, holding his leg in a fetal position.

"Ain't gon' be no fuckin' heroes up in here today." Junior pointed his gun at the others. "Drop your guns on the floor before I make another one of you cripple."

They did as they were told, pulling their guns out and letting them drop to the floor. Junior kicked all but one to the side. That one, he picked up, now pointing two barrels at them.

"You . . . you can't do this," Jimmy choked out. "We're protected."

"Protected by who? Because I'd love to have a conversation with them," I shouted, squeezing his neck harder. He stayed tight-lipped. "Now, I know what you and your people did to the Hellfire Club, and I'm gonna make sure your death is as painful as I can make it. Just like you did those girls."

"Aye, we had nothing to do with that, man!" Jimmy gasped for air. "I sw–swear! It wasn't us. W–why would we kill them?"

"I don't know, maybe to get rid of the competition, you sick fuck. Now, I wanna know every person involved."

"What? I don't know what you're talking about." He continued playing stupid.

"I'm tired of this. I bet I know what will make you talk." I let his neck go and started pistol-whipping his ass. He raised his arms to try to defend himself, but that only made my blows harder. Soon, my hands were covered in blood, just like his face. A thick gash had formed on his cheek, and one of his eyes was swollen shut.

"Jesus, Vegas, chill out." Junior grabbed my arm. "If you kill him, we won't find out anything."

"Fuck that. He's playing dumb." I placed the pistol to the center of his forehead. "I'm gonna bring him the same pain that he brought Marie and the girls. It's payback time, Junior."

"Stop! He knows nothing about Marie or the girl's death, and neither do I."

The voice belonged to an older woman, and when I glanced up, I saw her step out from behind the other men. I'd seen her when we came in but didn't pay her much mind. Her hands were in the air as if to show me that she wasn't armed. Still, I turned my gun on her, and she stopped in her tracks.

"Who the fuck are you?" I asked.

"My name is Bly. I am the owner of this club."

I tightened my grip on Jimmy's neck. "Now, that's awfully funny, because Jimmy here just said he was the boss."

"It's partly true. Jimmy manages things around here for me when my hands are tied up in other things, but I am the owner and person responsible."

"So you're saying you're responsible for what happened at the Hellfire Club?"

"No, of course not." She looked appalled. "What happened to Marie and the girls was unforgiveable and twisted. I hope whoever did it burns in hell. The truth is, I'm scared. We are all scared."

"Scared of what?" I asked.

"Whoever did that moved like a ghost and killed *all* of her girls. That shit is scary to all of us in this business. We deal with all kinds of whack jobs and crazies, but never has anything like this happened before. Nobody knows what the hell is going on."

I stared into her eyes, searching for a lie, but I couldn't find one. Still, that didn't mean that she was completely innocent. I averted my gaze back to Jimmy, who was teetering back and forth on the floor. I lowered my gun, and he fell to the ground, fighting to stay conscious. My fists clenched, and I let out an angry sigh.

"Give me one reason why I should believe you."

She chuckled. "It would appear Marie talked to me more than she did to her lover, Vegas Duncan."

"What the fuck is that supposed to mean? And how do you know my name?" I did not like being at a disadvantage.

"I make it my business to know all of the heavy hitters in this town. Of course, it did not hurt that Marie was my friend and my silent partner. She owned twenty percent of this place. Which, evidently, she didn't share with you."

"If that's true, then no, she didn't." I'd be lying if I didn't admit it pissed me off.

"She was supposed to buy me out by the end of the year. So I want you to ask yourself, why would I shoot the golden goose? I'm not a young woman. I needed that money for my retirement," she said simply and to the point.

This woman had me questioning everything me and Marie had.

"Well, if you didn't do it, who do you think did?" I asked, letting down my guard a little because I was starting to believe she was telling the truth.

"Marie had a lot of people who didn't like her. That comes with the territory, but the two people who hated her the most were Bobby Two Fingers and—"

"Bobby Two Fingers?" Junior interrupted. He turned to me, and our eyes met. "Isn't that the guy Bryant wanted us to check out?"

"Sure as hell is." I nodded slowly.

"You think he's our guy?"

"Maybe, but let's not jump to any conclusions." I glanced over at Jimmy, who was now sitting in a chair, a bloody mess. I'd fucked him up pretty bad and apparently for no reason. I was going to have to slow my roll and get back to myself, stop letting anger consume me.

I turned to Bly. "You mentioned two people. Who's the other one?"

Bly hesitated as if she wanted to say something but wasn't quite sure if she should.

"Look, you said you're Marie's friend. Well, she's fucked up, and the cops aren't doing shit," I told her to give her some incentive to talk. "Me and my family are the only ones who give a shit and are capable of getting to bottom of this. We just need a little help."

Her expression softened a little. "Marie told me all about you and her trying to have a baby. I'm sorry it didn't work out. She loves you. You know that, don't you?"

"I thought I did until I found out there are secrets she's kept from me."

Bly sighed heavily. "We all have our secrets, but they don't stop us from loving who we love. Marie was a very complicated woman, and you, Vegas Duncan, are a very complicated man."

"What are you trying to say?"

"You're smart. I would have thought you'd figure it out by now. But then again, you men are blinded by flesh."

"What are you talking about? Figured what out?" She was starting to aggravate me with all her cryptic talk.

"Nobody hates Marie more than your child's mother, Consuela Zuniga." With that being said, the room went silent, and out of the corner of my eye, I could see even my brother Junior nod his agreement. "You do know she threatened Marie three days before the attack on the Hellfire Club."

Deep down, I hoped Bly was mistaken, but I could not rule out Consuela and her out-of-control jealousy. Hell, it had crossed my mind once or twice as well, though I hadn't wanted to go there for Nevada's sake. Now I found out she had threatened Marie, and I was pissed. If she had something to do with this, then even that mother-son bond might not be enough to save Consuela's ass.

"Come on, let's go, Junior. There's nothing here."

Nevada

9

Friday finally came, and regular classes were canceled for Elites for special training with Brother Elijah. Our instructions were to wear our dorm-colored sweatsuits and wait in the school's library until somebody came for us. There were almost fifty of us in total and of course, Ivan was there, but he had opted to sit far from me, which I appreciated. Natasha was also there, and despite her head being buried in a book, she was still as captivating as ever.

"You should go over there and talk to her," Clem encouraged me when he caught me staring over at her. However, I was not staring at her for the reason he suspected.

"Talk to who?" I gave him an innocent look, but it wasn't working.

"Who else? Natasha." He glanced over at Raheem, who shook his head. "Don't play stupid. We can see you looking at her."

"No, I'm not. Why would I do that?" I asked with mock indignation.

"Duh, because she's the hottest girl in the school and she's your girlfriend," Clem responded. "Oh, and because she makes delicious strudel. Let's not forget that."

"She's not my girlfriend," I snapped.

"Nevada, I swear to God." Raheem finally chimed in. "I don't understand you. She saved your ass, made you fucking strudel, is willing to give it up, and you're getting upset because she's calling you her boyfriend. What the fuck is it that I'm missing?"

A part of me wanted to just shout out, "My girlfriend's dead! That's what you're missing!" but now wasn't the time or place. I didn't know if I could control my emotions, and although the three of us were fast becoming friends, I wasn't ready to talk to them about Kia, especially not her death.

I let out a frustrated breath. "Fellas, you just have to believe me. I have my reasons."

Raheem eyed me for a moment, "Not that it matters, bro, but are you gay?"

"Not that it should, but no, I'm not. I like girls."

"And that's such a shame." I looked up, and there was Richard, Arielle, and another girl. "So, what this all about?" Richard asked.

"Nothing. Just a conversation among mates," Clem replied, understanding that it was best to end it now that we had company. "It's over. Why don't you have a seat?"

"Hello, Nevada," Arielle said as she sat down in one of the empty chairs at our table. The girl she was with sat down next Raheem and smiled at us. Richard, for some reason, chose to stay standing.

Arielle introduced us to her companion. "This is my best friend, Demi. Demi, this is Nevada, Raheem, and Clem."

"You like her *that* much that you would actually be her bestie?" Clem feigned a look of shock at Demi. "She's a spitfire, this one. A true troublemaker."

Demi giggled. "She's not that bad when you get to know her."

Judging from her accent, Demi was a Spaniard. Her hair was blonde, but I knew it was dye, because the brunette was starting to show at her roots. Her eyes were hazel, and her nose had a small hook in it, but that didn't take away from the cuteness of her face. She was petite, like Arielle, and about the same height. They were both dressed in burgundy sweatsuits, which, I learned from know-it-all Clem, made them part of the Grail. They shared classes with us but were a step below Elite.

"So, what do you guys think our first lesson with the assistant headmaster will be?" Clem asked, changing the subject quickly. "I hope we'll get to shoot an AR57. Or maybe we'll learn how to disarm bombs or—oh! Build them."

"On the first lesson? That's a little heavy, isn't it?" Demi raised her eyebrow at him. "My brother said that the first lessons are always hand-to-hand combat. Plus, guns are only an extension to where our fists can't reach."

"You sound like my father." Clem groaned and put his head on the table.

"But she is right!" A deep male voice took us all by surprise, but me more than any because I recognized it.

Demi and Arielle looked at the person over our shoulders, while Clem, Raheem, and I spun around in our seats. Standing behind us and in the middle of two bookshelves was a short Muslim man. His brown skin was very dark, and he looked to be in his late fifties, although I knew for a fact he was almost eighty.

"Minister Farrah," I said with a smile. He needed no introduction; we all knew who he was. His picture was plastered throughout the entire school, although I was most likely the only student who had met him. There had been a rumor that he was returning to the school as temporary headmaster.

"Nevada Duncan, it is good to see you again, my son." He walked up to me, and we embraced tightly.

"It's good to see you as well, teacher," I replied.

"Indeed." He released me, patting me on the back. "I see you decided to grace us with your presence. How are you adjusting?"

"Just fine, sir. I take it the rumors are true? You've returned to the school?"

"Yes, I've returned temporarily until we find a replacement for Headmaster Starks."

"I was sorry to hear about his death—despite being happy to see you."

"My thanks. His death was very unfortunate. COVID-19 has taken many good men—and women," he replied.

I turned to the group. "These are my friends, Arielle, Clem, Demi, Raheem, and Richard."

"A fine group," he replied. "Welcome to the school. I look forward to teaching you all and one day pinning you."

"Thank you, sir," they all said in unison and bowed. Minister Farrah returned the bow with a smile.

"Nevada, we will talk soon. Stop by the headmaster's cottage for tea on Sunday." He nodded at us all then walked away.

When I turned to my friends, I realized that they were all staring at me in awe.

"Dude, you know him?" Raheem finally broke their silence, though he still looked mesmerized.

"Yeah," I replied.

"Like, you *know him,* know him. He invited you over for tea."

"Yeah, he's a family friend. He's part of the reason I came here." I didn't want to brag or anything, but Minister Farrah had been privately training me for years.

"Why didn't you tell us?" Clem asked.

"We've been here like a week, and you guys all seem to know my life story. I didn't think I had to fill you in on the small stuff."

"Holy shit. You just earned my newfound respect," Richard said. Arielle and Demi nodded their agreement. Clem and Raheem were still just plain flabbergasted.

We watched Minister Farrah walk up to the front of the room, where Brother Elijah was standing. He began to speak.

"First, I would like to formally introduce myself and apologize to you for my absence until now. My name is Minister Alfred Farrah. I have returned to the school as your interim headmaster until a new headmaster is appointed. I hope you, the one hundredth Elite class of Chi's Finishing School, are ready and willing to learn all that there is to be taught, so that when you are done here at the school, you can put your teachings to good use. Now, let us get down to business. There is one reason and one reason alone that you chose the school, and that is to train you for a world that not many get to be a part of. If you all will grab anything you brought with you and follow Brother Elijah, we will begin."

LC

10

Junior, the twins, and I stepped out of my Bentley into a neighborhood where people like us weren't exactly welcomed with open arms. The stare-down we got from the wannabe mobsters on the sidewalk were meant to intimidate us, no doubt, but these guys had no idea who we were. In about five minutes, they wouldn't be feeling so superior. Of that, I was sure.

I checked my watch as we approached the building that housed the social club, where we were met by two Italian thugs in cheap suits. One was about the size of the twins, and the other was about five foot four with an obvious Napoleon complex.

"Can I help you, Grandpa?" Little Napoleon asked in a thick Brooklyn accent.

"I'm here to see Bobby Two Fingers," I replied.

"Oh, yeah? Bobby's a very important man. Why would he wanna see you?"

I felt something inside of me flare. Now I understood why Junior suggested we leave Vegas behind, because this little punk would have been on his ass by now and things might have gotten a little tricky. "First, that's above your paygrade, young man. Secondly, why don't you go ask Bobby yourself?"

"I'm asking you," he said.

"You just don't seem that important to me to have to explain *shit* to," I told him.

"Then you have no business here."

"I obviously wouldn't be standing here in front of your short ass for no reason. If I walk away?" I paused and briefly looked away with a small laugh. "If I walk away, I guarantee you'll have a problem. Now, I don't have all day."

The bigger one whispered something in his ear. He clenched his jaw tightly before stepping back and motioning for the man with him to lean down. I watched him whisper something in his ear.

Seconds later, he said, "Who should I say is askin'?"

"Tell him LC Duncan is here."

Both men shrugged. They still had no idea who I was, but the big one disappeared then returned a minute later, whispering to little Napoleon, whose expression transformed from dismissive to shocked.

"You can come in," he said begrudgingly, "but we're gonna have to frisk you. The others can stay outside."

"He doesn't go nowhere without me," Junior said.

The two men looked at each other and shrugged again. Finally, Little Napoleon said, "Frisk him too."

We'd left our weapons in the car, knowing they would do this. The big guy checked us, and then we followed little Napoleon to the back of the club to a room marked OFFICE. Little Napoleon opened the door and a tall, skinny Italian man stood. He eyed the man who had brought us back, and then peered down his beaky nose at us. After a few seconds, he nodded and then stepped aside, granting us entrance. Sitting at the desk was none other than Bobby Two Fingers. He took a last puff of his cigar and then set it in an ashtray.

"So, you're LC Duncan?" He didn't get up out of his seat, but he did gesture toward two chairs. "I've heard a lot about you. Sit! Sit!"

I took a seat. Junior didn't. "All good I hope?"

"Depends on who you talk to," Bobby said, clasping his fingers together. "So, tell me. To what do I owe this pleasure?"

"I need some answers about Marie Hernandez."

Bobby sat back in his chair. No doubt the question had struck a nerve.

"I don't know no Marie Hernandez." He followed up his obvious lie with a weak shrug.

"Well, I have proof you do," I replied.

He couldn't conceal the flush that spread across his face. This wasn't a man who was used to people doubting him, especially in his own place of business. He glanced around the room at his associates.

"You calling me a liar? Because I don't have to answer to any nigger." Bobby made a shooing motion with his thumb and forefinger. He didn't know it yet, but he was going to pay for that comment.

"But you do have to answer to me, Bobby." Everyone, including me, turned their heads to see who had spoken, and instantly the climate in the room changed. Bobby's men stood up straighter and began to fidget.

Standing at the doorway was Don Fredricko, the leader of the Fredricko crime family. I'd known him for thirty years, long before he had his own family. Although the two of us weren't best friends, there was a mutual respect. Beside him were two men holding automatic weapons and leering at everyone in the room, almost daring them to make a wrong move. The Don slowly walked behind the desk, and Bobby jumped up to give him his seat.

"Bobby, what the fuck is going?" the Don asked after taking a seat.

"These muthafucking niggers just waltzed in here demanding shit, boss. Don't worry about it. I was about to handle them," Bobby said with bravado.

Don Fredricko held up a hand to silence him. "First of all, they are not niggers. They're African Americans, you got it? Now apologize to Mr. Duncan."

"Sure thing, boss." Bobby turned to me forcing a humble expression on his face. "Sorry, Mr. Duncan."

I nodded but did not say a word.

"Now, Bobby, what's going on?" The Don stared at him until Bobby got so nervous he cast his eyes down to the floor. "Is there anything you want to tell me? Anything at all. Like . . . something that wouldn't make me very happy?"

"N–no, boss." Bobby shook his head nervously.

"Are you sure?"

"Yes," Bobby answered, sounding less than sure.

The Don sighed deeply. "I was trying to give you a chance to be a man and speak on how you really feel, you scumbag."

"I–I don't understand, boss."

"My friend LC here has brought it to my attention that you been talking a lot of shit about me and the family."

"No, boss! I would never do that. I swear on my mother." He raised his hand like he was taking an oath, all the while glaring at me.

"Really." The Don chuckled. "Benny!" he yelled.

Benny, a young kid in his twenties, walked in wearing head-phones around his neck and carrying a black electronic wand.

"What you got?" the Don asked.

"We found five so far," Benny replied.

"Check this place out," Don Fredricko said, sweeping his gaze across the office.

Benny placed the headphones on his ears and began mov-ing around the room, waving the black wand over surfaces.

Don Fredricko turned to me and explained, "Benny here went to MIT. He's an electronic genius, and that shit he's waving around is the best bug-detecting equipment money can buy."

"That's pretty impressive," I said, watching Benny do his thing. "You ever think about loaning him out, I've got a few places I'd like swept."

"For the right price, anything is doable. You can't put a price on safety." Don Fredricko knew, of course, that I already had a guy to do the same kind of security checks for me, but he appreciated the flattery, nonetheless.

"Or peace of mind," I replied, glancing at Bobby. He looked scared to death.

Ten minutes later, Benny had six small electronic devices in his hand. He dropped them in a glass of water and took off his headphones.

"It's clean now." Benny placed the glass in front of the Don.

The Don turned to Bobby. "Still got nothing to say?"

"I fucked up, boss. No way anyone should be able to get a wire in here. I'll do whatever I gotta do to get back in your good graces. But I didn't know these things were here."

The Don studied him for a few moments, as if he were looking for a lie. I was doing the same thing. I didn't like it, but nothing Bobby had said seemed out of place.

"You know what, Bobby? I believe you. But what I don't be-lieve is that you weren't talking shit about me and the family. Tapes don't lie." Don Fredricko turned his attention back to me. "Thank you for the information you've provided me with. I have some more business to conduct with Bobby here." He made a motion with his hand, and the two men that had come with him grabbed Bobby tightly by the arms.

"Don, Don, I haven't done anything!" Bobby shouted. They dragged him out of the room, his cries for mercy falling on deaf ears.

"So what now," I asked?

"Now me, Bobby, and a few of the boys have a little sit down," the Don said nonchalantly.

I leaned in close to him. "I'd like to be a part of that sit-down."

He leaned back in his chair. "Sorry, I can't do that. This is a family matter. I'm sure you understand. But if anything else comes out during my . . . interrogation about the incident at the Hellfire Club, I promise I'll let you know right away."

"Thank you. I'd appreciate that, Don." I rose from my seat and exited with Junior on my tail.

Nevada

11

I trailed closely behind Brother Elijah with Raheem and Clem and the others as he led us out of the library. As we walked through the school courtyard, I wondered if there was some sort of secret basement where we would get to train. If so, the barriers would have to be soundproofed, so as not to bother the other students' studies. I was thrown for a loop, however, when we were led outside of the school common area to the visitors parking lot, where six black Mercedes Benz Metris vans were waiting for us.

"Where are we going?" Clem asked. "I thought we would train inside the school. At least I thought my brothers did."

"They and many of our other students did train inside of the school's walls. However, with this being such a special Elite class, we thought we'd try something different. Don't worry. You'll like what you see." Brother Elijah winked at us. "Trust me."

There was something about the mysterious wink that made me even more curious to see where we were going. We all piled inside of the vehicles, and I was the only one who buckled my seatbelt. Arielle smirked at me, and I shrugged my shoulders.

"Safety first, right?" she said and buckled her seatbelt too.

I smiled and turned my head to look out the window. I thought we were going to head toward the entrance gates, but the driver sped right for the school's field.

"What the f—Aaaagh!" Clem exclaimed when the van drove over the curb and into the grass.

He wasn't the only one. Everyone let out cries of shock as they bounced up off their seats. I couldn't believe how fast the van was moving. It seemed like we were headed directly into the woods behind the school—that was, if we didn't crash into the line of trees first, I thought in a panic. The other vans behind ours were going just as fast in the same direction, and I envisioned a pile-up of Mercedes vans and bleeding Elites.

"Hey!" Demi shouted to the driver from her seat near the front. "Hey! Are you trying to kill us?"

"Yeah!" Clem cosigned. "You're going to drive us right into those trees! Stop the van!"

The driver ignored them, and I swear it felt like he increased his speed even more. I was nervous, of course, but Minister Farrah had told us to trust him. Maybe we were all being tested, I thought. Maybe the driver was going to slow down at the last minute and take us to our real destination.

I tried to convince myself of that until it looked like we were about five seconds from making contact with the trees. That's when I knew we were all about to die, and my voice joined the others in protest.

"Stop the van! Stop the—"

I threw my arms up over my face and braced for impact . . . only we never hit the trees. We drove right through them, and when I glanced out the window, I saw that we were passing through a tall black wall, not a forest. Putting my forehead on the glass, I looked down and saw that we were driving on concrete, not grass anymore.

"What?" I breathed, trying to make sense of what had happened.

The driver finally slowed down as he drove up a long driveway that curved in front of a giant all-white facility with enough land behind it for a small neighborhood.

"Can somebody please tell me what just happened?" Demi asked. "Because I really feel like we're supposed to be dead right now."

"I don't know, but I'm getting out of this van right now," Clem said once the door opened.

He was the first one out of the van, and he moved onto the sidewalk as far away as he could. I went to stand next to him and watched everyone else piling out of the vans. When everyone else came out of the vehicles, they looked just as shaken up as I felt. Minister Farrah took a look at all of us on the sidewalk and started laughing so hard that his shoulders were jumping. Finally, he wiped the tears from his eyes and smiled at us. I wondered if the others were struggling like I was to keep a scowl off my face. I didn't see anything funny about what we'd just been through.

"Now, did you really think that I would drive all of my star pupils to their deaths? Not on the first day of Elite training, at least." He turned away from us to start toward the tall glass doors of the white building. "The far woods that some of you can see when you look out of your dorm or classroom windows are nothing but a hologram projected against a tall, soundproof wall—with an opening wide enough for our vans to pass through. I'm surprised that you, of all people, were frightened, Demi. After all, your father designed the wall." He glanced over his shoulder at her.

"My father doesn't share much with me about his inventions," Demi said shyly. "Not anymore, anyways."

"Ah, I can understand. Sometimes knowing certain things can put you in places that you don't want to be," Minister Farrah said with a head nod.

Inside the building, he stopped walking and faced us. "To the left of us, students, is the Combat Room. This is where you will study and practice your martial arts. On the floors below this one is where you will practice use of weaponry and have live simulations. Behind this facility in the large field that I'm sure you couldn't have missed is where you will practice your marksmanship. But you will only be able to shoot after learning about the guns in the weaponry room, understood?"

"Yes, Minister Farrah," we all said in unison.

"At the end of each course, I will send each of you on a mission. If you refuse, then you will be asked to leave the Elite program."

"Like, a real-life mission with real danger where we can actually die?" Clem asked.

"Yes."

"Dope," Clem said, and I tried to hide my grin.

"Danger is funny to you, Mr. Duncan?"

"No, Minister Farrah."

"Are you sure? Because I got word that you've gotten into your first school fight already."

"Ha! You call that a fight?" Ivan's voice came from behind me. "If it wasn't for your girlfriend sneaking up behind me, you'd be sporting two black eyes."

"You snuck that punch in after I knocked you back," I tossed over my shoulder. I didn't respect him enough to give him eye contact. "Whatever your issue is with me, dead it."

"What are you going to do if I don't? Call your Amazon girlfriend?"

"Ivan, a true warrior does not need to sneak for a hand-to-hand combat. That is a weak attribute to have," Minister Farrah said.

I smirked, but it was soon wiped from my face.

"However," Minister Farrah continued, "a true warrior also knows to be ready for anything and to never turn his back on his opponent. How about you two gentlemen settle your scores like men?"

"Settle the score?" I asked.

Minister Farrah pointed to the combat room. "I'll be the first to tell you that I do not like quarrels, but they are inevitable, and there is only one way to solve them. Let's see who the big bad wolf really is, shall we?" He parted the sliding doors to the Combat Room.

I could feel the energy in the group of students change. Even if I didn't want to be at the center of this, it was obvious that everyone else wanted to see combat, including Minister Farrah—which was confusing, because he knew what I was capable of since he was one of the people who trained me.

I walked inside the Combat Room. It was about the same size as a high school gymnasium, but the padded mat on the floor was where the similarity ended. Instead of basketball hoops on the wall, there were racks that held all kinds of knives and swords. This was like no school gym I'd ever seen.

Minister Farrah instructed me and Ivan to remove our shoes and socks and follow him to the middle of the room. The other Elites stood on the sidelines, completely silent. I wondered how many of them were just glad it wasn't them being called out to the mat like this on our first day.

Minister Farrah stood between Ivan and me as we faced each other. "I would rather my students work together, and not against each other. Whatever the problem is, leave it here today. May the best man win, and the loser learn from this lesson. No weapons will be used for this fight. If you find yourself in a detrimental situation, then you must tap the mat, and I will end it."

"Got it," Ivan said with his lip curled up at me.

"Got it." I returned Ivan's scowl.

"All right, on my command." Minister Farrah backed away from us on the red mat. "And . . . fight!"

I may not have looked intimidating at five foot nine, a hundred and fifty pounds, but with two black belts, I was not afraid to defend myself. The way Ivan put his fists up, I assumed that he was all power and no technique. However, that could still be bad news for me if he struck me the way he had on the stairs. All of my wind had been knocked out of me, leaving me vulnerable to another attack. I didn't want to think about what could have happened if Brother Elijah had not stepped in. Still, that wasn't going to happen this time. I wouldn't allow it.

We circled each other, waiting for the perfect time to strike. I wanted him to throw the first punch, and it seemed like he wanted me to do the same thing. He got tired of waiting, I guess, because the next thing I knew, he was hurtling toward me with an aggressive scream.

He started with a three-piece combo and followed through with an uppercut. I blocked his blows and dodged the uppercut, jumping back out of his reach. He came at me again almost instantly with another punch combo and a spin kick that caught me in the chest. I flew backward to the ground, looking up just in time to see him leaping in the air with his fist pulled back. I rolled to the side just before his fist made contact with the spot on the ground where my head had just been. He wasn't trying to spar with me; he was trying to cause some real damage. That's when I decided that it was time to go from Judo, a defensive martial art, to Taekwondo, a more aggressive or offensive martial art.

"Get him, Ivan!" I heard one of his German friends cry out. "That's how you do it!"

I didn't let the noise from the sidelines distract me from my opponent. I knew what I was doing. Ivan attacked again, and it confirmed what I had been thinking.

His left. He always starts with his left.

I dodged him, and we went back to circling one another. All I needed to do was to find a window of opportunity. I blinked once, and the entire room became a background blur. I envisioned myself and Ivan going at it as I calculated every move that I could possibly make against him.

No, he'd still be able to fight after that. . . . No, that might kill him. . . . Yeah, that's the one.

I blinked again, and the room returned to normal. I'd found my window, and it was time to act on it. The next time Ivan came at me, I was ready for him.

"Come on! Fight me!" he shouted. "Stop acting like a punk!"

As I predicted, he started with his left, so I went right, hitting him with a blow to his side. He groaned in pain, stumbling back, and I followed through with a tornado kick to the face.

He fell but got up quickly, trying to block my next moves. He was big and powerful; however, speed was not one of his strong points. I easily broke his block and mimicked his first combination as well as the upper cut. When I felt my fist meet the bottom of his chin and saw his body lift in the air, I knew the fight was over before he even hit the ground.

"You're done," I said, still in my fighting stance, just in case he didn't know when to quit.

Ivan spit out blood on the mat and looked at me with fire in his eyes. "Arrrrrrgh!" he yelled out in pure anguish. Jumping up, he went to one of the walls and pulled down a wooden samurai sword, then ran full speed in my direction.

"I'm going to kill you, Duncan!" He was so focused on slicing me to pieces that he didn't see Minister Farrah moving calmly toward him.

"Enough!" Minister Farrah grabbed Ivan by the arm when he was in mid-stride.

Then Ivan did something that made everyone gasp. He swung the sword at Minister Farrah.

Minister Farrah moved with a speed unheard of for a man his age and dodged the attack. He took Ivan by the wrist and pressed it with his fingertips. The move looked way too gentle for the situation at hand, but whatever point he pressed caused Ivan to drop the sword. Once he was disarmed, Minister Farrah delivered a powerful chop to the side of Ivan's neck. Ivan dropped to his knees.

"A student who cannot accept a fair defeat amongst his peers is a student I cannot teach." Minister Farrah glowered down at Ivan, who was clutching his neck. "I allowed your father to talk me into letting you back in my school, but it is only the first week, and I see that you are already up to your same tricks. You're expelled from the Elites."

A hush fell over the group. No one dared to move.

"You can't expel me," Ivan said, gasping to catch his breath.

"You are not expelled from regular courses. From here on out, you will be like the other students who attend my school. However, if your father wants you to receive Elite training, he will have to do so on his own. You are unteachable, and I fear that you will use this kind of training for unthinkable evil."

"My father will burn this place to the ground if you don't train me to be pinned!" Ivan yelled.

Minister Farrah raised his voice, but his body remined still and calm. "Your father will do nothing of the sort. He will be thankful to know that I did not expel you from school as a whole, which, although difficult, still leaves you an opportunity to be pinned. Now, put your shoes back on and head to the vans. You will be taken back to continue your regular coursework."

Ivan sulked out of the room, but not without shooting one more sinister look my way. I felt pure hatred emanating from that kid when it came to me, and I still didn't know why. I'd never met him before last week, but he'd had it out for me since I stepped foot in the school.

When he was gone, Minister Farrah announced, "Well, then, let us continue the rest of our tour. Nevada, put your shoes back on and join us in the hallway."

Everyone else followed him out—except for Brother Elijah. I was tying my shoes when I felt him looking over me.

"I saw what you were doing out there, and I'm impressed." Brother Elijah held out a hand to help me up. "You were calculating your moves. Most students would have thought to go at someone Ivan 's size with all of their might, but not you."

"That would have been one way to go about it, but one wrong move and it would be over," I explained. "I didn't want to hurt him, but I also didn't want to be hurt."

"Very tactful. Those are the traits that I look for in all of my squad leaders. I need groups of people who work well together."

"Unlike Ivan."

"Ivan . . ." Brother Elijah sighed. "Ivan hasn't had a kind life. I tried to help him last year, but he doesn't trust anyone and would rather go at everything alone."

"He hasn't had a kind life? Is that why they let him stay at the school?"

"In part," Brother Elijah said as we walked toward the sliding doors. "Like you, Ivan has the potential to be great. Did you know he delayed going to MIT to return to finish elite training?"

"Ivan got into MIT?" I was blown away.

"Yes, and he's also a prolific artist."

"Wow. Who would have thought?"

I expected him to say more about it, but he didn't.

"Nevada, may I ask you a more personal question?" Brother Elijah's voice became profoundly serious. "One that we will keep between us?"

"Yeah, sure."

"How is your cousin Sasha?"

I raised an eyebrow. "You know Sasha?"

"Intimately—" He paused awkwardly. "Well, not intimately, but yes, I do know her." He was tongue-tied, which felt weird to me.

I didn't know what to say in response, so I just started walking out of the room.

"I know most of your family," he said when he caught up to me.

Then I realized the connection. "Oh, you're Elijah! The Muslim that helped keep Sasha alive when that crazy Brother X kidnapped her and then went after my Uncle Junior and Aunt Sonya. During the X Wars."

"Is that what they are calling it now, The X Wars?" Brother Elijah chuckled. "Yes, I'm that Elijah. So understand, you are amongst friends."

Consuela

12

It had been three days since I'd seen Vegas, and I could still feel his presence in my soul. Nobody, and I mean nobody, had ever made love to me the way he had. I could still feel the anger and punishing passion he exuded during our lovemaking between my legs, and my body yearned for more. Unfortunately, it wasn't going to be quite that easy. Vegas wasn't like most men, who were easily manipulated by the lure of pleasure and sex. I guess that's what made him so damn interesting. However, I wasn't a stupid woman, and in the long run, I always achieved exactly what I wanted from a man.

As I rode in the back seat of my Maybach, contemplating my next move, a thought came to mind. If the seduction of sex alone wasn't going to get Vegas in my bed, perhaps appealing to his appetite might do the trick. I picked up my phone and called to invite him to dinner at his favorite restaurant. I hated Red Lobster, it was so ghetto and the food tasted processed, but he loved it and had gotten my son to love it too. I can't tell you how many times I'd offered to hire a private chef to cook Sunday dinners with caviar, freshly flown-in lobster, and Alaskan king crab legs only to be vetoed by the two of them so they could get an Ultimate Feast. But right now, as horny as I was, I would gladly sit in that ghetto restaurant and eat those overrated biscuits if I could get Vegas in bed tonight.

Of course, Vegas's phone went straight to voicemail. No matter. I left him a message. I'd be at my office in twenty minutes, so hopefully he'd checked his messages before then. Vegas had a bad habit of ghosting me lately, so I sent him a text message as well. This way, he'd have no excuse when I finally caught up with him.

I turned to Natalia, my personal secretary and bodyguard, who was sitting next to me. "Make an eight o'clock reservation for two at the Red Lobster at Green Acres Mall."

"Si, Consuela," she replied, pulling out her phone.

When I arrived at my high-rise office, Vegas still hadn't called or texted me back. I hoped he wasn't still caught up in his feelings about me putting that gun to my head. Yes, it was a ballsy move, but I'm a ballsy woman, and desperate times called for desperate measures. I needed him to concentrate less on Marie and more on me. I hadn't planned for it to go that way, but the circumstance presented itself, and let's be honest; it worked. I was a master when it came to schemes to help me get my way. For the past several years, I'd been using our son to help navigate our relationship and keep Vegas in check.

When my driver let me out, I rolled my eyes at him. "That took ten more minutes than it usually does, Roman. Find a better route next time."

"Si," he said, nodding obediently.

"Natalia, are you coming?" I asked.

"Yes, Consuela. I'll be right there," she replied, a phone to her ear. "I'm trying to confirm your reservation for eight o'clock. You may have to do nine thirty."

"I said eight. What's the problem? It's not like you're trying to book dinner reservations at the Ritz Carlton."

"I know, but this is a very popular place."

"Just get it done."

My cherry red heels stabbed the concrete as I walked toward the tall double doors of my building. When I walked through them, it seemed like everyone bustling around stopped breathing, which was exactly how I liked it. I was a giant to them.

The elevator took me to my office on the fifth floor. My bodyguards should have been the only people on that floor, but I could see someone moving around in my office through the stained glass windows. My hand inched closer and closer to the Chanel bag hanging on my shoulder, just in case I had to pull out my gun, but when I walked inside, a pleasant surprise was waiting for me.

"Vegas!"

He turned around at the sound of my voice.

"You must have gotten my voicemail . . ." My voice trailed off as I looked around my office. Everything was out of place. Drawers had been pulled out, their contents strewn across the floor. That's when I realized that he was standing in front of my office safe.

"What are you doing?"

"I should be asking you that," Vegas growled, throwing me off guard. I wanted to think he was joking, but the hateful eyes he was giving me matched his tone.

The next events were a blur. He was moving so fast that I didn't have time to react. Before I knew it, Vegas's strong hand was around my neck, and I was pinned to the wall.

"V–Vegas!" I choked and gasped for air. "What are you doing?"

"I know it was you. I know you had something to do with what happened to Marie and the girls! Bitch!"

"You're crazy!"

"Only because you're making me this way!" He squeezed my neck tighter. My hand went for my purse, but Vegas snatched it off my shoulder.

"What are you up to, Consuela? I know you're up to something."

"Nothing," I barely choked out.

"You don't know how lucky you are to be the one who carried my son into this world. That's the only thing that's saving you this time."

Our eyes locked, and I clawed at his hand through my lightheadedness to get some relief. Believe it or not, I wasn't scared as much as I was uncomfortable. I knew that despite all his bravado, he couldn't kill me because of our son. I was proven right when, finally, right as I was about to pass out, he let me go.

I doubled over to catch my breath.

"What are you up to?" he yelled.

I was not about to let him see that he'd upset me, so I answered him with sarcasm. "I'm not up to anything, and if this is foreplay, you have to let me know these things ahead of time. I would have worn sexier panties."

"You don't have to worry about foreplay or nothing else from me. We're done."

His words hurt because I knew he truly meant them.

"We will never be done. We have a son," I snapped at him.

"Yeah, well, let's see how our son feels when I see him and tell him what I know." He exited my office, slamming the door on his way out.

I waited until I heard the ding of the elevator to poke my head out to be sure he was gone. Then I walked over to my safe, which was still locked. I punched in the combination and quickly went through its contents. I realized something was missing.

"Fuck!" I picked my purse up off the ground, took my phone out, and dialed.

"Hello, love," a male voice said sweetly after the third ring. "How are you today?"

"Not well at all."

"What can I do?" he asked calmly.

"I need you to call me if you see Vegas Duncan."

Nevada

13

Weekends were the only time we were allowed to leave the school grounds and explore France. Clem, Raheem, Demi, Arielle, Richard, and the rest of the Elites had already left a few hours before. I'd stayed behind because I needed to talk to Natasha and break our date, which I was on my way to do now.

My sigh carried down the long hallway to Natasha's dorm room. As I approached her door, I tried to put what I was thinking in the right context and then hopefully the right words. Some people took rejection hard, and the last thing I wanted to do was hurt her feelings. I didn't really know her well, but she seemed like a nice enough girl. Besides, I had enough enemies with Ivan and his crew of cronies. I did not need Natasha in that camp too.

I knocked, and the door swung open. Natasha stood before me with a big smile on her face. She looked gorgeous in a black dress that clung to her shape. Her long hair had been brushed back into a sleek ponytail, and I could see that she was wearing just a touch of makeup. She seemed genuinely happy to see me, which made what I was about to do feel even heavier.

"A little underdressed for dinner, aren't we?" she asked, glancing at my casual attire. "Or perhaps I'm overdressed? I'm sorry it took me five hours to decide on this dress."

"No, you look nice. Really nice," I said and felt myself getting nervous. I took a deep breath. "So, yeaaah, about tonight . . ." My mind raced as I struggled to find the right words. I thought I was prepared to do this, but the way her eyes lit up when she saw me and continued to sparkle when she stared at me erased all the words I'd planned to say.

"What about tonight?" she asked.

Once again, nothing came out of my mouth. I didn't know what was so hard about telling her the truth. I barely knew her. Why was I considering her feelings so much?

Finally, I decided to just say it, and however she took it was on her.

"Natasha—"

She held up a hand to stop me. "Nevada, it's okay, I already know."

"Wait . . . you do?" I was so confused.

"Yes, your friend Clem already told me." She offered me a kind smile.

"Told you what?" Fucking Clem. Why could he not mind his business?

"That you're nervous about going out with a pretty girl like me. And that you're a virgin. But don't worry. It will be fine. I have taken many boys' virginity."

"But I'm not a—"

"Good. All the better." She cut me off again. "You might not know this, but I'm nervous too."

"You are?" *Why would she be nervous?*

"Yes, I really like you. You are very respectful and nonaggressive. I mean, I can be comfortable with you. I guess what I'm trying to say is that you make me feel safe. You're not like the other boys around here. Of course, I understand you have needs—"

This time, I cut her off. "Natasha, we need to talk."

"Yes, we will talk at dinner." She closed her door and began to walk down the hallway. "Come. We have reservations. I don't want to be late."

I followed her, trying to think of what my dad would do in this situation. Then again, my dad had been involved with my mom, even though he really loved Marie, so maybe his approach wouldn't be the best. Oh, well. I'd think of something before the night was over, and in the meantime, dinner wouldn't be a bad time to explain that I couldn't be her boyfriend.

Outside the dorm, I took out my phone.

"What are you doing?" she asked.

"Ordering an Uber."

She laughed as she walked over to a scooter parked at the bike rack outside the dorm. She placed a helmet on her head and got on. Starting up the engine, she maneuvered the scooter in front of me. Damn, even with a helmet on she was pretty.

"Let's go. It will take almost an hour for a uber to get here." She reached back and handed me the other helmet.

Once again, I did what I was told without a real plan in mind yet. I got on behind her, wrapping my arms around her waist. The perfume she wore smelled like a garden.

"Hold on tight." She hit the gas, and we were off.

Twenty minutes later we were in a quaint town with cobblestone roads and architecture that looked centuries old. Natasha pulled the scooter in front of a small building and headed for the front door. I followed her.

"I lied about the food being expensive. I wanted to know if you were cheap," she said as we entered the small building.

"You didn't have to do that."

"Some things are necessary. To find out a man's character," she said with a shrug. Her eyes traveled over the interior of the restaurant as if she were looking for someone. "The woman who owns this restaurant is from my country."

A middle-aged hostess greeted us. Natasha kissed her on both cheeks, and the two of them had a brief conversation in Hungarian. Then Natasha turned to me.

"Nevada, this is Anna. Anna, this is my boyfriend, Nevada."

I wasn't sure how much English this woman understood, so I just smiled and, like my grandpa had taught me, stuck out my hand. When in doubt, offer a strong, steady handshake, he always said.

"Pleasure to meet you, Anna."

"Nice to meet you." She took my hand and smiled at Natasha. "He is very handsome, this one." Apparently, her grasp of English was better than I had suspected.

I have to admit that her compliment made me blush a little. I couldn't help it. Between Anna's flattering words and Natasha's proud smile, I was putty in their hands.

Anna led us to a table and took our drink order.

"Thank you," Natasha said very sincerely to me when Anna left.

"For what?" I asked.

"For being a gentleman and not embarrassing me in front of Anna. She is from my village and will report back to my mother." From her tone, I could tell there was a story behind that.

I unfolded my napkin and placed it on my lap, looking down at the menu. "Are you close to your mother?"

"As close as one can be when your mother is a Gypsy whore."

She said it so nonchalantly I dropped my menu. I had no idea how to reply to something like that.

Thankfully, she filled in the blanks without me having to ask the questions. "I am not a whore. My mother is, and her mother was, and her mother, but I am not a whore, despite how I gained entry into the school."

Anna stepped up to the table just as Natasha finished. If she'd heard the last sentence, she didn't let it show on her face. "I bring you both tea and gyümölcsleves," she said, placing two cups in front of us, along with two bowls of what looked like red soup.

My mind was still consumed with Natasha's declaration, but with Anna hovering over us, I couldn't ask Natasha to elaborate on this shocking news.

I politely tasted the soup and was overwhelmed.

"You like?" Anna asked.

"Yes, very much. This is amazing." I dipped my spoon back in, slurping up some more.

"Good." Anna smiled at me. "I will bring you pörkölt?"

Natasha nodded. "She likes you. She likes it when people enjoy her cooking."

"Well, I'm a fan. This soup is amazing,"

"That is nothing. Wait until you taste the pörkölt. It is out of this world."

I looked up from my half empty bowl. "I don't know what that is, but if it's as good as this soup, then I can't wait."

"I cannot wait to make love to you tonight."

The seductive gaze she gave me snapped me back to reality. I'd almost forgotten what I was supposed to be doing. I exhaled into my now empty soup bowl, then looked up at her. She was grinning, but my somber face must have alerted her that something was wrong.

"What? Did you forget the condoms?"

"Not exactly." I placed my spoon on the table. "Natasha, I didn't bring any condoms."

Her face went pale. "Nevada, I cannot afford to get pregnant. We must stop and get them before we go to the hotel."

"No, we shouldn't. We're not going to a hotel."

"Why not? You do want to have sex with me, don't you?" She looked confused.

It was time for me to say what I'd been trying to say all night. "To be honest, no, I don't think I'm ready."

The look of bewilderment on her face was intense and only softened when Anna returned with two steaming plates of what looked like stew that she placed in front of us. Natasha gave her a smile, but the sparkle was gone from her eyes, so it looked fake. I was sure she was pissed and waiting on Anna to leave so she could lay into me.

"You taste," Anna said, standing over me.

I picked up my fork and speared a piece of the meat. To say it was stupendous was an understatement. "Holy cow. The flavors are amazing. What did you season this with?"

"It is an old family recipe," Anna replied pridefully.

I ate a few more mouthfuls with Anna watching over me, then kept shoveling the food into my mouth after she left because I didn't want to look up at Natasha.

Eventually, I got up the courage to raise my head, and I saw Natasha's eyes welling up with tears. This was bad. I hadn't even broken up with her yet, and she was already crying.

She tried to blink away her tears, but they began to fall freely from her eyes. What the hell had I done? I hated to see women cry.

"Are you okay?" I asked, even though she obviously was not.

She sniffled back tears and took a deep breath, then spoke in a shaky voice. "I am not a whore, Nevada."

My eyes opened wide. "I didn't say you were."

"Then why do you not want to have sex with me? Is it because I told you I come from a family of Gypsy whores?" She stared at me with red-rimmed eyes. "I am trying to be truthful. You are my boyfriend."

"No, I'm not." I shook my head. "Natasha, you're a really nice girl, and any guy would be lucky to have you as his girlfriend, but I'm not looking to be yours or anyone else's boyfriend. My girlfriend, Kia, was murdered two months ago, and I still love her. Very much. I'm sorry."

There, I'd said it, and she could be cool with it or not. At that moment, I really didn't care. Unfortunately, now my eyes were filling with tears.

The two of us were caught in a staring contest, until she finally spoke. "I am such a fool. I should have known a man like you would never dishonor yourself. I am truly sorry."

"It's okay. You didn't know. No one at the school knows," I wiped away the tear that had rolled down my cheek. "I'd appreciate it if you kept this between us."

"Of course. You have my word. However, I would appreciate if you would not tell anyone about my mother. It will be hard to find a decent boyfriend if it gets out."

"Your secret is safe. But why do you need to find a boyfriend? You can have any man you want."

"I am not like the rest of you, Nevada. My parents are not rich and powerful. I was not sent to Chi's to learn how to be a general, a head of state, or even a crime boss. My mother sent me here to seduce the sons of the future leaders of the world and the men behind these walls.

"I gained entry into the Elites by having sex with Dean Wilensky in the admissions office. He helped me to forge the documents and letters of reference required to gain admittance. I seek a boyfriend like you whose family has deep roots in the school and will protect me from his advances. I do not want to have sex with him anymore."

Fuck! I stared at her for a brief moment, trying to ascertain if she was serious. From her tears and shaky voice, I'd come to the conclusion that she was being honest. I felt deeply saddened for her. Like me, she was just a young adult trying to find her way, and instead of helping her, Dean Wilensky took advantage of her. Part of me wanted to go straight back to school and punch him in the mouth.

"Natasha, you can't sleep with that man anymore." Just the thought of them together made me want to poke out my own eyes.

"Believe me, I am not proud of it. He is old and vile, and he smells of rotten teeth, but it was my only way to become an Elite. Thankfully, he has not made any more advances toward me since word has gotten around that you are my new boyfriend."

As I began to put things in perspective, I became angry—at the dean and at her mother. These were adults who should have been protecting her, not using her body like a commodity so that she was forced to seek protection from me, a guy she barely knew. Although her situation was not exactly like Kia's, it was close enough to make me wonder just how many pretty young girls are preyed upon this same way.

"Yeah, I'm sure he knows about my family's closeness with Minister Farrah. Would you like me to speak with the headmaster?"

"No! No!" she said in a panic. "Please, Nevada. I cannot take a chance that Minister Farrah might expel me from the Elites for lying on my application."

"Natasha, you can't keep sleeping with that pervert."

"Without a powerful boyfriend, I don't think I have any choice." She sounded so defeated.

I wanted to help her, of course, but she was tying my hands by not wanting to involve Minister Farrah. I thought for a moment, and then an idea came to mind. "Natasha, have you ever heard of kayfabe?"

"No, I have not. What is this?"

"Well, kayfabe is a professional wrestling term that means *putting on an act*. The wrestlers know what they're doing is fake, but the audience does not. It's kayfabe."

"I don't understand. What does that have to do with me and Dean Wilensky? If I do not have a boyfriend, he is sure to pursue me. He's said so in so many words."

"Natasha, I can't be your real boyfriend, but I don't think I'm dishonoring Kia's memory if I become your *kayfabe* boyfriend."

She took a moment to take consider my words, her eyes widening as it dawned on her what I was suggesting. "You would do that for me?"

"Sure, us eating meals together, walking to class, and hanging out will be fun. Kind of like tonight." I picked up my fork to skewer another bite of the stew. "But you have to promise to bring me back here to eat."

"I promise." A smile crept up on her face, and she leaned over the table and quickly kissed me on the lips.

"What was that about?"

"That was *kayfabe*. Anna is watching." She waved at her, and Anna turned her back as if to pretend she hadn't been observing us all along. "And also, a thank you. You are the nicest man I have ever met by far, Nevada Duncan."

Natasha

14

Nevada and I spent the rest of the night getting to know each other, laughing, joking, telling each other stories about our families, and eating Anna's great cooking. Although I had latched onto him so quickly simply as a means of protection and would have done so no matter what he looked like, I found myself genuinely attracted to him. Despite his state of mourning, I got the sense that the attraction was mutual—although now that I think about it, outside of his confession about his girlfriend's death and his explanation of kayfabe, I did most of the talking.

He was a remarkably interesting, if not confusing boy, this Nevada, not like any other I had ever encountered. I understood his reason for not wanting to have sex, although I must admit, in some ridiculous way, I liked the challenge. Seducing him over the next few months would be fun.

By the time we left Anna's and arrived on campus, we were not just a kayfabe boyfriend and girlfriend, but had begun what could be a longtime friendship, or, if I was successful, perhaps even a romance.

I let him drive my prized scooter back to school, where we were met by Clem, Raheem, Arielle, Richard, and Demi when we pulled up to the dorm. I stepped off the scooter, and Nevada handed me his helmet so I could lock it up. Perhaps I was paranoid, but I could feel Arielle and Demi staring at me. I had never gotten along well with women, mostly, I suspected, because they were intimidated by me. If only they understood that my looks were a curse that brought me unwanted attention from all the wrong kinds of men.

"Well, if it isn't the happy couple. Everyone have a good time tonight?" Clem teased, giving Nevada a knowing look. I'm sure his mind was in the gutter, where it should have been if Nevada had brought condoms and things had gone the way I had originally planned.

"You have a good time?" Arielle's sarcastic tone didn't surprise me. I could see Demi discreetly nudge her in the side as if to say, "Cut it out."

"We had an amazing time." I linked my arm through Nevada's and snuggled up against him affectionately. "I have the best boyfriend in the world. I am going to sleep like a baby." I gave him a kiss on the cheek, but Nevada looked a little tense. I would have to explain to him later that while our kayfabe arrangement was for my protection, I wouldn't mind if he played along in front of jealous girls like Arielle, too.

Raheem slapped Nevada's back so hard I could feel it. "Taught him everything he knows," he joked.

Nevada didn't appreciate his humor. "Come on, Natasha. Let's go inside." He took my hand and we were about to head into the dorm when we heard a commotion nearby. Somebody was shouting, and then we heard a thud and what sounded like a scuffle.

"What's that?" Richard asked.

"Sounds like a fight," Raheem said. "Let's go check it out."

They all headed in the direction of the skirmish. Nevada tugged at my hand, and we followed behind them.

"Dad, please stop!" I recognized that voice. It was Ivan.

We all sped up around the corner, and there was Ivan, doubled over and clutching his stomach on the ground. His nose was bleeding. In front of him, with his fists balled, was an older man who had to be Ivan's father. His face was twisted up and red with rage. It was also pretty obvious he was drunk. The moment Ivan stood up, he swung and hit him again, catching him hard in the jaw. It was not a pretty sight.

"You worthless piece of shit!" he shouted. "I return from Paris to this? Did you think I wouldn't hear ya got yourself kicked out of the Elites?"

"It's not my fault," Ivan said, coughing up blood.

"It's never your fault, just like it wasn't your fault that you got your ass kicked by a girl in the dining hall." I think he was talking about me. "You didn't think I'd hear about that either, did you?"

Ivan's father waited less than two seconds for a response before he started kicking him. "You're a disgrace! A fucking disgrace!"

"I'm not a disgrace! She snuck up behind—"

"Worthless piece of shit! I can't believe you're my son."

When his father finally stopped kicking him, Ivan managed to get back on his feet. He was staggering a little, but he didn't fall. He was a tough boy; I had to give him that, although I couldn't help but wonder why he didn't fight back, or at least block his father's blows. Ivan was just taking this beating like a defenseless puppy.

"Don't say that, Dad. Please don't—" His father's fist connected with the side of his face before he could finish his statement.

"Help him," Demi pleaded.

"For what?" Clem replied. "That's his dad. A father has a right to beat his son."

Raheem and Nevada glanced at him. I'm sure neither one of them were in favor of that.

"So what? He has no right to do that. He's beating him to death!" Demi replied.

"She's right. We gotta do something," Nevada let go of my hand and moved closer.

I don't know what came over him, but it was very arousing to watch him rush over there without thought for his own well-being. Ivan's father was pulling his arm back and getting ready to hit his son again. Right as he swung, Nevada moved quickly between them, bodychecking the older man and blocking his blow from connecting with Ivan's head. I'm not sure if he would have been able to do that if Ivan's father was sober, but it was sexy as hell.

"That's enough!" Nevada shouted. He was now in a karate stance, ready to strike if Ivan's father made the wrong move.

Clem, Raheem, Richard, and I rushed to flank him on each side. I glanced back at Ivan and saw that Demi and Arielle had rushed over to help him stand upright.

"Is he all right?" Nevada asked.

"We need to take him to the infirmary," Demi replied.

"Oh, so you're with them now?" Ivan's father said as he struggled back to his feet. He glared at Nevada. "The Duncan boy and the bitch that kicked your ass?"

How did he know about the incident in the dining hall? I wondered with a pit in my stomach.

Ivan's father turned to Nevada, who also looked taken aback. "Yes, I know who you are, Nevada Duncan"—he turned his evil gaze on me—"and that gypsy whore too."

I wanted to run up and punch him in the face for calling me a whore, but that man was huge and could squash me if I tried it.

"Go on with them, you big pussy. But don't think I'll be helping you to get a pin. You're going to be the first Igor not to have one in a hundred years." He walked away from his son.

"Dad!" Ivan called. "Dad! Please, I'm sorry."

"For Christ's sake, man, let him go!" Clem said. "He just tried to kill you."

Ivan watched his father round the corner, and when he could no longer see him, his shoulders dropped in disappointment.

"No. He's just angry. He wasn't trying to kill me. He was trying to teach me," Ivan argued.

"Are you sure about that, mate?" Richard asked, pointing to the bruise forming underneath his eye. Ivan looked pretty beat up, and he was holding his ribs like one might be broken. "Because that's a lesson I personally could skip."

"Richard's right. We should bring this to the headmaster and get Ivan to the infirmary," Nevada added. It was sexy how he just took charge, and I could see from Arielle's smirk that she saw it too.

"No," Ivan looked at us as though he were seeing us for the first time. "This is none of your fucking business. What are you doing here anyway?"

"We came to help you, Ivan," Demi said.

He glanced around at us, probably surprised we'd come to his aid, but only for a brief second. "Fuck off. I don't need your help," he said, turning his head to look Nevada directly in the eyes. "Especially not yours, Duncan."

"No problem." Nevada raised his hands in surrender. "Sorry I got involved."

"Unbelievable." Arielle shook her head as we watched him walk away. "Next time, we should just let him get his ass kicked."

"Yeah, maybe," Nevada said, but I didn't believe he meant it. Something in his eyes told me he felt sorry for Ivan.

"Come on. Let's get back to the dorm, guys," I said, taking Nevada's hand and smirking at Arielle's jealous ass when I noticed her staring at our intertwined fingers.

Vegas

15

I'd stayed away from the Clayborn Institute for most of the week at the suggestion of Marie's psychiatrist. Dr. Jacobs thought it would be better to let Marie get adjusted to the facility, but I couldn't stay away any longer. Not just because I needed to lay my eyes on her and reassure her that I would always be there for her, but because I needed some answers, and Marie was the only person who could give them to me.

Once at the hospital, I had to do the song and dance with James Fester, the hospital security chief, who was eager to inform me that it was not visiting hours. As always, it came down to a payoff before I was finally escorted to the maximum-security psych ward on the fifth floor. I had to admit the place was kinda creepy. It reminded me of my time in lockup, only worse. In prison, only half the guys were crazy. Here, it was like the people were so crazy you could feel their disturbed energy in the air. I was told they had Marie on this floor because of her constant attempts at escape.

The guard escorted me to the nurses' station and let the sister behind the desk know I was there to see Marie Hernandez.

"She's down there, poor thing." She pointed at a lone woman standing at the end of the hallway in a hospital gown, looking out the barred window. Her back was turned, but I could tell it was Marie despite the fact she looked like she'd lost some weight.

I made my way down the hall and called her name gently so I wouldn't scare her. Maybe I was too quiet, I thought, because she stayed completely still. I said her name again a little louder.

"Marie? I brought you a lily like you asked." I held the flower out in front of me.

"Leave the plant and go away, Vegas." She finally answered me, but she didn't turn her gaze away from the window. "You've already proven you don't give a shit about me by locking me up in this place."

"I brought you here for your own good." I didn't know what else to say.

"Does this look like it's for my own good?" She finally turned around, and I couldn't believe what I was seeing.

One of the most naturally beautiful women I'd ever seen now looked like a female Klingon from Star Trek. Half the hair on her head from her forehead back was gone, along with her eyebrows and lashes. The raccoon bags under her eyes made her look twenty years older, and her lips were so dry they looked like cracked cement. I didn't get it. What the hell was going on?

"What the fuck! Who did this to you?" I asked between gritted teeth. All she had to do was point me in the right direction, and I was going to rain holy hell down on that place, starting with head of security James Fester.

"I did this to me," she replied with a blank expression as she slowly reached up to her head and then yanked out a few more strands of hair. "Pain is the only way I can stay up at night after they shove those sleeping pills down my throat. I don't know why they want me to sleep. If I sleep, they'll get me."

"Oh God, Marie. Nobody is going to get you." I reached out and pulled her into my arms, relieved when she didn't resist.

"You think I'm crazy, don't you?" She sobbed into my shoulder.

This was getting out of hand, especially now that she was mutilating herself. I had put her here for her own benefit, but she seemed even worse than when I'd brought her in.

"I'm not crazy, Vegas."

"No, I don't think you are, Marie. I just think you've been through a lot." I gently took her by the arm and guided her into a nearby chair. "Here, sit down. Stop crying." I wiped her tears away with a bandana I carried in my leather jacket.

"I'm not the woman you fell in love with anymore, am I?"

"I fell in love with the woman in here." I touched her chest with the palm of my hand.

She shook her head. "I'm different there too. I don't think I'll ever be the same. I–I have to get out of here, Vegas. I've lost so much, and I don't want to lose anymore."

"I know you're in pain, Marie, and I hate seeing you like this. Both you and my son lost people you care about, and I swear to you I'm going to make this better. I'm going to find out who—"

"Nevada! Oh my God, I forgot all about him. Is he okay? Where is he? Jesus, how could I forget that sweet boy?"

"He's fine. He's at school."

She let out a thankful sigh. "That's right. He's at Harvard. They wouldn't dare go after him there. He'll be safe there."

"He's not at Harvard. He took a gap year, so he's in Europe at Chi's. But like I was saying, he—"

"No! He can't be in Europe! Europe's not safe," she blurted out, sounding terrified. "You have to bring him home now! Europe's not safe."

"He's fine, Marie. You just take care of yourself and let me worry about the rest, okay?"

"He's not fine," she snapped. "They live in Europe."

"What the fuck am I missing? Who lives in Europe?" Was this some paranoid delusion, or did Marie really know something that could help me catch the killers?

She stared at me blankly, like she was retreating back into a shell.

"God dammit, Marie, talk to me." I grabbed her shoulders probably a little harder than I should have and forced her eyes to meet mine.

She pressed her lips together tightly. Even in her crazed state, she was standing her ground. It was frustrating me to no end, because I'd gone there to find *something* out, and so far, I had nothing. I exhaled a long breath to calm myself before I spoke again.

"Why are you so afraid? They let you go. Why would they come back for you?"

"They didn't let me go, Vegas." Tears began to roll down her face. "I lied. I'm sorry, but I lied to you for your own good."

"Lied about what?"

"About everything. They didn't let me go." She let out a shaky breath. "They gave me time to find it."

"Find what?" I snatched my hands away. "What the fuck are you talking about?"

"Don't be mad. Let me explain," she pleaded.

Suddenly, Marie looked behind me and gasped. The look of fear on her face was even more intensified.

"Oh God! Vegas! They're here! They found me!" Marie's voice was frantic, but there was something in her tone that resonated with me. Fear. Real fear. Not the kind that came from having PTSD after trauma, but the kind that came when you honestly believed bad shit was about to happen. "Run, Vegas, run! It's them!"

I turned around to see what had spooked her, and the only person in the corridor was a tall, redheaded orderly walking toward us, carrying a tray with medicine. Marie's words were so convincing and her fear so real to me that my mind and body just went into autopilot, snatching the guy up and pinning him to the wall. Marie took off running down the hall.

"Who the fuck are you?" I growled, pulling my fist back to pulverize him. "And why are you here?"

"I'm John Wilson. I'm a nurse," the terrified man replied. "I—I was just bringing my patient his meds. Please don't hit me."

"He's telling the truth," a woman said from behind me. I looked back and saw the nurse that had directed me to Marie. She looked scared too. "He does work here."

I let go of him, and he slid down the wall. I was so embarrassed I didn't even offer an apology or help him up. I just walked away to find Marie. Once again, I'd let my anger and emotions get the best of me.

Nevada

16

"Hey, Nevada, you have a minute?" Demi asked.

I'd just walked Natasha to the dining hall, holding her hand like she insisted. She was taking this whole kayfabe thing pretty seriously. I was about to head over to the head's parsonage to have tea with Minister Farrah when Demi shouted my name. She said goodbye to the girls she'd been talking to and headed over in my direction.

"Sure, but I have to meet Minister Farrah for tea in a minute." I checked my watch.

"This won't take long," Demi said, closing the space between us. She looked nice in a traditional Indian sari, and I was surprised to see a large diamond earing in her nose that she didn't wear during the week. We didn't have to wear uniforms other than for training on the weekends, but I'd decided to wear mine to have tea with Minister Farrah.

"What's up?"

"I wanna know what your thoughts are about him." Demi pointed across the small lake at the dirty blonde figure sitting on the bank.

"Ivan? I have no thoughts. Why? He hasn't been bothering you, has he?"

Ivan looked like he might be fishing. Why Minister Farrah didn't just expel him completely, I didn't know. In spite of the beating he took from his father that earned him some sympathy for a minute, I still thought that guy was bad news and I didn't trust him at all.

"No, Ivan would never bother me. I think you need to talk to the head on his behalf," she replied.

I took a step back. "Why would I do that?"

"Because you're the voice of reason around here and it's the right thing to do. Everyone knows your Minister Farrah's favorite. You just said yourself you're going to have tea with him. If anyone can convince him to reinstate Ivan to Elite status, you can."

I kept staring at her in disbelief. She was crossing quite a few lines.

"You sound like you think I'm some sort of teacher's pet." I liked Demi, but I was a little offended by her innuendo. "Minister Farrah is a family friend. He used to train me back in New York. My invitation to tea has nothing to do with school. I will not be talking to him about Ivan Igor."

"Why not?" She was not going to give up easily. "Ivan would still be in Elite training if it weren't for you. You're responsible. You ruined his life."

"Really, Demi? Really? You wanna blame somebody, blame the guy kicking the crap outta him last night. Who, by the way, we saved him from." I was irritated. As far as I was concerned, I would have been happy to have never met Ivan Igor, and now somehow I was responsible for this guy's whole existence?

Demi's face softened a bit. "You don't know Ivan the way I do. We grew up together. He's not as bad as he seems. He just . . . he just had a tougher life than most other kids. You can't imagine what it's like to grow up in fear of your parent."

"What are you, his lawyer or something?"

"No, I just—"

"Oh my God," I interrupted. "You like him, don't you?"

My words changed her entire demeanor, and she would not make eye contact. "He's not as bad as you think he is. He doesn't get time to be happy or have fun like the rest of us. He has no control over who he wants to be. All that matters is him getting a pin. It's all he ever talked about, all he ever wanted. He needs this place way more than any of us, and if you're going to be our leader, it's your responsibility, whether he fails or succeeds." She didn't answer me, but she answered me. Demi had a thing for the big lug. Who would have guessed?

"Be your leader?" I laughed. "Demi, I'm not an instructor or teacher here, I'm just a kid trying to find his way, just like everyone else."

"Don't be naïve. You're not like the rest of us. Whether you want to recognize it or not, you're a natural born leader, and it doesn't have anything to do with your family. Everyone can see that. The students, the teachers and staff, everybody. The only one that doesn't see it is you."

LC

17

I walked along a small path toward a park bench with a newspaper tucked under my arm. Settling on the bench, I watched a group of young kids trying to fly a kite but mostly just wrecking it. Off in the distance, I could smell all-beef hot dogs from a food truck, and I promised myself I would have one when this was all over.

The normalcy of the day was what made it easy to blend in. I flapped open the newspaper and aimlessly flipped pages for a minute until someone sat down next to me.

"You're late," I said, not putting the paper down.

"I was at a funeral. It went longer than I expected," Don Fredricko responded. He'd contacted me and said we needed to meet face to face, although he hadn't shared any details. I was hoping he had some information about the Hellfire Club.

I lowered the newspaper. "My condolences. Anybody I know?"

The Don leaned back on the bench and removed the dark shades from over his hardened eyes. The way his jaw slightly clenched and unclenched gave me an off feeling. Don Fredricko, who usually kept a poker face, was wearing his unease like clothes. "Bobby Two Fingers."

"You sound a little emotional. Isn't that what you wanted?"

"To be honest, no, that's not what I wanted. Bobby was old school, and there aren't many old school guys like him around anymore." He shook his head. "But his death was inevitable."

"Then why the long face?"

The Don turned and gave me an intense look. "Because my people didn't do it."

This sounded like bullshit. "I don't understand."

"Neither do I. And I'm almost embarrassed to tell you what happened."

"Well, I'm sorry if it makes you uncomfortable. But you called me here for a reason, so what is it? What does Bobby Two Fingers' death have to do with me?"

Don Fredricko was silent for a minute, and I wondered if he was going to just get up and leave.

"Don Fredricko, don't waste my time. We're old friends, aren't we?"

Finally, he shrugged and told me his story. "After you and your people left, Bobby tried to plead his case. He said he had something at his house that would make up for all his fuckups. Something to do with that gal Marie that I'd have to see for myself."

I leaned forward, my senses on high alert now that I knew this might be valuable information. "What did he have?"

"I don't know. I sent him with a few of the boys to his place, but they didn't get five steps out the building before the feds pull up in two big-ass SUVs and take Bobby away."

I leaned back on the bench. "You gotta be fucking kidding me. Bobby knows a lot about your organization, doesn't he? Do you think he'd talk?"

"It crossed my mind, you can be sure of that. But anyways, there was a silver lining to this cloud."

"What's that?" I asked.

"Those feds that took Bobby, they weren't really feds."

"Keep going."

"About two hours after they took him, a couple of cops on our payroll found Bobby's body in a ditch in Staten Island. His throat was cut from ear to ear."

An alarm went off in my head. "Shit, like the girls?"

"Yep, like the girls."

"You're right. Those weren't feds." I rubbed my temples to ward off the headache I felt developing. "But who the fuck are they?"

"I don't know, but Bobby was a pretty tough son of a bitch, and from the bruises on his knuckles, it's pretty evident he put up one hell of a fight." Don stopped and pulled something from his pocket. "Cops found this clenched tight in his hand."

"Let me see that." I held my hand out, and he placed it in my palm. It was a pin, one I recognized right away. "Do you know what this is?" I asked.

The Don shook his head. "I was hoping you could tell me."

I held it up. "This is a Chi's Finishing School pin. Four of my kids have them. And when I say it's their most prized possession, I'm not exaggerating."

"It's a fucking pin. What's the big deal?"

"All I can tell you is that pin is the key to getting into one of the most exclusive secret societies in the world. To replace it costs over 100K, and I know because my flighty daughter Paris lost hers three years ago." A lot of things were running through my mind, but I knew I needed to get to Vegas and Junior as soon as I could. "What would a piece of shit like Bobby be doing with this? He didn't go to the school."

"I'm thinking he snatched it off of whoever was killing him. Bobby wasn't no graduate of Chi's, but he was a tough son of a bitch," The Don said with admiration in his voice.

"Hmm, he had to be to get a pin off a graduate of the school."

"Do you think the people who killed Bobby are the same ones responsible for what happened at the Hellfire Club?"

"There's a strong possibility."

It was time to pay a visit to Chi's Finishing School to check on my grandson and get some answers.

Nevada

18

In spite of Demi's attempt to wrangle me into saving Ivan, I reached the headmaster's cottage on time. It was my first visit there, and from the outside, it reminded me of a medieval cottage with its heavy wooden door, which was slightly ajar, clay siding, and steep roof.

"Come in, Nevada," Minister Farrah called out from inside before I even had a chance to knock. The house looked old, but I'm sure it had the most modern surveillance equipment surrounding it.

I pushed the door open and found him sitting on a sofa, sorting through some paperwork. He was wearing a long, colorful dashiki and a matching kufi cap. I approached him, and he got up, shook my hand, and motioned for me to take a chair across from him.

"My wife is in the process of making us some hot fudge sundaes. I know I invited you for tea, but it's a warm day, and ice cream seems more appropriate."

"You'll get no complaints out of me, teacher." I sat down, looking around the room at all the antique weaponry and Chi's Finishing School memorabilia he had displayed. His place was like a museum.

"Your home is amazing," I said.

"Thank you. A hundred years' worth of history in this room." Minister Farrah glanced around proudly. "So, how are you getting along? I know it's a little tougher on you Elites who come from outside our system."

"I'm adjusting," I replied.

"I'd say you're doing more than that," Minister Farrah said with a slightly raised brow. "I've heard nothing but good things. Wasn't it you who led the group who protected Ivan Igor from his father's drunken attack last night?"

I could not hide my shocked expression. "You heard about that, huh?"

"Not much I don't hear about when it comes to this school and its Elite members."

"Ivan didn't deserve that treatment. His father was being abusive," I replied.

"From what I hear, his father was upset about him being removed from the Elites. Some would say he was teaching Ivan a lesson."

"There is no lesson that can come from beating someone who has already submitted. You taught me that," I retorted.

He chuckled. "So, my lessons have not gone on deaf ears."

"No, sir."

"Good, because you will need them. Tomorrow, you will be offered the position of squad leader." Did he just say what I think he said? Being asked to be a squad leader was like being promoted to a battalion commander at Chi's. It was one of the highest honors that could be bestowed on an Elite.

"But I just got here. There are students that have worked the past three years to obtain that rank," I said.

"Yes, it's quite a bit of responsibility, but none of them have been accepted into Harvard University, had your family background or lineage, and more importantly, none have been trained by me. You are well deserving and ready to lead, I believe."

His wife, a very reserved woman who looked to be in her sixties, entered the room carrying a tray with bowls of ice cream and toppings. She placed it on the coffee table in front of us.

"Thank you, Mrs. Farrah," I said.

"You are welcome, Nevada. It is good to see you again."

"You as well."

She kissed Minister Farrah's cheek and took her leave.

"You have a nice wife," I said.

"Thank you. A good woman can take you far in this world, especially if she's your friend first." Minister Farrah picked up his bowl of ice cream, pouring hot fudge on it as he glanced at me with knowing eyes that told me he knew everything about Natasha and me. "Now, let's not change the subject. I have all the confidence in the world that you can be one of the best squad leaders this school has ever had, and this school has had some good ones—most of whom you are related to. But I will not sugarcoat it. Being squad leader with your last name will not be easy. All of the other squads will be coming for you, and you will not have many true friends outside your group."

That didn't sound too appealing, but something told me I was not being given a choice to decline. "Do I get to pick my own squad, or is it picked for me?"

"You will get to choose. But understand, the choices you make may come back to haunt you. A squad has many parts and many personalities. In many ways, you are their friend, their brother, and at times their father. They are your responsibility. So, are you up to the challenge of leadership?"

"It's a little intimidating, but yes, I think I can rise to the occasion," I replied, leaning forward in my chair. "So, if called, teacher, I will accept."

"Good. Now let us finish our ice cream before it melts." He began digging in, and I grabbed the hot fudge and poured a generous pool onto my ice cream.

I enjoyed the rest of my visit with Minister Farrah, and I learned a lot of things about the politics and inner workings of the school. It felt good to be treated like an adult and someone with intelligence. He made me feel like he trusted me with the valuable information he was sharing.

"So," he said as he walked me to the door, "same time next week?"

"I'd like that."

A photo hanging by the door caught my eye, and he noticed. "I take it you know those men?" He handed it to me.

"I've never seen this particular picture, but I think this is my father's squad."

"Yes, indeed. The greatest group of Elites I ever had the pleasure to teach. They saved the school from the Black Hand, literally."

"So I've been told. But who are those people? I know Uncle Junior, Daryl Graham, and of course my dad, but who are these other four?" I pointed at the two white men, a Latin man and a woman.

"The man to the right of your father is Jason Starks, our recently departed headmaster. He was a very capable man, destined for greatness. It saddens me to think that something as simple as COVID-19 could kill him."

"Wow. I didn't know he was on my father's squad. And who is that?" I asked, pointing to the Latino man.

"The man on the right is Raul Hernandez, the illegitimate son of Pablo Hernandez, the Colombian drug lord. Raul died protecting the school from our greatest enemy, the Black Hand."

I could see the sadness in Minister Farrah's eyes, so I moved on.

"And who is this?" I pointed at the other man, who was so muscular he looked like he was on steroids.

"That's Demetri Igor," he said, and my tongue almost fell out of my mouth. "He and your father were very close at one time. He would have taken a bullet for your father, and vice versa."

"Ivan's father?"

"Yes, Ivan's father." Minister Farrah nodded.

"He looks so different. What happened to him?" In the picture, he looked to be my dad's age, but the man I'd run into last night looked closer to my grandpa's age.

"The years have not been kind to Demetri. His wife stole his inheritance and then left him and his child for another man. He's raised Ivan the best he could, but the bottle became his best friend. I gave him a job here at the school so Ivan would get a good education before I left for retirement in New York. I personally feel that his biggest mistake was choosing his wife over your father's friendship," Minister Farrah said sadly. "Vegas was Demetri's moral compass."

"What about her? Who is she?" I pointed to the woman in fatigues and black-and-green camouflage face paint. She looked familiar.

"Ah, yes. She was one of the most capable women the school has ever produced. I'm surprised you don't recognize her."

"Do I know her?" She really did look familiar.

"I believe so. You do know Marie Hernandez, don't you?"

"Wait a minute. Are you talking about Ms. Marie from the Hellfire Club?"

Minister Farrah nodded, and I lifted the picture to get a closer look.

Oh my God, it is Ms. Marie.

"I didn't know she was a student here, let alone that she was an Elite."

"Yes, she was for a while, but she left the school before she could complete her training after her brother died at the hands of the Black Hand."

"How come no one told me about this?"

"I can only believe that it was a shameful and hurtful time in her life. From what I've been told, she and your father did not speak for more than a decade."

"I'd never heard that, but it makes sense." I tried to hand him the photo back to hang on the wall, but he shook his head.

"Keep it," he said. "That picture is a part of your family history, and as a squad leader, it may give you strength and help you one day."

Vegas

19

Sunday dinner was not something you missed in my family, not unless you were doing something mighty important. Sunday was my mom's day, and none of us wanted to deal with her wrath if you weren't there. That went double for me since I'd been spending all my time hunting down the people responsible for the massacre at the Hellfire Club. So, despite the many questions about the investigation and Marie I knew I would hear from my family members, I arrived an hour early for dinner. This gave me the time I needed to talk to Pop about his sit-down with Don Fredricko.

I found him right where I expected, sitting in his favorite chair, puffing on a cigar. Junior was sitting beside him, and on the table that separated them was a half-empty decanter of Pop's favorite brandy.

"Didn't think we were going to see you tonight, but I'm glad you're here." Pop placed his cigar in an ashtray and lifted the decanter. "Drink?"

"Yeah, I'll take one."

He filled a glass halfway and handed it to me. I took a seat on the sofa across from them.

"The plan was to stay at the hospital until Marie went to sleep, but that didn't work out quite the way I expected, considering I got myself banned from the hospital."

Pop sat up in his chair, glaring across the coffee table at me intensely. "You got yourself what? What the hell happened?"

"It's a long story, but I almost beat the shit out of an orderly." I took a sip of my brandy, which was smooth and very much needed. "Long story short, let's just say anything we get out of Marie is going to be suspect. She's got a long way back to recovery."

"Sorry to hear that, son. I know how important she is to you."

"Yeah, she is," I said solemnly, then changed the subject to avoid sinking into my feelings. "So, how'd your meeting go with the Don? He get anything out of Bobby?"

"Well, kind of like you, it's a long story and complicated, but the bottom line is Bobby Two Fingers is dead."

"Did he talk before he died?"

"From what I'm told, he said he had something on Marie, but that's when the fake feds showed up and took him away," Pop explained.

Junior and I shared confused looks.

"Fake feds?" Junior asked.

"Yep, evidently they're the ones who killed Bobby. Cut his throat from ear to ear just like they did the girls at the Hellfire Club."

"Damn. This isn't some Mickey Mouse operation. You've got to be pretty sophisticated and have a lot of balls to walk up to Don Fredricko's people masquerading as the feds," I said.

"Well, son, it gets even deeper and a little more personal for you and your brother." Pop pulled something small from his pocket. I could see from the troubled expression on Junior's face that it was concerning. Pop reached over and handed it to me.

"Shit. Where the fuck did you find that?" I was sitting on the edge of my seat now.

"The cops found it clutched in Bobby's hand. They think he snatched it off whoever killed him."

"It's a Chi's Elite pin," Junior said.

That pin was more valuable to an Elite graduate of Chi's than a crown was to a king. They weren't an everyday fashion statement, though. Usually the graduates only wore them in situations where they expected to be around other Elite graduates, to identify their common background. In this case, I wondered, was it a graduate wearing it on a mission to murder an informant?

"Fuck," I groaned. Chi's was a special place to my family, a source of pride. To think that another graduate of the school could be responsible for Marie's and my son's pain made it feel worse than it already did. "You said Bobby was picked up by feds, plural. If one of them was wearing a pin, I wonder if they all were."

"Well, this situation certainly isn't getting any easier." Pop gulped down what was left of his drink. "We may have to call in some of our family and friends from down south."

Junior told us, "I don't know if this is significant or not, but Detective Bryant confirmed one of the killers at the Hellfire Club is a redhead."

Junior's comment caused me immediate alarm. "You sure about that?"

"I met up with him about an hour ago. The autopsies came back, and one of the girls had a short red hair embedded in her wound. They think it's from her assailant."

"Are we sure that hair didn't belong to one of the other girls?" Pop asked.

"None of them had red hair," Junior replied. "Initial forensics says most likely from a man."

"How long until they get a DNA back on it?" Pop asked.

"It's going to take a while. There was no root on the hair. But even if they extract DNA, we all know that doesn't mean there's going to be a match."

People trained at Chi's were very good at avoiding any permanent record of their existence, even if it meant having a person on the inside who could wipe your fingerprints and DNA from law enforcement databases.

"Well, it's not much to go on, but it's all we've got right now," Pop said. "In light of this, I think I need to go to Chi's to see what Minister Farrah knows that could help us."

I had heard everything they said, but my mind was still stuck on the pin. Marie's warnings about Nevada plagued my mind. I had cast them off as a crazy rant, but now I knew that someone from Chi's was involved, and her words took on new meaning.

"It appears Marie's not as crazy as I thought," I said. "Let me go to Chi's, Pop. I think my son might be in danger."

Marie

20

"Twinkle, twinkle, little star. How I wonder what you are . . ."

I heard my voice singing, but I couldn't say that I felt my lips moving. The only thing I felt was the comforting sting of my fingers plucking out my hair, one by one, strand by strand. I was sitting cross-legged on my bed, staring out of the barred window. The moon was pretty that night. So were the stars. Oh! The stars. They made me want to sing. But wasn't I already singing? I couldn't remember. Just in case, I started over.

"Twinkle, twinkle, little star. How I wonder what you are. Up above a world so high . . . so high . . . so . . ."

What were the lyrics again? It was becoming harder and harder to think straight. I was so sleepy. I hadn't been to sleep in two days, because I couldn't sleep. If I did, I was dead, and I knew it. I had to stay awake. I had to stay awake. I just had to.

"I can't go to sleep," I murmured to myself as I plucked a few more hairs. "I have to stay awake. They'll kill me if I go to sleep."

I wanted so badly to go to my happy place inside of my head, to escape this madness. It was the place where my girls were waiting to see me, so I could tell them how beautiful they were. The place where they told me they forgave me and loved me. But I knew if I went there, I would become complacent and comfortable, and eventually, I would go to sleep. So I hadn't seen my girls in two days. I knew they missed me, but they would understand. I had to be the one to survive. They would forgive me for my absence.

Knock! Knock!

My body jolted at the sound of a knock on my door, and I peered meekly over my shoulder. I watched the door open slowly and my heart raced. Had the time finally come? Was my life over?

It was Beth, but even the sight of my usual nurse didn't comfort me. I didn't like her old ass. She was always trying to put me to sleep.

"Time to take your medicine," she said in her usual annoying sing-song voice.

"I'm not taking those fucking pills!"

"You have to, dear. We've gone over this."

"Fuck. You." I folded my arms defiantly.

"Marie, between you being so grumpy and those hideous bags under your eyes, you need to sleep." Her tone had more edge to it now, revealing the inner bitch I always knew was there.

"I don't wanna! I'm not gonna!"

She sighed. "All right, have it your way. If you don't want to take the pills, I have a nice shot waiting for you. Is that what you want?" She gave me a malicious grin, and I knew she would enjoy giving me that shot.

The thought of being held down while a needle was jabbed in my arm scared me. There would be no fighting my sleep then.

"Fine," I said finally. "Just give me the fucking pills."

"Good girl." She handed me a small cup with two pills in it.

I tossed them back and took the other cup filled with water. I swallowed a big gulp and opened my mouth so she could see that the pills were gone. She gave me an approving nod.

"Good girl," she said again like I was her pet. "You'll get some good sleep with those. And maybe tomorrow we can talk about doing something with your hair. You're so pretty. It's a shame what you've done to yourself." She yawned. "Gosh, I feel like I need a nap myself."

When she left, I waited a few moments to make sure she wouldn't double back. Then I stuck my finger in my mouth and fished the two pills out from where I'd stored them in my cheek. I'd made a small incision in my pillow, and I stored those pills with all of the others that I'd pretended to take.

"The bitch wants to talk shit about my hair," I mumbled to myself and sat cross-legged again. I faced the door and began to rock. "Nobody . . . nobody said anything about her fat-ass stomach. Yeah, I should have. I should have told the bitch maybe she should take the sleeping pills. Maybe then she'd skip a few meals. Bitch . . . always . . . always trying to put me to sleep. I can't sleep. I have to stay awake."

My fingers found their way to my head again. A lot of my hair was gone, but I still had plenty of good strands left to go. I plucked and rocked and plucked some more. The brief pain that came when each hair was pulled from my scalp was now almost a pleasure. A delicacy. It was one of the only things that I could control since Vegas had put me in that hellhole.

"Vegas."

I wonder if he had thought of me. He couldn't have. He said he loved me, but the only time I seemed to see him was when he wanted to ask me fifty million questions. Never to take me home.

Home . . . I didn't have one of those anymore. I couldn't go back to that club. I wouldn't. The last things I saw in there were buried deep in my memory. The Hellfire Club had once been my place of business, but also my sanctuary. Now it was my hell. I never wanted to step foot inside of it ever again. The devil could have it.

"Marie . . . Marie?" I could hear someone calling me, and I tried to reply, but nothing came out of my mouth. That's when I realized I was dreaming.

I had to wake up! Sleep was not my friend.

"Time to go home."

Upon hearing the word *home,* I blinked open my eyes. It didn't take but a second for me to wish I'd kept them closed, because hovering over me was my worst nightmare—the nurse with the red hair who called himself John Wilson. Gone was the look of fear he'd worn when Vegas had him pinned against the wall. What replaced it was an intense glare. He stared at me like he despised me.

My breathing turned slow and shallow, and I couldn't bring myself to make a noise, let alone to move. *What the fuck are you going to do now, Marie?* I felt trapped.

"What are you doing here?" I croaked out.

The bastard didn't answer, just gave me a sinister smile.

"Get out! You can't be here," I screamed, praying that some-one would recognize my panic above all the screams coming from the other loony patients and come rescue me.

"Where's Beth? Where's my nurse?"

He stared at me with blank eyes for a while. I couldn't tell if he had even heard what I said, or maybe he just didn't care. I uncrossed my legs and scooted back toward my pillows.

"She's taking a nap." He finally answered me, leaning in closer. "Something you'll be doing soon as well if you don't tell me where it is."

There was confirmation of what I'd suspected all along. He was one of them.

"I told them I don't have it. It was stolen," I whispered.

"I guess we'll have to find it ourselves." He lifted his shirt, exposing a knife.

Tears welled up in my eyes because I'd seen a similar knife in the past, right before all of my girls were gutted. I was about to die.

"And without it, you're no good to us anymo—"

I realized that I wasn't ready to go. Not yet.

When he reached to yank me off the bed, I used that op-portunity to knee him square in the nuts. The beautiful thing about being a madam all these years was that I'd had a lot of practice. In fact, I'd gotten my technique down to a science. Most people think a swift kick in the balls is good, but it's nothing compared to the driving force of a knee connecting and driving his nuts through his groin and practically out his anus.

His face turned as red as his hair, and his eyes bulged. While he was gasping for air, I jumped off the bed and grabbed the medicine tray that Beth had left behind. He tried to grab me again, but he was still too winded and hurt.

I brought the tray crashing down on his head twenty times before I stopped. Then I smashed his head with the flowerpot Vegas had given me. I heard a crack. I was not sure if it was his head or the pot, but I didn't really care.

Instinct took over from that point. I went into survival mode, and my head felt clearer than it had in weeks. I reached into one of his pockets and took all of the money he had in his wallet. I reached in his other pocket and found car keys with a tag from a car rental company.

"You'll have to ditch the car once you're far enough away," I told myself, clutching the keys in my hand and stashing the knife on my waist.

On the front of his work jacket was a key card that all of the staff wore. I'd watched them use it to open locked doors in the building. I snatched the key card and ran to the door, leaving behind the flimsy slippers they gave to their patients. I was better off barefoot.

I was scared, but adrenaline was pumping through my veins, so I pushed on. This was a window of opportunity I might never get again. I placed the card by the sensor on the wall, and I heard the soft buzz as my room door unlocked.

"Yes, yes!" I cheered in a whisper when I was able to turn the doorknob.

I stepped into the hallway and saw that it was empty. The night nurses were either in other patient rooms or napping behind some desk, I assumed. Either way, it gave me an opportunity to get out unseen.

"Okay, okay. Which way? Which way?" I hit myself in the head with my palm, trying to remember the way the orderlies had walked the first time they brought me there. The white walls were so confusing. I didn't remember. I couldn't . . . *Yes, you can, Marie. Think!*

When we first came in, we walked down the hallway and made two lefts at the end of every hall. And then we made a right at the water fountain. I looked at the end of the hallway outside my room and saw the same water fountain from my memory, which meant I had to make a left and then two rights.

"Okay. Okay. Go, Marie. Go!"

I willed my legs to carry me as fast as they could. If anyone saw me, they would sound the alarm and try to take me right back in the room. I would slice and dice them all before I let that happen.

I was out of breath by the time I reached the elevator, scanned the card, and pushed the button. When the elevator chimed and the doors opened, I jumped in and jammed the button for the first floor repeatedly, willing the doors to close faster. Finally, the elevator started to descend, and I was one step closer to freedom.

I almost jumped for joy when those elevator doors opened and I saw the double doors. Then my elation deflated just as fast when I spotted the security guard at the front desk by the door. His back was to me, and he seemed to be engrossed in something on his phone. I was surprised that the ding of the elevator hadn't drawn his attention, but then I crept closer and noticed that he had ear bud in his ears.

I was prepared to slice his throat for my freedom, but as I wrapped my hand around the knife handle, a snore escaped his mouth. He was sound asleep. I relaxed my grip on the handle and tiptoed away from him. When I was close enough to the door, I ran faster than Angela Basset did out of that hotel room in *What's Love Got to Do with It.*

I welcomed the cool night air smacking me in my face. I ran all the way to the parking lot, hitting the unlock button on the key in my hands as I pointed it toward random cars in the lot. Finally, the lights to a Nissan Altima flickered and the horn beeped. I got inside and zoomed away from the hospital. I was free!

Nevada

21

"Dude, your girl Natasha is over there kicking ass on the rifle range." Clem pointed my attention in her direction. Natasha was lying on her stomach and had drawn a crowd with her skills with a sniper rifle. "She's seven for ten at three hundred meters. That's the second best shot in the school."

"That's pretty impressive. I only got five. That's a long shot. Guess she was serious when she told me her goal was to be a hitwoman."

I glanced over in her direction and caught her eye. She winked, and I winked back. Natasha seemed happy, and that made me happy. We'd been kayfabe for almost a week, and everyone seemed to be buying it.

"Here's a question for you, Clem. If she's second, then who's number one?"

"That would be me." Raheem stood up from the bench where he'd been talking to Cassie, a girl he'd been trying to hook up with. He walked confidently past us. "Just like I'm going to be number one in handguns. You boys coming, or are you afraid?"

We had all been waiting for our turn on the pistol range. Every month, the Elites had mandatory handgun, rifle, physical training, and hand-to-hand combat evaluations. It wasn't a competition, but the competitive nature in all of us made it one. Everyone knew who was on the bottom and who was on top in each category. Because I'd started the semester late, I'd missed the initial evaluations, but that didn't mean I was any less competitive.

Raheem and Richard walked over to the gun range, both choosing 9 mm Glocks.

"Come on, Nevada. Might as well get it over with. He's going to kick our asses anyway." Clem rose from the bench and I followed him. He chose a Glock, while I chose a Smith and Wesson M&P 2.0, the gun I used at home.

Brother Elijah, our weapons instructor, gave us a few safety instructions and some basic tips and then said, "You each have ten shots. Your evaluation will be based on those ten shots, and please remember, this is not a competition. You are all going to get better with practice."

"You can't get better than this, Brother Elijah," Raheem joked, putting on his noise-deafening headphones. He sure was confident.

Brother Elijah shook his head, looking amused. I'm sure he was used to the overconfidence of the Elite students, like most of our instructors were. Instead of scolding us about it, they usually just waited until the challenges they put before us knocked our egos down a few pegs.

When we all had our headphones on, he said, "Begin."

I went into a zone. Imagining I was in my basement at our home firing rage, I zeroed in on the target and listened for my grandmother's voice. She had taught me to shoot. *Lift your shoulders, straighten out your back, aim, and pull the trigger like the gun is a piece of you hand.*" I squeezed the trigger ten times.

We removed our headphones and put our weapons away while Brother Elijah retrieved our targets, then brought our results back to us.

"Raheem, eight out of ten." Brother Elijah handed him his target. "You continue to be consistent."

Raheem smiled and gave a shrug, trying hard to look humble, although he was far from it. He sat down next to Cassie again.

Brother Elijah handed Richard his target. "Richard, four out of ten. You're going to need more after class instruction."

Richard looked disappointed. I was going to have to help him.

"Clem six out of ten, an improvement of one. I can see you've been practicing. Well done."

Clem pumped his fist in the air.

Brother Elijah walked over to me. He stared down at the target, then back up at me. "Nevada, a very impressive nine out of ten. Well done, young man! I look forward to seeing how you do with moving targets." He offered me his hand.

I heard some applause, and that's when I realized that the crowd that had surrounded Natasha was now behind me.

"That's my man," I heard Natasha shout.

Clem came running up behind me, and then Natasha, Demi, and Arielle surrounded me too.

"Congratulations, Nevada." Arielle gave me a nod of approval. "Number one at hand-to-hand combat, PT, and handguns. That's pretty impressive."

"Thanks, but like Brother Elijah said, it's not a competition," I said, even though of course I was proud of what I'd accomplished.

I could feel Natasha move closer to me and take my hand.

"Clearly you're new around here," Arielle joked. She tossed a glance at Natasha and as she walked away, I heard her mutter, "Everything is a competition around here."

It took me a second to realize her meaning, but Natasha clearly understood the jab. She squeezed my hand tighter and whispered, "Jealous bitch," at Arielle's back.

Clem smirked like he was amused by the muted cat fight, but at least he didn't try to egg it on further. "I'm just trying to get better," he said with a shrug.

"Students!" Brother Elijah's voice boomed. Instantly, everyone stopped what they were doing and faced him. "I am very pleased with your training today. Most of you have shown quite a bit of improvement. As the weeks and months go by, you will hone your skills until you truly become the best that you can be. And with that said, I have recommended to the head that you are all ready to be placed in squads."

Excited whispers erupted, and even I was a little thrilled. I hoped that Clem, Raheem, and I would be on the same squad.

"First, I will name the squad leaders, and they will have the remainder of the week to add the other members to their squad, which will be comprised of five Elites and two Grails," Brother Elijah explained. "The leaders are as follows—Margaret, Muhammad, Simon, Alice, Raheem, Nevada . . ."

After I heard my name, I stopped listening to the others. True to his word, Minister Farrah had made me squad leader. I wanted to jump and shout, but I knew that was not what a leader would do, so I straightened my back and stood, silent and proud.

"All right. Once you have been assigned to a squad, your squad leader will report back to me." Brother Elijah looked at all of us, but his eyes fell on me. He nodded his head slowly, then took his leave.

Raheem came to stand beside me. "Congrats. I'd hoped we were gonna be on the same team. The way you shoot, you would have made me one hell of a wingman," he said, looking genuinely bummed out. "I guess I'm going to have to get my rocks off kicking your ass."

"You can try." I offered my hand, and we embraced. "I'm happy for you, Raheem."

"Happy for you too, bro. Let's turn this place upside down."

"I'm happy for the both of you." Clem slapped us both on the back. "Really I am. But me? I wouldn't want all that pressure."

"Your ass would lead us to our deaths every time, Clem," Raheem joked, and we all laughed. "However, I could use a good wingman."

"No offense, Raheem," Clem told him, "but I gotta go with Nevada—if he'll have me. Our families kinda go back."

"You're my first choice. You know that," I said. We shook hands, although I did feel bad for Raheem.

"Well, then I'm about to go talk to Charlie O before someone snatches him up. His evaluations were pretty high. I'll catch up with you guys later."

Once Raheem was gone, I barely had a second to breathe before Natasha was hovering over me. She had a determined look in her eyes, and I already knew what she wanted. I just wasn't sure if giving it to her was the best thing for her or me.

"What about me?" she asked.

Before I could even open my mouth, Arielle and Demi approached me as well. Were they all just going to put me on the spot at once?

"Nevada Duncan!" Mrs. Farrah, who also doubled as Minister Farrah's secretary, called my name as she headed my way. She had no idea how grateful I was for the distraction.

"Yes, ma'am?"

"Nevada, the headmaster would like to see you in his office immediately."

"Of course." I turned toward the girls. "Hey, why don't we all get together over dinner and chat?" I gave them a quick smile then followed behind Mrs. Farrah, grateful to have just earned some time to think how to put together a team without hurting anyone's feelings.

Vegas

22

I placed a cup of tea on the edge of the desk and sat back in the leather chair. Despite how comfortable the chair was, I was nervous, and I was sure it showed. There weren't many men other than Pop who could make me feel that way without saying a word. Regrettably, Minister Farrah was one of those men, and he was sitting right in front of me, staring a hole through my chest.

"You do understand that this is highly unusual." Minister Farrah finally spoke in a grim voice. He had a cup of tea in front of him as well, but he hadn't touched it since I'd broken the news to him. "An explanation would be helpful."

"It's personal, a family matter, sir," I replied, suddenly wishing I'd brought Pop or Junior with me. The man had a way of sizing you up that was truly uncomfortable.

The door opened, and Nevada walked into the room wearing his school uniform. I could tell he'd really grown up in a very short time, and for that, I was proud. But I could also tell my son had that same nervousness when it came to being around Minister Farrah. I don't think he even noticed I was in the room at first.

"They said you wanted to see me, sir?" The familiar voice made me smile.

"Yes, actually, it was your father who wanted to see you." Minister Farrah gestured toward me.

"Dad?"

"Hey, son." I rose from my chair, and we embraced. "Boy, you have no idea how good it is to see you."

"Good to see you too," he said. "But why are you here? Did something happen back home? Are Grandma and Grandpa okay?"

"Yeah, they're fine. Everybody's fine."

"Then why are you here? Uncle Orlando handles the international part of the business now. It was him I expected to pop up. I wasn't expecting to see you until Gala."

"Your father is here to take you back home, Nevada," Minister Farrah chimed in, letting his displeasure be known in his snippy tone. "Perhaps you can change his mind."

Nevada glanced at him then me. "Is this true? You want me to go home?"

"There's no easy way to say this, son, but yeah, I'm taking you home," I said with no further explanation. "Now say goodbye to Minister Farrah. I'll meet you outside." I just wanted to get out of that office. I loved the man, but he had a way of taking me out of my comfort zone. I took a step toward the door.

"But Dad—" Nevada grabbed my arm, something the old obedient him would never do. He really was growing up. He looked over at Minister Farrah as if he could save him. I may have had a healthy fear for the man, but this was my kid, and that fear stopped when it came to his safety. "Teacher."

"Don't look at him. He's not your father. I am," I reminded him, pulling my arm free. I had no problem with Nevada asking me questions, but as much as I loved Minister Farrah and the school, I could not trust him until I was sure who that pin belonged to.

"What's going on? Did something happen to my mom?" I guess my tone scared him.

"No, son, your mother's fine, but we have some family business to handle. Now, let's go! I'll explain on the plane."

I turned to Minister Farrah. "No disrespect, Minister, but this family emergency needs to be addressed, and there is no changing my mind."

"He is your son. Do as you see fit," he said with a nod and then I left the office.

Natasha

23

"He's gone!" Clem ran out of the dormitory toward me and Richard with a look of horror on his face, sending my anxiety through the roof. After being called to the headmaster's office, Nevada seemed to have just disappeared. A fast-spreading rumor claimed that he'd been kicked out of school for drugs. I did not believe it, and neither did most of his friends, but his sudden absence was cause for concern.

"Are you sure? Perhaps he went for a walk or a run?" I said, trying to reassure myself. "He likes to run."

"No." Clem shook his head. "All his things are gone, Natasha. He's gone, gone."

I wanted to grab him by the shoulders and shake him. *He can't be gone. He just can't.*

"Who would have thought, Nevada Duncan, campus king-pin." Richard stood there snickering like a gossip columnist. "You can never trust the quiet ones, my old man used to say. They're the sneakiest."

"Don't say that! That's not true," I snapped back at Richard. "Nevada didn't do drugs or sell them. When did you ever see him with drugs? He didn't even drink alcohol, and he would not leave without even saying goodbye." I was trying keep it together.

"Hold on there, missy. Don't kill the messenger. I like the guy personally, but everybody knows his family's involved with drugs. And if it walks like a duck and quacks like a duck, dammit, it's usually a duck." He was laughing, but Clem and I wore identical somber expressions. I noticed Clem flexing his fist like he might be thinking about punching him in the face. Now I understood why so many people disliked Richard. He just never had anything good to say.

"You know what, Richard? You're an ass," I said angrily. "And you wouldn't be saying this shit if Nevada was around, would you?"

"Of course not, because he'd kick your ass." Clem stepped up to him. "But you keep talking like that and I might do it myself."

Richard took a fearful step back, quickly deflecting the conversation in another direction. "Hey, there's Arielle. Maybe she knows something."

Arielle, who supposedly had connections in the front office, walked over to us with a grim face.

"You find anything out?" Clem asked in hurry.

"Yeah." She sighed. "I just left the administration building. I'm sorry to say, he really is gone."

"Shit," Clem murmured.

"What do you mean he's gone? Nevada would not just leave without saying goodbye. He's not that kind of person." I couldn't control the emotion that took over my voice.

"His father came and got him. Some type of family emergency," Arielle said.

That was actually a relief to me. He didn't leave by choice. He left out of duty. "When is he coming back?" I asked.

"From what I was just told, he's not. They're already talking about naming a squad leader in his place."

This was terrible news. Our relationship might have only been kayfabe, but I felt like Nevada and I had formed some sort of bond, and now I might never see him again. Then Arielle said something that reminded me of an even worse consequence of Nevada's sudden absence.

"Oh, Natasha," she said, "Dean Wilensky is looking for you. He said it was imperative that he see you."

At the mention of Dean Wilensky, my knees became weak, and I found it hard to breathe. "Oh my God. He can't do this. Nevada can't just leave me like this."

"Calm down, girl," Richard snapped. "We know you and him was all booed up and everything, but you look like you're about to hyperventilate over the man. Take a deep breath."

They did not understand.

I am not a whore. I am not a whore.

Nevada

24

"How long until we're in the air, Rob?" my dad asked as we boarded our family jet.

"Twenty minutes tops," Rob replied from the cockpit. "They're fueling us up now."

Dad and I took our seats. Neither of us had spoken since we left the school, and there was an uneasiness between us that I can't ever remember feeling. He didn't even give me a chance to say goodbye to any of my friends, so I was pretty pissed at him at the moment. Ironically, Ivan was fishing on the side of the moat, so he was the last person from the school I would see. I still couldn't believe I was being forced to leave school just as I was settling in and making new friends, and my dad still hadn't given me an explanation. I'd tried to ask him twice since we left Minister Farrah's office, but he raised his hand to silence me both times. "I'll explain on the plane," he had said. Well, we were on the plane, so it was time for some answers.

"Dad, what the hell is going on? Who knows what my friends are going to think now that I basically disappeared. I was supposed to be a squad leader, you know." My tone was probably not as respectful as it should have been, but I wasn't sorry for that. I wasn't a little kid anymore, and I felt like I was owed some answers.

He turned his head to look at me and I could see from his expression that he was stressed out. "I know, and I'm sorry about that, but I had to get you off campus. I couldn't take a chance that Minister Farrah would hear us on one of the hidden cameras or listening devices around campus."

"They have listening devices?" I probably shouldn't have been surprised that a place with fake forests surrounding the property would also have plenty of other security features hidden in plain sight, but the idea that there were listening devices and cameras watching us around campus was a little creepy.

"State of the art surveillance throughout the campus," Dad confirmed. "Why do you think he knows everything?"

"I just thought he was really smart," I answered, suddenly feeling pretty stupid.

"He is. That's why he put up the cameras and listening devices," Dad replied, chuckling. "The man's responsible for over three hundred children of the most powerful people in the world. He has to have eyes and ears everywhere."

What he was saying actually made sense, but I don't think my fellow students would have liked it any more than I did. I wished there was a way I could go back and warn them.

We were getting off subject, so I steered us right back in. "That's all interesting, Dad, but it doesn't explain why I'm on this plane."

"You're on this plane because I've gotta keep you safe." His expression was intense. I still didn't understand what was going on, but Dad's demeanor was so somber that it almost made me forgive him for pulling me out so abruptly. He wasn't one to make rash decisions, so I knew something had him seriously concerned.

"Safe from what?" I came back at him with the same emotion. "Will you stop beating around the bush? I just wanna know what's going on. I deserve to know what's going on, Dad!"

His eyes widened, probably surprised by my tone, but he didn't get angry. "You're right. You do. I couldn't say it in front of the minister, but the school's not a safe place right now."

Now that surprised me. It also piqued my curiosity. "Why not? Chi's is one of the safest places in the world. You said it yourself—the school can fight off almost any attack."

"It can, unless that attack is coming from within."

I hesitated to think. "I don't understand. Are you saying Minister Farrah is a potential enemy?"

Dad bit down on his lip. "I'm not ruling it out. I'm not ruling anyone out at that school. Son, there's a lot of things about the school, good and bad, you won't find out about until after you're pinned."

I sat back in my chair, folding my arms. "No, not Minister Farrah. He taught and prepared me for this. He even made me a squad leader today. You may not, but I trust him."

"I'll admit him making you a squad leader is a good sign. And, son, I love Minister, but somebody affiliated with the school had something to do with what happened at the Hellfire Club. We have reason to believe that you could be a target for whoever it is."

"Why? I'm just a kid. Who gives a crap about me?" I asked.

"I do, for starters, and because we're getting closer to who did this. Real close. I can feel it." He reached in his pocket and pulled out a piece of gold jewelry. "Have you ever seen one of these before?"

"Yeah, it's a Chi's pin. You guys keep yours in the safe," I answered.

"Well, this one was found in the hands of a guy by the name of Bobby Two Fingers. He ripped it off of one of the people who slit his throat from ear to ear. That sound familiar?"

I felt my stomach tighten with anxiety. "Yes, too familiar." It was all starting to make sense. Dad thought it was possible that Kia's murderer was somehow affiliated with the school. "So that's why you didn't want Minister Farrah to know?"

"I love the guy, but we don't know who we can trust. Whoever's responsible for the deaths has a connection to Chi's, and maybe on the inside."

I sat up in my chair, trying my best to be the adult I wanted to be at that moment. "Dad, let me stay, please."

"Son, did you hear anything I said? This is not a game. This is serious. People are getting killed."

"You mean like the woman I love? If I was anyone else, you'd hand me a gun and tell me to handle my business."

He knew I was right, but he still shook his head. "Well, you're not anyone else. You're my son. It's too dangerous, especially with this redhead motherfucka running around and we don't know what they're looking for or who's their next target."

"Redhead?"

"Yeah, at least one of the killers has red hair. We know that for a fact."

"Dad." I leaned in a little closer to him so he could see the emotion that was behind my eyes. "I respect and love you. We have a very special relationship, wouldn't you say?"

"Yeah, definitely."

"So, I want you to ask yourself something. Did you tell Grandpa what you were planning when you and your squad went up against the Black Hand to save the school?"

"Hell, no! He would've killed me. I would have been on a jet faster than—" He stopped midsentence and shook his head.

I sat there and stared at him, and he stared back at me, "I'm not going behind your back. I'm looking you in the face and telling you what needs to be done, man to man. I'm not a little boy anymore. I can help! I'm the only one on the inside of Chi's that you can trust."

"Nevada, it's my job to protect you." For the first time that I could remember, I heard my dad's voice crack. He continued to study me for a while, probably because he knew I was right that we needed an inside man. "You understand, I'm not gonna be there to cover your ass?"

"I'm a Duncan. I can do this," I whispered.

Dad leaned over and looked down the aisle. "Rob!"

"Yeah, boss?" Rob stepped out of the cockpit.

"Open the doors. Nevada's getting off," he said, then turned to me. "But I need to know where you are at all times. Here. Put this on." He handed me his watch. "It's got its own wi-fi, so I'll be able to keep tabs on you. You can also use it to text me, even if you're a hundred feet underground or thirty thousand feet in the sky." He unbuckled his seat belt and grabbed me. "Check in twice a day or you're going to see me the next morning. Don't take any chances. If something were to happen to you . . ." He let his voice trail off.

"It won't, Dad. I'll be careful. And I'll tell you everything I find."

"Okay, but one last piece of advice. You need to put together a team you can trust. Fuck winning competitions. Pick people who will cover your ass and have skills to do it." His voice was dead serious. "I'll be back in three weeks for the gala, but hopefully we'll catch these bastards by then."

He kissed my cheek and let go of me. I grabbed my knapsack and headed for the exit with my head held high.

LC

25

"Move! Move! Trauma patient coming through!"

I entered the Clayborn Institute and was barely able to step out of the way in time as doctors and nurses rushed by with a stretcher. The patient was in pretty bad shape, covered in so much blood it was hard to tell where it was coming from. The entire hospital seemed to be busy, and all I wanted to do was make it to the elevator.

"Pop! Over here," Junior called from the other side of the lobby. He was holding the elevator, and I rushed across to get in. "He text you too?"

"Yeah. Any idea what this is all about?"

The elevator door shut, and Junior pushed the button for the fifth floor.

"Nope. He wouldn't say anything over the phone." Junior answered.

I shook my head warily. "I don't like it, Junior. This situation with Marie is getting out of hand. Did you take a look outside? There are way too many cop cars in front of this building. And why the hell are we meeting Bryant here? He's not supposed to even know Marie is at this hospital."

"I know, Pop. I was thinking about that the entire ride over here."

When we finally stepped off the elevator, Detective Bryant was standing there waiting for us. The corridor was filled with police officers, and from the hustle and bustle, there was no doubt in my mind this was an active crime scene.

"What happened?" I questioned Bryant.

"Your girl Marie happened," he replied.

"Oh God, she's not dead, is she?" I glanced down the hall at the men and women wearing blue coroner's jackets. Damn it, the last thing I wanted to do was explain to Vegas that something had happened to Marie on my watch.

"No, but she did leave a body," Detective Bryant said, motioning for us to follow.

"Jesus Christ, this is just going from bad to worse," I mumbled as we made our way down the hall.

"Open it," Bryant demanded when we reached the gurney.

The coroner unzipped the black body bag, and the first thing I saw was the red hair. The man's face was swollen badly, and I could tell that his jaw was broken.

"Marie did this?" Junior commented once we were in the hallway again. "I guess she still got it."

"Yeah, she did a number on him. He died from blunt force trauma to the head."

"Do you know who he is?" I asked.

"His hospital ID says John Wilson," Bryant replied.

"But you don't believe that, do you?" Junior asked, picking up on Bryant's tone.

"Nope, his ID and credit cards are a fake. There is no John Wilson on record. He's a ghost, but I know you saw what I saw."

"The red hair."

"Yep. We're gonna run his DNA through the lab and see what we come up with, but I'm pretty confident we found our guy."

"Why? Just because he has red hair?" Junior asked.

"No, because we found a fifteen-inch knife next his body that I'll stake my pension on matches the knife that killed Bobby Two Fingers."

"Hmm . . ." It wasn't adding up. "And where was the staff when all of this was happening?" I asked.

"This is the shit that's going to blow your mind," Bryant said. "They were all asleep. Every last one of them, including the security guard at the front desk."

"Get the hell outta here," Junior replied. "So you think he drugged the floor with doughnuts?"

Bryant threw up his hands and started to laugh. "Bingo! We watched the surveillance video. This guy strolled in here with three dozen doughnuts, handing them out to everybody like he worked at Krispy Kreme. An hour later, they were all knocked out."

"Passed out 'sleep? In a mental institute?" Junior asked incredulously.

"He knocked out the entire staff so that he could go and kill Marie."

"And I'm sure he planned to wipe all the security footage before he left. He made one wrong calculation, though," Junior said. "He wasn't counting on Marie being a fighter."

"That's for sure," I said, looking back at the room where his body lay. "So, what's next, Bryant?"

"The most important thing is we find your girl Marie before she does something stupid. I'm pretty sure I can make any charges against her go away. She's pretty much the victim here, but we don't need her on the loose."

Bryant walked away and left Junior and me alone. I let out a deep sigh as we walked to the elevator.

"What's on your mind, Pop?" Junior asked.

"I was just thinking—which one of us is going to tell Vegas Marie's on the loose?"

Nevada

26

As the SUV approached the castle and began to cross the moat, my body was filled with all kinds of nervous energy and my mind was consumed with a jumble of thoughts. Dad's advice had been to put together a squad based on skills, not on winning competitions. If things got dangerous, who would I trust to have my back? And who had the necessary skills?

I still couldn't believe my dad had allowed me to return to school. One thing I'd learned early on was, like my grandpa, my dad was not a man who was easily swayed or convinced about anything, unless he respected you. The fact that I was on that bridge spoke volumes about our relationship and the newfound respect he had for me as a man, a Duncan man. I was not going to let him down. My first objective was to assemble my squad and find out who owned that pin.

"Pull over," I told the driver.

He looked in the rearview mirror and frowned. "Sir?"

"I said pull over, right here."

He gave me a look of uncertainty as he pulled to the side of the road. I hopped out and walked to the driver's window. "Take my things to Paris Hall."

Again, he gave me a doubtful look. "I can't leave you here. I was instructed to take you back to school, and that's what I'm doing. I'll wait here."

I reached into the backpack that hung on my shoulder and took out a crisp bill. "Here. It's a hundred euros. Just leave my bags by the entrance. There's something I have to do."

After a brief pause, he took the money from me, then drove away. I waited until he crossed the small bridge before making my way over to the bank, where I found Ivan, who was still fishing. He remained focused on the water. I wasn't sure if he was ignoring me or if he hadn't realized I'd joined him, so I spoke first.

"Catch anything?" I asked.

"What the hell are you doing here, Duncan?" He didn't turn around or seem surprised by my voice.

"I was thinking about trying my luck, so I came over to see if I could find a good spot." I sat beside him.

Ivan finally looked at me and frowned. "I didn't ask for any company. I'm busy here."

I motioned toward the empty pail sitting on the opposite side. "Busy with what? Doesn't look like you're having much luck."

He rolled his eyes and said, "Fishing takes patience. I don't have nowhere else to be. I got kicked out of the Elites, so I have plenty of time."

"That's what I kinda wanna talk to you about, Ivan," I told him. "I wanna call an armistice."

"For what? I ain't at war with you. I just don't like you. And I'd appreciate it if you left me the hell alone—before I give you a beating."

"Really? How'd that work out for you last time?" I stared at him, and he turned back toward the water, looking ashamed. "You're a smart guy, Ivan. You do know violence and fighting is not the answer to everything? Guys like us have to use our brains, not our brawn."

"You don't know anything about me, Duncan." He shot me an angry glance. "And I'm nothing like you."

"Dude, you knew what armistice meant without thinking about it. You got into MIT, for God's sake. Admit it. You're smart." I sighed.

"So what? I got into MIT. Who gives a fuck about that? You think anybody around here cares that I got into a prestigious school?" Ivan shook his head and stared back into the water. "All they care about is getting pinned."

"They, who? Your father? Because where the hell did that pin get him?" I asked, knowing that I was taking a chance by insulting his father like that. He had a scowl on his face, but he didn't hit me, so I figured it was safe to continue. "That pin doesn't mean shit if you don't understand the meaning behind it. This place isn't just about learning how to fight. It's about learning how to live and the lifelong connections that go with it. Being pinned is about joining a lifelong brother and sisterhood of friends. People that have your back."

"Go away, Duncan."

"Damn, I guess you're not as intelligent as I thought you were, Ivan. That's disappointing." I shook my head. "I guess you're not like me."

"I can assure you my IQ is higher than yours," he shot back.

"That can't be true. Because if it were, you'd be hell bent on continuing what the guys in this pic started at this place." I reached into my backpack and took out the picture Minister Farrah had given me.

"What the hell is this?" Ivan's eyes went to the object in my hand, then back to me. I handed it to him.

"Look at it."

After he finally took it, I waited for him to study it for a few moments before I spoke again. "This is what I know we're capable of. But we can be better."

Ivan handed the picture back to me.

"You came here to be pinned like all the great men in your family, right? Isn't that why you're here?" I asked.

"Yeah, and?"

"You ever thought about something more than that?"

Ivan turned his head toward me. "What do you mean, more?"

"I mean continuing what these men started. Greatness." I held the picture up again. "My father, Darryl Graham, your dad, Jason Starks, and this guy right here, Raul Hernandez, he died a hero. They weren't here to just earn a pin, Ivan. They were here to be great."

Ivan pointed to his father. "Yeah, well, that dude right there doesn't think I'll be anything. I'll never be great to him. And my destiny is to follow in his footsteps as a drunk."

"Do you have greatness in you?" I asked. "Because I know I have it in me. Hell, Ivan, you gotta have something in you too. This is the second time you've gone through the program, and you still haven't given up. If that's not greatness, then I don't know what is."

"That's resilience, Nevada. And determination."

For the first time since meeting, Ivan called me by my first name. Perhaps I was making headway with him. "All components of great men, as far as I'm concerned. Which is why I want you on my squad."

His eyes widened for a second, then lowered. "Even if I wanted to be, I can't. I'm not an Elite anymore."

"The question is, do you wanna be an Elite, Ivan? If you do, then meet me on the field at six tomorrow morning." I stood up. "If you're there, I'll do the rest. It's up to you. I do have one rule, however."

"What's that?"

"Loyalty."

Ivan didn't say anything else. His attention was on the photo.

Having said all that I felt needed to be said, I turned to make my exit. I saw a slight movement in my peripheral vision. I paused.

"Hey, Ivan."

"What?" Ivan looked up.

I pointed to the water. "You got a fish."

Ivan grabbed the pole that he'd laid on the ground and began reeling it in. I didn't wait to see what was on the line. I needed to get back to campus and assemble my squad.

Marie

27

I drove with one hand on the steering wheel, and the other on my arm. The adrenaline in my system had worn off, only to be replaced by the overwhelming urge to sleep. The headlights of the oncoming cars weren't enough to keep me alert, and neither was the fear of crashing. I kept pinching myself as hard as I could to stay awake.

"No sleep. No sleep. Gotta stay awake," I mumbled to myself.

I knew where I was going, I just had to get there. I had to. My eyes just felt so . . . heavy. I had to close them, just for a second—

The sound of a horn blaring made my eyes snap open just in time to notice that I had swerved into oncoming traffic. I swung back into my own lane, barely missing a head-on collision with a Dodge Ram. My heart pounded at the near miss. I shook my head vigorously to wake myself up.

"That would have been very bad. Very, very bad," I said to myself. "Stay awake. You're almost there. You're almost to that motherfucka's house. Just stay awake."

I didn't know how long I'd been driving. Ever since I was locked away in that institution, I couldn't keep track of the passage of time. Things seemed to just blend together. Sometimes I didn't even know what was real and what wasn't.

I'd been to my destination a few times before. Even though it wasn't so long ago, it felt like another lifetime or another dimension, when I was a different person, a boss. Now I was just a fragment of my former self who didn't care to be pieced back together. One thing I did know was that Bobby Two Fingers was a piece of shit. When I finally parked beside a curb outside of his apartment, I hoped he was inside so that I could say it to his face.

"Fucking shitbag," I said, getting out of the car.

When my feet touched the cold concrete, I remembered that I was barefoot, and I still had on the white pajamas provided to me by the Institute. I checked my surroundings then walked fast into the building. A young black couple was exiting as I headed in. I kept my head down, but I could feel their eyes on me.

"Goddamn, what the fuck happened to shorty's head? Bitch looks crazy as fuck!"

I ignored him and kept going up the stairs. I was there for something, and I wasn't going to leave until I got it.

Bobby's apartment was on the third floor at the end of the hall. When I got there, I checked over my shoulder to make sure I hadn't been followed. I raised my hand and banged on the door. After a few seconds when nobody came to answer it, I banged on it again.

"Bobby, I know you're in there, you son of a bitch! Open the door!" With each word coming from my mouth, I felt my energy drain a little bit more. "Bobby!"

Still nothing. I placed my ear to the door and tried to listen for any sign of life. Nothing. Not even a footstep. I didn't have the skills or the patience to pick the lock, and I didn't have any more energy to bang on the door. Something told me to just try the knob. I was surprised to feel that it turned with no problem.

I pushed the door wide open and stared inside the empty apartment. The only light on was the one in the dining room, and it lit everything in the front of the home. I stepped inside and shut the door behind me, making sure to lock it.

"Bobby?" I moved slowly throughout the home. "Is anybody here?"

It was completely empty. In fact, it was so neat that it looked like nobody lived there. I went to his bedroom and saw that his bed was made. There wasn't so much as a wrinkle on the comforter. Maybe he was just a neat freak, I thought. Either way, he wasn't there.

"Where the fuck is that bastard?" I asked myself. "I don't know where it is without him. Where is it?"

I started rummaging through the things in his bedroom—his drawers, his closet, under his pillow and his bed. Nothing. I couldn't find it.

"Where is it? Where the fuck is it?" I shook my hands on the sides of my face in frustration. I didn't know where he would have hidden it.

Damn him! Damn him to hell. No one is going to believe me without it.

Turning off the light in the bedroom, I went to the kitchen. Maybe it was in there. I went through every cabinet and every drawer, but still nothing. I groaned loudly and slammed the last cabinet I'd gone through. It was useless. I wouldn't be able to find it without him.

Maybe—

My thought process was interrupted when my eyes rested on a box of Cap'n Crunch sitting on top of the fridge. My stomach gave a low growl, alerting me that I was hungry. I barely ate the slop they served at the Institute. I didn't know if they were trying to poison me or not. So right then, the cereal was looking as good as a steak.

Before I knew it, I had poured a bowl of cereal and milk. It didn't take long for me to scarf it down and pour another bowl. When my belly was full, I put the cereal and milk back where I got them. I set the bowl and spoon in the sink for Bobby to clean whenever he got there.

My eyes grew heavy again, and this time, there was no car horn to wake me up. My legs carried me to one of the living room couches, and I just collapsed. My body had finally been pushed to its limits. It needed rest. I needed to sleep. . . .

After my time at the Institute, I was on high alert at all times. Even the smallest noise would wake me. That was why I jolted awake at the sound of keys jangling and voices I didn't recognize outside of Bobby's apartment.

I heard the muffled voice of a man. "I thought you said Liam left this door unlocked."

"I thought he did too. But then again, he had a few shots of whiskey that night," another man said.

"Yeah, yeah. Just open the fuckin' door."

I jumped to my feet in a panic when I saw the doorknob turn.

No, no, no! Nobody could find me. Terror filled my entire body. *Where can I hide? The bathroom! No, they might come in there. The closet? Under the bed?*

I ran back to Bobby's bedroom, and I spun in a circle, frantically trying to figure out where to go. I grabbed one of his old shirts, sliding into it. They still hadn't gotten the door open, but it was just a matter of time. Shit!

"Open the fucking door! I have to piss!"

I nearly wet my own pants right then and there. I knew that voice. I could never forget it. It was him; it was the bastard who had held a knife to my throat as I watched his henchmen slice my girls to death.

"I don't know which goddamn key it is! Hold on, you unruly motherfucker."

Fear ran through me, but it hadn't taken over yet. I didn't have much time. My eyes went to the bedroom window and the fire escape outside of it. I ran to the window, lifted it open, and climbed out. As I stood on the fire escape and turned to close the window, I heard the front door opening. I dropped to my knees and moved my body out of view.

Bobby's cheap windows enabled me to hear everything that was going on inside. After a minute, I summoned the courage to lean over and peek inside the apartment. My hand flew to my mouth to silence my gasp when I saw a tall man coming out of the bathroom. My eyes immediately went to the disheveled red hair on top of his head. There was no doubt that was him.

"I almost pissed myself," he yelled.

"Well, maybe you're getting to old for this. Ya need to start wearing Depends." The other one laughed. I could see now he was a redhead too, but much younger.

"Very fucking funny," the madman replied. "Now, let's do what we came here to do and torch the place."

"I thought we were supposed to wait until Liam got the information from that bitch at the loony hospital."

"Yeah, but no harm getting the place prepared, just in case she doesn't talk."

Good. Good. They didn't know what had happened to their partner in crime yet. But that didn't mean I was out of danger. I had to get out of there, but how? I knew if I stood up while they were in the living room, they would see me.

My body began to shake in fear. I looked back toward the stairs on the fire escape and thought about just taking my chance. But—

"We would have gotten the information out of Bobby if you hadn't killed him."

"The son of a bitch was stronger than I thought. He wouldn't let go. So I did what I had to do and gutted the bastard." The madman laughed.

Shit! Shit! Bobby is dead? They're not going to believe me if I don't have proof.

Wait, I had to focus. This wasn't the time to zone out.

Keep it together, Marie. Keep it together.

"Hey, who the fuck left a bowl in the sink?"

Shit.

"Who was the last person here?"

"I don't know. It wasn't me. And it wasn't Bobby, that's for sure." There was a pause. "Maybe that's why the door was locked." Another pause. "Shit, you think those Mafia bozos were here? Bobby may have told them where to find it."

"If they were, we'll just have to pay them a little visit."

The younger one pulled out a phone. "Hold on a second, Da. This is Connor."

"Good. Hopefully him and Liam have the information and we can go back home."

"What's up?" The younger spoke into the phone.

I could see his demeanor deflate as he listened.

"Ah, no, no!" He hung up the phone, staring at the madman. "Fuck!"

"What?"

It took the younger one a moment to say, "Liam's dead. That bitch killed him."

The madman didn't say anything, but I was surprised to see sadness on his face, although it transformed pretty quickly into intense rage.

His fist went right through the wall. "I'm going to kill that bitch!"

"What do we do now?"

"First, we make arrangements to steal Liam's body from the morgue and take him home. Then we go see the kid."

Kid! What kid? Oh God, did he mean Nevada?

"No! I gotta get to him." The words escaped my lips before I could stop them.

"Hey, did you hear that?"

I saw them both remove guns from their waistlines. I didn't have a choice. I had to run. I stood to my feet, and the sudden movement caught their attention.

"Somebody's on the fire escape!"

They wasted no time in releasing their bullets. I screamed when the window shattered as I ran for the stairs. I stepped on a few of the shards and felt them slice the bottom of my feet, but I didn't care. That pain was the least of my worries, because they were trying to climb out of the window after me.

I half ran, half jumped down the metal stairs then, where they ended, I let the ladder down and started climbing. Bullets ricocheted off the metal around me. I flinched, which caused me to lose my grip on the ladder halfway down. I fell onto the pavement in an alley on my back. The wind was knocked out of me.

"Go," I told myself. "Go!" I hadn't parked too far from the alley. All I needed to do was get to the car. I struggled to my feet, thankful that their aim was not better as bullets whizzed by me.

When I heard their guns click, I knew they were out of ammunition. They paused to reload, and I used that window of opportunity to run to the car, speeding off as fast as I could from another near-death experience.

Natasha

28

I am not a whore! I am not a whore!

I didn't bother to try to disguise the level of disgust I felt as I sat across from Dean Wilensky. His office was old, faded, and dingy, much like him as he sat smirking at me from behind his desk. His thinning hair and horn-rimmed glasses made him look even creepier, if that was even possible. As much as I wanted to jump up and run out of his office as fast as I could, I knew it would do no good. He would always find a way to get to me, especially now that Nevada was gone.

"So, you haven't been to see me in a while, Natasha." He raised one of his thick, bushy eyebrows.

"I've been busy. With my *boyfriend*."

"Ah, yes, I heard about your relationship with the Duncan boy, but I also have heard that he is no longer with us," he sneered.

Nevada had only been gone a few hours, and the old pervert already had me in his sights.

I'm not a whore. I'm not a whore.

"He will be back," I responded, determined not to let him intimidate me. "He's just gone temporarily for a family emergency, that's all."

"No, I don't think so. I spoke to the headmaster myself. He's been officially withdrawn from the school." He smiled at me with stained teeth.

I deflated slightly. I had prayed Arielle was wrong and that Nevada would only be gone for a few days, a week at the most. Now, it seemed like he was going to be gone forever. I was right back where I started. I had no one to protect me.

"Now we can get back to normal." Dean Wilensky slid something across the deck toward me. When he removed his pale, weathered hand, I saw the shiny key. "Here you go. You can go ahead to my bungalow and get ready. I hope you're wearing one of those thongs?" The old bastard was so excited he started having a coughing fit. "I'll be there in thirty minutes."

I stared at the key for a moment without moving or speaking. The memory of his hands touching my head, forcing me lower until his wrinkled penis was in front of my face, sickened me.

I have to kill him. That's the only way to put an end to this nightmare. If not, I'll have to keep doing this.

"And what if I refuse?" I asked, even though I knew trying to reason with him was hopeless.

"You won't. You enjoy being a student here too much," he said, staring at my breasts with his mouth open. "You're too smart to jeopardize your place here. Besides, you have a wonderful future in front of you."

He was right. Leaving school was not an option for me, and I had been willing to do anything to stay. That was how I'd ended up here in the first place. But now, I was going to have to do something else in order to stay, and I was sure Dean Wilensky wouldn't like it.

Too bad for him. All the training I'd received since being at school was going to be put to good use. *I'm going to kill this bastard.*

I reached across the desk and picked up the key. "I will see you back at your bungalow. Don't forget to take your pill."

"I won't. I have it right here." Dean Wilensky stood and walked around the desk. He pulled me up and began caressing my hair. I held my breath to avoid the stench of his breath that was a mix of cigarettes, stale coffee, and who knows what else. "You're so pretty. You know that? So damn pretty. Maybe we should do it right here on my desk."

His fingers caressed my neck and began traveling lower. I glared at him.

I'm not a whore. I'm not a whore.

Dean Wilensky's hands stopped traveling when there was a knock at the door.

"I'm busy! Go away!" he yelled, resuming his vile fondling.

The unexpected visitor remained vigilant, knocking even harder.

"I said *go away!*"

The knocking continued until he let out a frustrated grunt as he finally removed his hand from my breast and stepped toward the door.

He swung it open. "Didn't you hear what I said? I'm busy! What do you want?"

"I'm here for my girlfriend, Dean Wilensky."

I turned around to see Nevada walking into the office. His eyes met mine, and I was finally able to exhale.

He's here. He's here for me. I'd never been so happy to see someone in my life. Nevada had come for me. My heart leapt.

"Young man, you need to leave, *now*! Do you hear me?" Dean Wilensky turned red. "Do you know who I am?"

His threats meant nothing to Nevada, who grabbed my hand and led me toward the door. I could hear the yelling continue as we exited the office and rushed down the hallway.

"Are you okay? When they told me he sent for you, I knew what that meant, and I came as fast as I could." He looked worried. "He didn't hurt you, did he?"

"No, I am fine." I was relieved that I didn't have to murder the dean in order to stay in school. I was safe, at least for now.

"Good." Nevada smiled.

I stopped walking and looked at him. "Your timing was perfect. I'm so glad you're back."

"I am too." He hugged me tight. It felt good being in his arms. I didn't want him to let go.

"Come on, we gotta go," he said when he released me and stepped back.

"Where are we going?" I asked, slipping my hand back into his.

"We've gotta assemble the squad." He said it with such authority that I knew he meant business.

As we ran hand in hand across the campus to meet with our fellow classmates, I felt an elation that I'd never felt before. I knew I liked him from the start, but now I was falling in love with him.

Nevada

29

The fog was heavy as Natasha, Clem, and I walked onto the west end field just after daybreak. After the incident with Dean Wilensky, Natasha was so distraught, that I'd allowed her, with the permission of Clem and Raheem, to stay the night in my room. She slept in my bed while I spent most of the night contemplating who I would select for my squad. I finally fell asleep in the chair at my computer.

One thing I'd learned from my grandfather was that proper planning prevents piss-poor performance. He applied that rule not only to choosing suppliers and methods for his business, but to the people he surrounded himself with. That's why he kept things mostly in the family, the people he could rely on and trust the most. Being selective about your inner circle is important and could mean the difference between life and death.

"Who's that?" Clem asked, noticing a group across the field. "Are they with us?"

I squinted at the group of shadows. "Nah, they aren't."

"Who did you choose?" Natasha asked. She and Clem had been trying to get me to reveal my final decision all night, but I'd refused. I didn't want to be influenced by anyone else.

"You're about to find out." I pointed to two shadowy figures approaching. "Here come our Grails."

"Good morning," Arielle and Demi said at the same time. I couldn't help but notice Natasha's cheerful grin fade slightly when she saw Arielle.

"Ladies, welcome to the team." Clem nodded his approval. The three of them exchanged high-fives. They seemed excited to be together.

"We're going to kick ass," he said.

Natasha moved closer to me and asked, "Okay, who else is supposed to be here?"

"Pardon my tardiness, but I could hardly see through this dense fog, which, by the way, is doing nothing for my skin." Richard strolled up.

"Maybe if you take those sunglasses off you could see better," Demi suggested.

He peered over the top and smirked at her. "These are Gucci, honey. They're not just sunglasses. They are a statement."

"And just what exactly are they saying? You're stylish but visually impaired?" Arielle quipped, and even Richard laughed. It was just good-natured teasing, and he gave it right back to her.

"No, they say I'm too focused on my life to be bothered by peasants." He fanned the air as if he were shooing away an insect. "Now, exactly what are we doing? And why did we have to be here this damn early?" Richard folded his arms.

"Obviously, we're here because Nevada picked us, dummy. The real question is, what are you doing here?" Clem sighed, turning to me. "You do know he's the one who started the rumor about you being a drug dealer?"

"That was you?" Arielle squealed.

Richard looked like the cat that ate the canary. "I wouldn't exactly say I started it. But I did tell a few people."

"You mean like everyone on campus?" Natasha spat.

Richard turned to me and opened his mouth to offer some explanation.

"Save it, Richard. I don't need your bullshit excuses." I turned to my new squad and launched into my introductory speech. "Now, you're here because I want you to be, but that can change at a moment's notice." I looked at each of them. "I picked each and every one of you for a reason. Because you're the best. You possess a unique skill, talent, or expertise that no other Elite possesses, and you bring something to the team that we are going to need."

"I do enjoy being the best," Richard commented.

"Good, because that's exactly what we're gonna be," I told him as I reached into my backpack and took out my iPad. I opened the document that contained the plans I'd been working on. "Now, Clem, when we're out in the field, you're in charge of ammunition and artillery."

"Can do." Clem nodded.

"And when we're not in the field, you're my wingman, my second in command."

"I got your back, cap'n." He gave me a high five.

"Good, I'm going to need it," I said, "Arielle, you're in charge of logistics. With your connections with administration, you're gonna be our eyes and ears on the inside."

"Sounds good." Arielle smiled.

"I'm not trying to be rude, but everyone knows that if it's information you need, I'm the one to get it." Richard sucked his teeth, and even though he had the shades on, I could see his eyes rolling.

"Which is exactly why you're our espionage specialist." I turned to him. "You, somehow, have the capability of finding out everything about everyone everywhere. It's your job to procure anything we need and keep us informed on what's going on everywhere. I just don't need you to embellish it. I need facts, not bullshit."

"I understand." Richard beamed with pride, unashamed that I was calling him out for his gossiping. I needed to put him in his place.

"Good." I stepped toward him, so we stood face to face. I grabbed him by the collar and lowered my voice. "Now, on a personal note, if you ever lie on me again, or include me or anyone on this squad in your gossipy bullshit, you'll be wearing those fucking shades permanently, because I'm going to blacken both your eyes. Are we clear?"

Visibly shaken, Richard slowly released the breath that he'd been holding while I was speaking. The guy who always had a sarcastic response or snappy comeback nodded meekly. "Crystal clear."

"Excellent." I smiled, then released him, smoothing out his shirt. "Because your gift of gab and good looks are gonna be critical to this squad. You're a charmer, Richard, and that's gonna be one of our secret weapons."

The fearful look on his face dissolved into a prideful smirk, a clear indication that he was pleased with the assignment I'd given him. "I'm officially excited."

"Glad to hear that." I turned to Demi. "Dem, you're our tech engineering guru, the McGuyver of the team."

"What the hell does that mean?" Natasha asked.

"It means she can fix anything we need. And if she can't fix it, she'll make it," Arielle said sarcastically. "Haven't you been paying attention this semester? She's the one who fixed the air conditioner in the dining hall."

"And the Elite pool? Don't forget the pool," Clem added.

"I got you, Nevada." Demi rubbed her hands together like a mad scientist.

"And lemme guess, fearless leader," Clem volunteered. "You're gonna be our computer guy, right?"

"Actually, I'm not," I said.

They all looked confused.

"We need a computer person," Arielle insisted.

Natasha said, "Don't look at me to do it. I do not know the difference between a Mac and a PC."

"And there are only six of us. Aren't we supposed to have seven members? We need one more person," Demi pointed out.

"We have one," I said.

"Who?" Arielle asked.

"Him." I nodded my head toward the person who'd been standing a short distance away from us.

They all turned to look.

"Where? The only person over there is Ivan." Natasha raised an eyebrow at me.

"Ivan?" Clem spat, his eyes the size of silver dollars.

"Yes, Ivan," I replied.

"Have you lost your mind?" Natasha asked, the others nodding their agreement with her assessment.

"Nope. Have any of you gotten accepted into MIT?" I asked them. They cast their eyes downward. "Well, he did."

"Ivan got into MIT? As in Massachusetts Institute of Technology? *That* MIT?" Arielle turned to Demi.

"Uh-huh. He's really smart, you know," Demi said.

"Nevada, bro, say it ain't so," Clem moaned. "He's not even an Elite. He was kicked out, remember?"

"He is now. I convinced Minister Farrah to have him reinstated."

Ivan was obviously aware that the other squad members weren't thrilled about his presence. I could see it in his body language as he walked over to our group with his head down low.

I reached into my bag and handed him a folded piece of paper. He opened it and began to read. He'd been reinstated, thanks to a little pleading on my part to the headmaster, under the condition that I be personally responsible for him.

I looked at Ivan. "I guess you're my responsibility now."

"I don't know what to say." Ivan shrugged.

"You don't have to say anything. Just do your part and stay loyal. From this moment on, everything that happened in the past between you and any of us is over. It's a fresh start for you. Everyone agree?"

They all nodded, except Richard.

"I'm not sure how I feel about being on a squad with him. There's a reason he got kicked out twice, you know, and I—"

"Fine, Richard, you don't wanna be on this squad, I'll be more than happy to go and speak to one of the other squad leaders about swapping you out for—"

"No, no, I'll stay." Richard stopped me, then turned to Ivan. "Let bygones be bygones, I always say. It's all cool."

"Welcome to the squad, Ivan." Demi shook his hand, and then the others did so, but with much less enthusiasm.

"And me?" Natasha stood with her hands on her hips. "What about me? What is my position?"

Arielle looked like she was about to say something, until I shot her a look.

"You're one of the best shots in the school. You're going to be our sniper," I explained.

"I can do that." She grabbed me for a hug.

"So, your girlfriend is a sniper. What else is she gonna do, carry around pom-poms and cheer for us?" The sarcasm in Arielle's voice didn't go unnoticed.

"No, she's gonna be in charge of transportation. I've been informed that we will be assigned missions all over France. We're gonna need a driver."

"Driver?" Clem laughed. "What's she gonna drive? Her scooter?"

Natasha's face turned red with heat, and I could see the anger and embarrassment in her eyes.

Before I could respond, Demi spoke. "No, I have a better option. Come with me."

We followed Demi across the field to the far side of campus, where the motor pool was located. The bodies of several junk cars and other random automotive parts were scattered in front of the large metal building. Ivan pulled the garage door open and revealed what had to be the biggest jeep I'd ever seen. Black, with oversized tires and an extended cab that looked not only large enough to fit eight people easily, but it had a bed of a pickup truck.

"It doesn't look like much, but this thing is powerful and can handle any kind of terrain. Can you drive a stick?" Demi asked.

"Of course. Can't everyone?" Natasha rushed over and climbed up in the driver's seat.

Demi tossed a set of keys to Natasha. "Crank it up."

Natasha turned the key with a grin. The loud engine erupted, then smoothed out and began to purr.

"Come on, get in," I told everyone.

Demi moved to the back seat as I got in and sat beside Natasha. Clem and Ivan sat in the farthest rear seat, while Richard and Arielle sat next to Demi. My squad was loaded and ready to go.

I looked at Natasha. "Well, where to?"

"Paris?" Natasha looked into the rearview mirror. "There is no better place in the world to explore and get to know somebody."

Everyone sounded excited. "Okay, then, Paris it is. I always wanted to see the Eiffel Tower in person."

Natasha put the jeep in gear and pulled out of the garage. I relaxed in my seat, satisfied that I'd made the right choices.

Marie

30

"Twinkle, twinkle, little star. How I wonder what you are . . ."

It was cold and dark, and I'm sure I smelled like a sewer, but I stayed in that cramped space for what seemed like hours, singing quietly and waiting. Eventually my waiting paid off when I heard the loud clanking of a metal door and then a very distinctive voice.

"Twenty-five. There are twenty-five of you no-good hookers, and none of you even thinks about taking out the goddamn trash."

A few seconds later, my space was flooded with the brightness of the alley lights. I sprang up towards the light, looking over the edge of the dumpster I'd been hiding in like a Jack-in-the-box.

"Bly?" I raised my hand just in time to stop the metal lid from slamming down on my head. She jumped back.

"Oh, shit! You scared the crap out of me!" She swung the white bag of trash she was holding at my head. "Get away from me, you freak!"

"Bly, please. It's me, Marie. Stop!"

She didn't hear a word I said. She just kept swinging that damn garbage bag at me until I grabbed it with my free hand. I must have really looked fucked up for her to react like that.

"Dammit, Bly, stop it!"

My tone was forceful enough that it snapped her to attention and made her hesitate. I think she finally recognized my voice.

"Marie?" she questioned me with frightened eyes. "You scared the shit out of me. And . . . your hair!"

"Yes, Bly, it's me."

"What the fuck happened to you? What the hell did you do to your hair?"

"I pulled it out," I moaned. I climbed out of the dumpster and fell on my face.

"Oh, Marie! Honey, what are you doing out here?"

"I was waiting for you."

"All right then, come on inside," she said, urging me to get up and directing me to the door.

Inside her office, she helped me sit down in one of the big pink plush chairs. "Whew! Now, when you catch your breath, I need you to tell me why the hell you were hiding in a god-damn dumpster. You stink, girl!"

She grabbed two water bottles from the mini fridge and sat beside me. I took one of the bottles and drank it quickly. I felt as if I hadn't had water in days. She handed me the second bottle, and I finished it just as fast.

I saw her staring at the bruises on my arms and the plastic bags I was now wearing as shoes. I could only imagine what she was thinking.

"I didn't mean to scare you," I said when I was done with the second bottle of water. "There were just cops driving up and down the street. I didn't want them to take me. I didn't know when you would be back here."

"What happened to you, Marie? I mean, after the girls were killed."

"Vegas took care of me for a little bit, but I guess that got to be too much for him. And I can't blame him. I . . . I couldn't handle all of the nightmares. Seeing what I saw, it changed me." I flinched as the image of bloody bodies strewn across the floor of the club replayed in my head.

"So, what did he do? Since it got too much for him. And don't tell me he put you in the streets, because I'll put a number on his head right now." I could see the anger in her eyes.

"He didn't put me out. And you and I both know he would send whoever came for him back home in a body bag." I didn't want any blame placed on the man I loved. He hadn't done anything to hurt me. "Vegas checked me into a . . . a mental institute. He said I was unstable. And all they wanted to do was put me to sleep, but I had to stay up. So I—"

"Pulled your damn hair out?" She'd been avoiding looking at my head, but now she couldn't stop staring. It must have looked hideous. "I know that I should be all sentimental and empathetic right now, but you look crazy as hell. Why the fuck would you do that shit to yourself?"

"Because they were there." I tried to remain calm, but my nerves were frazzled. My life was on the line, and Bly was more concerned about my lack of hair care.

"Who was there?"

"The redhead hospital nurse. He worked with the people who killed my girls. And he tried to kill me. So I killed him and escaped. They're still after me, Bly. I'm not safe here. I'm not safe. I'm not—" I began trembling. The tears I'd been holding back fell from my eyes.

"Shhh." She took hold of my hands. "You're always safe with me. In fact, I'm about to have you looking like the old Marie in no time. Hold on."

Bly went to the closet in her office. I watched as she pulled out a pair of jeans, a form-fitting T-shirt, and a pair of Nikes, along with a set of clean underwear and a washcloth. "These should fit. Go into the bathroom over there and clean yourself up."

I steadied myself as I stood, then went into the bathroom. Avoiding the mirror, I turned on the water, hoping the steam would soon make it impossible to see my reflection. I didn't want to see myself. I knew how fucked up I looked.

I was grateful to be able to wash up and have clean clothes to change into. Not wanting to waste any more time than needed, I quickly changed out of the dirty, torn hospital gown and plastic bags, tossing them into the trash. The clean underwear felt like a luxury after everything I'd been through.

I emerged from the bathroom, feeling and smelling ten times better.

"Well, it's an improvement. But we gotta cut that shit." Bly held up a pair of clippers. "And I'll give you one of my lace wigs and some glue. But *that* dead animal on top of your head has got to go."

"Fine." I was too exhausted to protest, and besides, I knew she was right about the state of my hair. I sat down in the desk chair, and she stood behind me.

"I'm not crazy, Bly."

"Yes, you are, but that don't mean I don't love you," she said.

After the haircut, Bly took it a step further and applied makeup to my face.

"There's my Marie," she said with a smile, admiring her makeover skills.

She handed me a compact mirror, and I finally looked at myself. It was still a drastic change from how I used to look, but it damn sure was an improvement.

"Thank you, but I don't think the Marie you knew will ever resurface," I said, passing the mirror to her. "Bly, I need your help."

"Anything." She stared at me. "What do you need?"

"I need to get to Europe, and I don't have a passport."

Nevada

31

The moonlight slipped through the cracks of the blinds and rested on my face. That wasn't what woke me up, though. Raheem having sex with some girl did that. The fact that I could hear them from my bedroom with the door shut was an indicator of how loud they were. Jeeez, what was he, some type of love machine? This guy had been at it all night.

I grabbed my pillow and pressed it over my face and ears to try to block out the noise. It didn't work. Sleep wasn't going to find me again that night. Of that, I was sure.

I groaned loudly and threw the pillow to the side. It was 5:18 a.m., and it would be light in another hour. Usually, we'd have PT in the morning, but it was Sunday, the only day Elites had no scheduled activities other than catching up on our rest. Thanks to Raheem, that was not in the cards for me. I needed to clear my head anyway.

I pulled on some school sweatpants and found a hoodie to wear. A run might do me some good. My feet hit the ground quietly as I passed Raheem's door. He was still going at it. I wondered if he was keeping Clem up as well.

The thought crossed my mind to knock on his door so we could talk it out, but I decided against it. I didn't really want to talk with him about what was on my mind. I wanted to sort it out by myself, because if I was honest, it wasn't just Raheem having sex that had me up. It was the fact that someone affiliated with Chi's had something to do with Kia's death. Whoever was behind it was not someone to be played with, and I didn't want to be hurt or get someone hurt.

Sure, I'd done what my dad had told me and assembled a squad of people I trusted; except I was starting to second guess my choice of a team. Not that I had put together a bad team. We weren't as strong as Raheem's squad—who I wish I could have recruited—or some of the others, but there were far worse teams. My concern came down to their dedication to being great, and of course, their loyalty to me and each other. With Richard's ego, Arielle and Natasha's rivalry, and of course Ivan in the mix, would my group really hold together and have each other's backs?

Running always helped me to think, and by the time I finished a run, I had usually worked out my problems. This time, I needed to clear my head to piece together the little bit of information we had about Kia's murderer. There wasn't much to go on, which was part of what had me so agitated. My dad had said that whoever was involved in the murders was missing their Chi's pin. Now I had to figure out how to use my squad to find the owner of the missing pin.

I knew that losing a Chi's pin was like losing a limb. I remembered my Aunt Paris going insane when she had simply misplaced hers before some event in the city. She was in tears. I wondered how the owner of the pin my dad showed me felt about losing it. If that person was here on campus, would I know it?

The shadows from the moon cloaked me as I passed the trees and statues. It was still and quiet on campus—or at least it was until I heard the sound of twigs breaking behind me. My senses were instantly on high alert. There were definitely footsteps behind me. Whoever it was seemed to be keeping pace close behind me.

I sped up, but the footsteps got closer and closer until—

Screw it. I stopped and turned quickly in karate stance. "Who's there?"

"I did not think I would see you out here this early, heifer," the familiar voice said, running out of the shadows.

"What the hell are you doing out here?" I said as my eye confirmed what my ears had told me. "Richard!"

"He's with me." Clem, of all people, came running to a halt behind Richard. I gave them both the side-eye. What the hell were they up to?

"Untwist your lips, mate. It's not what it looks like. You're more my type than he is," Richard snipped, but I was still confused. It was five something in the morning. What the hell were the two of them doing on a wooded trail on the other side of campus together?

"I'm your wingman, so I'm training him, Nevada," Clem replied.

"Training him for what?"

"To be a viable part of your bloody team. I heard what you said yesterday about loyalty, greatness, and having each other's backs. I want that. I need that," Richard said sincerely. "I know I'm the weak link, but I wanna be a part of this team. Your team. So, I asked your mate here to give me a little training, get me in shape, teach me to use the old fisticuffs, and shoot."

If he was for real, this could be good. I was impressed that Clem had taken the initiative as well.

"Hey, I also know I can be an ass, but I can't help it. It's a defense mechanism, a way of hiding my insecurities," Richard continued.

"How's he doing?" I looked past Richard to Clem.

"It's the first day." Clem kind of shrugged. "But it's Sunday, and he was downstairs waiting for me at oh-five-hundred, so it's a start."

It was a start, and I was impressed. I had walked out the dorm thinking Richard was the biggest of my mistakes, and it turned out he'd heard me the loudest.

"What are you doing up?" Clem asked.

"I couldn't sleep."

Clem laughed. "Yeah, Raheem's pretty loud. Or at least Leesha is."

"That's not what had me up. I'm trying to work our first possible mission through my head."

"Well, share, mate," Richard pressed.

"My dad got some information that one of the people responsible for a mass murder in New York is a pinned member of the school," I revealed.

"Are they on campus?"

"Doubtful, but the means to find them is here. Because whoever did it is missing a Chi's pin," I told them, and Richard's face lit up. "Why do you look so happy?"

"Because they lost their pin!"

"I thought that was a bad thing," Clem said.

"It is for them! But not for us," Richard said with a smile.

"I'm lost."

"The Chi Gala One Hundred is next month."

"Still lost," I said.

"The *Chi Gala One Hundred*. It's like having all of what you Americans call the Free Masons under one roof. And in order to get in, you have to have your pin." Richard gave us a look like, *Duh, how could you not know that?*

"And our guy doesn't have one." I was finally picking up what he was putting down, but there was a problem. "He'll have to get a replacement pin. And lucky for us, our girl Arielle has an in at . . ."

"The administration office!" Clem stated. "Brilliant."

"Sorry to burst your bubble, boys, but the administration office doesn't keep track of who lost their pins. The alumni office handles missing pins."

"Fuck," Clem growled. "The alumni office is in the castle, and none of their people work for the school. We don't have an in, and that place is like Fort Knox."

"Maybe between me, Ivan, and Demi we can bypass the alarm," I suggested.

Clem shook his head. "And break in? I'm not trying to get expelled, Nevada. Not yet, at least. There's gotta be a better way."

"I could always take one for the team," Richard volunteered.

"What are you talking about?" I asked.

"Gerald English."

"Mr. English, the art teacher?" Clem asked.

"One in the same, but he also doubles as the assistant director of alumni affairs, and he is totally infatuated with *moi*." Richard laughed, pointing at himself.

"Mr. English is gay? I thought he was married," Clem said.

"Ah, Clem, so young and naive." Richard seemed to be amusing himself. "He flirts with me every chance he can get. But don't worry. I only have eyes for you, Nevada."

"Great," I said sarcastically. "But just because the guy thinks you're hot doesn't mean he'll tell you who lost their pins."

"He doesn't have to tell me, because I'm going to be face to face with everyone who needs to buy one," he said, grinning mischievously. "I think it's time for me to get a part-time job, don't you think?"

Marie

32

"Sure you don't want me to stay? I can wait," Marco said in his heavy French accent as I stepped out of his pickup truck and onto the cobblestone street. I was close enough to the school that I could see the sun setting behind the castle-like structure.

I'd arrived in Paris the day before, broke but determined. Bly had given me one of her girls' passports and a thousand dollars, which I used to purchase a nonstop ticket to Paris. With all my hair cut off, nobody even gave me a second look at customs. They probably figured I was a cancer patient on chemotherapy. I only had about a hundred and twenty dollars left, which I exchanged for about a hundred euros. Unfortunately, the taxi ride to school was almost three hundred. Fortunately, being a madam, I'd learned a trick or two about how to survive. That's how I met Marco.

He'd driven me all the way from Paris, bought me dinner, a bottle of wine, and five packs of cigarettes, which I really needed for my nerves. In turn, I had given him the best blowjob he'd ever had. So good, in fact, that this Frenchman was sprung.

"No, I can make it from here. I'll call you," I replied, closing the car door.

I walked into a small convenience store, loaded up on chips, water, and the essential chocolate, then waited around until Marco had driven off. Then I found a hardware store, where I purchase a pair of bolt cutters and a flashlight.

The walk to the school was about a mile or so. Thirty minutes later, I found an old tree that I recalled from my days at the school. It was twice as big as I remembered, and it actually made me smile. The carving Vegas had dug into was still there: *VD luvs MH*, with a heart around it. This was our tree.

I traced the carving with my finger, then sat down beneath it to eat some chips. I needed to keep up my strength. I sang to myself to pass the time as I waited for night to fall.

Twinkle, twinkle, little star. How I wonder . . .

When it was good and dark, I made my way over to a wooded area at the northeast end of the castle. It would have been nice if I could have just walked up to the castle gates and say "Hey, I'm Marie Hernandez, a former student that didn't graduate," but that wasn't going to work, and most likely, they'd be waiting for me. Fortunately, I knew of another way in.

I began tapping the ground with the bolt cutters until I heard a clanking sound. *Bingo!* I got down on my knees and removed the leaves and debris until I uncovered the round vent.

"It's still here," I mumbled gratefully.

Our squad had used this vent to break curfew and sneak off campus to buy beer, wine, and weed a hundred times. I was surprised it had been undisturbed. I used the bolt cutters to snap off the lock, then shone my flashlight into the dark hole. Climbing onto the access ladder, I descended into the tunnel that would eventually take me under the moat to a damp ten-by-ten, rat-infested room that split into eight different tunnels. From there, if you knew where to go, you could get to any building on campus. I headed toward the castle.

Richard

33

When I entered the alumni office, Mr. English, who never missed an opportunity to catch a glimpse of me, had his back turned. It was late evening when I choose to stop by—a time when most of his staff was gone and I wasn't obligated to wear my uniform. I wore a tight-fitting pair of jeans and a skin-tight black T-shirt for this occasion.

I cleared my throat to get his attention. He turned around, and the annoyed expression on his face faded quickly when he saw it was me. In fact, he almost dropped the file he was holding; he was so enamored with what he saw. I watched as his eyes deliberately fell from my face to my chest to my crotch before making their way back up to my eyes again. It wasn't a big deal, I was used to it, but the fact that he was so much older than me made it awkward. He was probably the same age as my father, and as much as I liked turning out married men, old was not my type. Not to mention the fact that I was totally into black and Latino guys, and he was pasty white.

"Richard! To what do I owe this pleasure?" He was all smiles, leaning over the counter.

The look I gave him was far from innocent, yet subtle. Somehow, I'd perfected what I thought was my signature gaze: demure with a hint of intrigue. It worked every time.

"Actually, Mr. English, I'm glad I caught you before you left. Do you have a moment to talk?"

"Well, I'm trying to finish up for the day, but sure. I can stop long enough to chat with you. What can I do for you?" He couldn't help it. His eyes were all over me.

"Funny, that's what I was going to ask. What can I do for you?" I stared directly at his crotch without changing the expression on my face. I'm not sure if he thought I was trying to hit on him or not, which was exactly what I wanted. He was completely caught off guard.

He stood and paused for a moment. "Wha—what exactly do you mean, Richard?"

"Well, I know your office is swamped with the upcoming gala, and I was wondering if maybe you could use some extra help around here," I replied. "I had a lot of fun last year when we worked on the spring fundraiser together."

"Oh." He relaxed a bit. "Okay, I see."

"This time, I'd like to work more directly with you, Mr. English." Once again, I stared at his crotch. "I think we both can benefit from it."

"I'd like that." He looked curiously at me, as if he were trying to decide if I was sincere. The room became so quiet that I thought he was about to decline my request. Finally, he said. "What kind of work are you looking for exactly, and why? You don't seem like the work-study type. No offense, of course."

"None taken. Paperwork, filing, basic stuff. And since you asked, I need a job because I could really use the extra money. My father wasn't too pleased with the last credit card statement that showed I spent about two grand over the limit he gave me." I faked a guilty sigh. "As long as the charge goes through, I have no way of knowing I'm at my limit. He pretty much cut me off, but if I get a job, he'll see that I'm making an effort. Who knows? Maybe I'll even find some fringe benefits along the way, right?"

I put my hand on the counter and "accidentally" touched his as I gave him my signature look. His thick Adam's apple moved up and down as he swallowed hard.

He cleared his throat and said, "Well . . . I guess I can use the extra help. Between finalizing the gala plans and completing these orders, I am quite busy. You would think that former graduates would hold more carefully onto something that costs one hundred grand to replace."

"Orders?" I asked, although I already had a good idea what he was talking about.

"Yes. Their pins. You wouldn't believe how many graduates lose them."

"I couldn't imagine losing something that priceless." I smiled. "And I promise, I definitely won't let you down. I can start tomorrow after my last class. Will that work?"

"It does." He grinned, his hand now touching mine. "I look forward to having you help around here, Richard."

Now I swallowed hard. I had accomplished what I'd come in to do, but I hoped I'd never have to actually follow through with what he obviously had on his mind. As soon as I got the information Nevada needed, Mr. English would be working all alone again.

"Thanks, Mr. English. See you Monday," I said and was out the door before he tried to flirt some more.

Arielle

34

The entire squad had just left Nevada and Clem's dorm room. It had become our hangout, even when neither one of them was around. We weren't just a team; we were all starting to become friends. Well, almost all of us.

"Where are you going?"

I rolled my eyes when I heard Natasha's whiny voice talking to Nevada. It was puke-worthy, really. I didn't understand how he could be with somebody so needy. It was unbecoming of him. We were on our way to training, but Nevada began to walk a separate way. I glanced back and caught sight of her holding his arm hostage, prohibiting him from taking another step.

This bitch is controlling too? I found myself thinking. I shook my head. He could do so much better. I swore, when it came to Natasha, all the guys saw were her looks and her accent. Nevada needed to wake up.

"I'm going to have tea with Minister Farrah. I'll catch up with you guys later," he said.

"Okay, darling." Natasha kissed him on the cheek. I was confused. Why was she always kissing him on the cheek? If he was my guy, I'd be kissing him more passionately than that.

Nevada and I made eye contact for a second, but I looked away quickly, not wanting him to think I'd been watching long.

Demi was looking at me with a small smile.

"What?" I asked sheepishly.

"Why don't you just tell him?" she asked.

"Tell him what?" I asked. "The same thing you should be telling Ivan?"

"Shhh!" She grabbed my arm and pulled me to the side, checking to make sure the others hadn't heard. "Lower your voice."

"They aren't paying attention to us. Anyway, so what if I like him? He's with Natasha."

"Please." She sucked her teeth. "I don't know how long that will last. Nevada needs somebody who doesn't need him so much. That girl seems like she's under his ass twenty-four seven."

"I know. She's either the most in love woman I've ever met, or the most paranoid."

I looked back again and saw Natasha unlinking her arm with his. I didn't miss the annoyed look on his face when she walked away, and neither did she. When she noticed me looking, her skin turned red. I faced forward with a smirk on my face.

When we arrived at our training building, I went to take my usual seat by Demi in the combat room, but a hand on my shoulder stopped me. It was Natasha.

"You think I don't see you always staring at Nevada with little puppy dog eyes?" she asked, turning her nose up at me.

"I didn't know I could make puppy dog eyes. You'll have to take a picture one of these days and show me since you pay so much attention to me."

"Just back up off of him. He is my man." She tried to put some bass in her voice, but it was far from intimidating.

"Whatever." I waved her off and headed toward Demi.

"Welcome, students," Brother Elijah said. "We will be working on hand-to-hand combat, but today, we're going to be doing things a little differently. Only one match will go at a time instead of everybody at once. You will choose your opponent, and peers will observe you."

Richard raised his hand and asked, "Are we judging them?"

"No. You will be learning from everyone," Brother Elijah said. "Natasha, you're up first. Pick your opponent."

Natasha stood up and went to the center of the floor beside Brother Elijah and surveyed the room. When her gaze fell on me, a small smile spread across her face.

"I want Arielle."

Brother Elijah raised an eyebrow. "Are you sure you want to fight someone on your own squad?"

"Positive."

"Arielle, how do you feel about this?"

"Bring it." I jumped out of my seat. I knew Natasha would be hard to beat. I'd seen her fight others, including guys, but I wasn't going to let her punk me in front of the others. All I wanted to do was wipe the smug look off her face.

Brother Elijah stood between us and spoke to the whole group. "This exercise is to open your eyes. No face shots, and I want to see moves, not reckless punching. The purpose of these trainings is to make you better. Understand all circumstances?"

"Yes, Brother Elijah," we all said in unison.

"Good. Now, ladies, on my signal . . . match!" He pumped his fist and quickly stepped out from between us.

Natasha wasted no time. She drove her fist toward my chest, which I dodged, but I was so focused on not getting punched that I didn't see her foot coming my way. She kicked me in the side and sent me flying. Before I could steady my footing, she was back again with a barrage of punches and kicks. I dodged as many as I could, but once again, I ended up on the ground. I saw what she was doing. There was no better way to win a match than to make sure your opponent was always on defense.

"When I am done with you, you'll wish you never met Nevada Duncan," Natasha hissed at me. "He is strong. He would not want someone weak like you."

When she came at me again, I was ready for her. She swung her right fist, and I dropped to the ground and swept her leg.

"Ahh!" She shouted in pain as she fell to the ground, but then she quickly jumped back up.

"You are weak," she said furiously. That blow seemed to have supercharged her energy, and she swung at me wildly. I knew it would be her downfall. She wasn't battling me with her mind; she was battling me with emotions, and that was blinding her. I knew what I had to do.

"Weak? If I was weak, Nevada wouldn't have me on his squad. You don't want to admit it, but he sees me the same way he sees you. Except I don't annoy him."

"Bitch!" Natasha shouted loud enough for everyone to hear.

"Ladies, take it down a notch," Brother Elijah tried to tell us, but neither one of us listened.

We both were breathing heavily, but I wasn't going to stop until she was down, and she clearly had the same plan for me. I wiped some blood away from my nose just as she came at me again with her fists.

"He does not want you!" she growled.

"We don't know that, because I'm not as thirsty as you. I haven't tried," I shot back.

"And you will never get the chance to!" Natasha attempted to kick me in the groin.

I caught her foot, but she snatched it away. I moved quickly to the side as she extended her arm, trying to smash her fist into my chest.. I saw my opening. Grabbing her wrist, I spun it around behind her back. Once I was behind her, I kicked her knee, making her kneel, and wrapped my free arm around her neck.

I squeezed tightly, cutting off most of her air supply. She clawed at my arm with her free hand, but I barely felt it. I had her right where I wanted her.

"He doesn't want someone like you," Natasha said, choking out the words. "He's mine."

"Someone like me? You must be forgetting one thing. You're cute or whatever, but you will never be me. You will never understand the makings of him the way I can. To you, he's just a boytoy. To me, he's a strong young black man who will lead my people to greatness. Now, tap out so I don't accidently kill you."

To my surprise, she tapped the ground. When I let her go, I shoved her a little. Bitch. The nerve of her.

"Arielle wins!" Brother Elijah exclaimed, and all my peers applauded. Nevada, standing behind the crowd, was clapping the loudest.

Nevada

35

The sound of clinking glasses filled Anna's restaurant as my entire squad celebrated three wins in our first competition. We had excelled in the preliminaries against all the squads we faced. There was one squad we hadn't faced, though, and that was Raheem's squad. Sunday, we'd be going up against them head-to-head, and the winner would be recognized at the Chi's Gala in front of all of the alumni. It was a big deal, because no students were allowed at the gala. I wanted that win for my squad.

I looked around at all of them—Demi, Arielle, Clem, Natasha, Richard, and Ivan. "You all did good this week, and all of your hard work paid off. We did what nobody expected, including ourselves. Win or lose Sunday, I can't begin to tell you how proud I am of all of you."

"We should not celebrate too early, though, Nevada. It could be bad luck," Natasha pointed out. "Raheem's team has beaten all their opponents significantly."

"I agree, but I wouldn't be a good squad leader if I didn't give all of you your props. Clem, the way you rushed into that building and picked that lock in record time was crazy!"

"It was nothing." Clem shrugged. "My brothers taught me how to do that shit when I was a kid. Easy peasy."

"Raheem's team won't be easy to beat, but we can do it. The objective is to capture the other team's flag. It sounds simple, but if you know Minister Farrah, you should know it won't be."

I pulled out a rolled-up piece of paper. "Each squad was given a blueprint of the battleground." Clem and Ivan moved their plates out of the way so that I could unroll it on the table. I pointed at two towers on opposite ends of the battleground.

"This is where our flags will be." I pointed at all of the small buildings and cars in between. "We'll have to figure out the smartest route to their tower with the most coverage and defend our flag at the same time."

"It's not going to be easy," Clem said.

"Ivan?" I asked.

"Yeah?" he grunted.

"I'm going to need you and Clem to cover our asses to the other squad's tower and then cover our six. We can't do this without you."

"No one will sneak up on you," he replied.

"Demi? I need you to—"

"Crack the code at the tower. I know. Us smart guys have to stick together," she said with a wink, and I grinned.

"Natasha, I'm pretty sure Raheem will have some tricks up his sleeve, so I'll need you to take the high ground early."

"No problem, my golden lambchop."

God, I hated when she did stuff like that in front of everybody.

"Okay, well, what about me?" Arielle asked.

"You have the most important job of all. You'll be protecting our flag," I told her. "Arielle, your combat skills will come in handy on the ground. Natasha, you'll be sharp-shooting on the roof of this building." I pointed at a building close to our tower.

"Cool," Arielle said, cracking her knuckles. "I guess I do have a little bit of steam to let off since I've been so stressed about midterms." She turned to Natasha. "You better not let me get shot. Those rubber bullets hurt like a bitch."

"You will be in safe hands," Natasha assured her. Ever since their hand-to-hand contest, the heat between them wasn't quite as intense. Still, I was sure Natasha would protect Arielle for the good of the team, not because she actually cared about her.

"What will Richard be doing?" Natasha asked.

"The most fabulous person at this table got his job days ago," Richard said, speaking about himself in third person. "I'm espionage. I've been spying on Raheem's squad for a week. Lira Gordina, to be exact. I guess she would be who I am for Raheem. All it took was a 'girls' night,' some wine, and me letting her take some selfies with my limited edition Gucci bag for her to spill tea. When she woke up, she didn't even remember our conversation. Their plan is to come at us with all of their force to draw us back."

"That's not smart. All they would be doing is bunching us together, and there is strength in numbers," Ivan said.

"True, but all of our focus would be on the fight, not on protecting our flag. If we're busy fighting most of them, we won't notice that *one* of them is missing, and then our flag is gone," I pointed out. "That's their plan."

"Wow, that's actually pretty smart," Clem noted.

"It is, which is why it's up to the twins to get us to their flag as quietly as possible. So while they're planning to attack, we'll already be behind them."

"Well then, Natasha and Arielle might need an extra set of hands to keep the other squad busy and buy you enough time," Richard said. "I'll stay and help them out."

"How noble of you," Clem said in a dry voice.

"Okay, now that that's settled—" I started.

"Well, well, well!" I was interrupted by a voice from behind me. "You guys celebrating being the second-best squad already?"

I knew who it was before I turned and saw him standing there. Raheem had a smug look on his face as his eyes fell on each member of my squad. His squad was with him.

"What are you doing here, Raheem?" I asked.

"We came out to eat dinner, and I remembered you said you and Natasha really enjoyed this spot. I figured me and my squad could celebrate Sunday's victory early."

He was obviously there to try to intimidate us. I'm sure he'd overheard me and Clem say we were going there.

"Loss. You mean your loss," I corrected.

"Why don't you put your money where your mouth is?" Raheem taunted nastily. "Your little makeshift squad doesn't stand a chance against mine. Only thing you got going for you is cute girls."

I didn't like his tone, his stance . . . actually, nothing about his presence was sitting well with me. Ever since he had been named squad leader, I had been noticing little things about him. He was very competitive, but not with the other leaders, only me. His whole vibe toward me had changed once he got his own squad, and it left me wondering if he had ever been my friend. I knew the difference between friendly competition and flat-out competition. There was nothing friendly about the way he was eyeing me.

"Go sit down, Raheem. Nobody is going to bet you," I said.

"A thousand euros," Airele snapped at them, stepping up.

"No, make it two thousand." Demi stood, folding her arms.

Raheem stared at them, and so did I, but I had to back my squad, win or lose.

"You heard them," I said. "Two thousand euros."

"What's wrong, Raheem? You intimidated?" Clem rose to his feet. "Would it make you feel better if I pretended to shake in my shoes?" He knocked his knees together in exaggerated fear.

"Shut up, Clem. You and I both know that the only reason he's a squad leader is because his family is close to Minister Farrah." Raheem's squad behind him laughed.

"What I know is that you've been jealous of him since day one, Raheem," Clem replied.

"Jealous of what? There is nothing to be jealous of."

"If that's the case, why haven't you ever been able to beat me in hand-to-hand combat or on the pistol range?" I asked, and my friends laughed. I could see that Raheem was flustered, but I didn't care. "I'm starting to think that the only reason you hung around me was because you thought it would help you climb up the ladder faster. But now that you've got your own team, your true colors are showing."

Raheem didn't have much to say about that.

"Now about that bet, what you going to do?" I asked.

"You got a bet," Raheem sneered.

"Good. Now, find a table somewhere else. This side of the restaurant is occupied."

I sat back down and went back to talking to my friends. I heard Raheem and his team walk away, but the look of disdain in his eyes stayed with me. Minister Farrah had been right. They were all gunning for me.

Vegas

36

From the moment I stepped off the plane, I was on edge. There was no doubt in my mind that Marie was somewhere in France, trying her best to make her way to the school to protect Nevada. But from what or who, I didn't know. Of course, looming over everything was the possibility that Marie was just crazy. However, deep down, I was starting to think that she was a lot saner than she let on. At this point, it was all to be determined, and all I could do was get to the school, look out for Marie, and keep an eye on my son until she or our mysterious enemy made their presence felt.

"Mr. Duncan?" I turned to the voice, where I saw a very unimposing old man in a tweed suit. "There's a car waiting for you outside. Right this way."

I gazed at the man for a moment. I hadn't ordered a car. However, I did want to know who had, so I cautiously followed him. He picked up my bag and walked out of the building to an older black Mercedes. He placed my bag in the trunk, and when he opened the rear door, I was surprised to see a familiar face.

"Demetri."

"Hello, Vegas. You are looking well. I guess it's true what they say." He picked up a half-filled glass from a cup holder in the center console and gulped it down as I slid into the back seat.

"I guess it's true what they say. Black don't crack." He laughed, and I joined, but not as enthusiastically.

"Drink?" He lifted a bottle of vodka and filled his glass.

I shook my head. "You're still drinking that shit, I see."

"Yes, it is a hard habit to break. I see you're still dressing like you're a model and not a killing machine." He looked down at my black sports coat, silk shirt, and loafers.

The old man got behind the wheel, and the car started moving,

"So, Demetri, where exactly are we going?"

"To the school. That is where you were headed, isn't it?"

"Yeah, but how did—"

"I know you were coming?" He grinned at me. "Someone made a reservation in room 602 in the castle. And there's only one reason anyone would request that room if there were others available. It's a shithole."

I'd heard he was a drunk, but he sure as hell wasn't stupid. Room 602 was a dump, but it was the only technology-secure room on the campus.

"I have informed the front desk to notify me whenever the room is to be occupied. Imagine my surprise when I heard that the reservation was under the name Michael Johnson. It was pretty obvious it was you."

Michael Johnson had been one of my aliases since I was a student at Chi's.

"Very astute. I guess that's the reason you were our logistics guy," I said.

"Why are you here, Vegas?" He gulped half his drink.

"Why is it any of your business? From what I hear, you're the head groundskeeper, not the head of security."

He narrowed his eyes but gave me an amused smirk. "Hmmm. Perhaps I should speak to the head of security. He might be interested to know that room 602 is the only room secure from his surveillance on the premises."

"I'd prefer you didn't," I replied nonchalantly. Demetri had always been a standup guy, but from what Nevada had told me, he was a pretty shitty human being toward his son. "I need you to trust me, Demetri. That room has been a squad secret for many years."

"Yes, it has, and it shall remain our secret." He poured himself another drink. "Is this about your son?"

"My son and my woman. You remember Marie?"

"Yes, I remember." He studied me for a brief moment. "You are a very interesting man, Vegas Duncan, and so is your son. Many people admire him, including my ignorant son. He is a natural leader like you."

"I'd like to think so. He's a good kid. Very smart." I watched him gulp down half a glass of vodka. "I'm told your son is very smart as well."

He shook his head. "My son is a complete failure. I'm embarrassed to say I sired him."

"He got into MIT. That doesn't sound like failure to me."

"I could give a fuck about MIT. He had to do a second year as an Elite, then he was kicked out of the Elites this year, as well. If it weren't for your son . . ." His voice trailed off, maybe because he'd had so much vodka by this point. "To be truthful, I'd keep your son away from him. He's just no good. He'll screw up your kid too. It's in his genetic material. He's a son of a bitch."

"You don't have to talk about him like that. I'm sure he's a good kid," I said.

He scoffed. "No, I really mean he's a son of a bitch. His mother is a bitch. I hate her. I should have—"

"Listened to me?"

"Yes," he replied humbly as he looked out the window.

All these years later, he was still hurting, and we hadn't addressed the elephant in the room. Her name was Raiel, and she was from Paris. She was unquestionably one of the most beautiful girls on campus with her long, silky blond hair. Everyone on our squad knew Demetri was in love with Raiel, so we barely looked her way.

Marie had left school after her brother's death, and about six months later. Raiel showed up at our dorm with an expensive bottle of brandy and a full-length coat. I should have known then that she was looking for trouble. She claimed she was looking for Demetri, but looking back on it, I'm sure she knew he was away in Ukraine for the weekend.

She offered to stay and share the brandy with me and Daryl, my other roommate, who accepted her offer right away. Halfway through the bottle, she removed her trench coat and revealed that she was completely naked.

"How about a threesome?" she'd suggested.

I'd be lying if I said I wasn't tempted, and I'm sure Daryl was too, but we did the right thing.

"You got to go, Raiel," I told her.

"Yeah, get the hell out," Daryl said as he took one last long look at her body.

We also did the right thing and told Demetri about it. She denied it, telling Demetri we were bold-faced liars. Demetri, of course, took her side.

He moved out of our dorm a few days after that, and we were never the same again. I hadn't spoken more than ten words to him since.

"I knew you weren't lying," he replied.

"Then why'd you marry her?" I was confused.

"Because my love for her was stronger than the lie she told," he replied. "What a bitch."

"Where is she now?"

"Dead, I can only hope. She cleaned out my accounts and left me with no money and a kid." He shook his head as he poured another glass of vodka.

"Ivan is a really good kid. I just want him to do well." His tone softened. "I'm . . . harder on him than I should be, but I don't know how to be any other way. I mean, look at me! I'm a fucking drunk wreck. I don't want him to be like me."

"Come on, Demetri. You have so much potential," I told him, remembering the way he used to be. "You're the only motherfucka in the world who could beat me in hand-to-hand combat. You remember that?"

"Yeah, and I remember what a good sport you were about it," he said with a fond smirk. "You would always get me to teach you my moves. Then by the end, you would kick my ass. That's why you were squad leader. You always wanted to get better."

He leaned back in his seat with his shoulders slumped. "That's how my Ivan is. He deserves better than me."

"So why don't you *be* better? You can start by putting that drink down and telling me why you've picked me up tonight."

Demetri suddenly sat up and looked cautiously over his shoulder. I could sense his paranoia, but what was causing it?

He set his drink on the center console and turned to me with a serious scowl on his face.

He leaned closer. "Jason Starks."

"Our old squad mate?"

"Yes, and the headmaster of the school."

"Yeah, I forgot about that. I heard he died of COVID," I said sadly.

Demetri shook his head. "Vegas, Starks did *not* die from COVID. Someone killed him."

His words came as a shock. "It would take a whole army to kill Starks," I said in disbelief. "I saw some recent pictures of him before he passed. He took that headmaster shit seriously. He was in tremendous shape. Hell, I was surprised to hear that COVID was what finally defeated him."

"You're not hearing me!" Demetri said, banging a fist on the seat. "He was killed. Not by a sickness, but by a person or people."

"Why do you say that?"

"Because it's true. I was with him the morning he died. We went boar hunting."

I'd been told Demetri and Starks had remained close.

"That doesn't mean he didn't have COVID."

He reached in his pocket and pulled out a phone. "Does this look like he had COVID-19?"

He forced a picture in my face, and I studied it. It was a picture of the two of them holding rifles next to a huge boar. He was right; Jason Starks did not look sick at all.

"Who the hell would want to kill Starks?" I asked.

"I don't know. That's why I am talking to you. I just know he did not die of COVID, and they are purposely covering it up. I have proof."

I wanted to believe him, I really did, but a picture he says was taken that day wasn't enough proof. Especially since I could smell the alcohol seeping through his pores. How could I trust a drunk?

"Okay, show me what you have," I said.

Natasha

37

I'd just put the finishing touches on my makeup when I heard a knock at my door. I jumped up from my desk and grabbed my sweater, taking a last-minute glance at myself before turning the doorknob.

"You've got to be the most punctual person I've ever met." I smiled at Nevada.

I had quickly learned that he was never late for anything: class, meetings, meals, or even dates like the one we were about to go on. When he had called and asked me if I was available for dinner, I was ecstatic. We'd been engaging in "kayfabe" for a while, but I wasn't pretending. I'd developed real feelings for him. I hoped he was feeling the same way. Him asking me out was a good sign.

"Time is the most valuable thing a man can spend," he said, looking handsome in his khaki pants and a brown sweater that was identical to his eyes. The coils of his freshly washed, soft curls glistened.

"You're also the most philosophical person I've ever met." I reached over and touched his hair gently.

"Nah, Brother Minister definitely has me beat with the philosophies."

"I think you might be right about that. The other day in the hallway, he told me that trees that are slow to grow bear the best fruit. I still have no clue what he was talking about."

"Patience. Basically, good things come to those who wait," Nevada explained.

I thought about how patient I'd been, waiting for him to make a move, or more importantly, for him to figure out that I loved him.

How much longer do I have to wait? I want him to know.

"I like that," I agreed, deciding that it wasn't time to tell him. I needed to wait a little while longer.

"The only person who might be just as deep is my grandfather. But that makes sense, because they're good friends," Nevada said. "Grandpa has as many adages as Headmaster and a story for every one of them."

"He sounds like quite the character."

"Believe me, he is."

I began putting on my sweater. Nevada, being the gentleman that he was, helped me pull it around my back and held it as I slipped my arm in.

I turned and looked at him. "I'd love to meet him one day. You always have such great things to say about your family."

"Uh, yeah, maybe one day." He shrugged nonchalantly. "You ready?"

"Yes." I made sure to stay by his side as we passed people in the hallway. Although it was a well-known fact, I wanted to make sure they knew that Nevada was off limits, especially Arielle. For the most part, she played it cool, but there was something about the way she looked at Nevada when she thought no one was paying attention that didn't sit right with me. And although we were teammates, I knew that she didn't care for me. Even if she didn't speak it out loud, I could feel her disdain every time she rolled her eyes at me.

We hopped on my scooter and drove into town. Instead of parking in my usual spot, I continued further into the neighboring city, until we arrived at what looked like a small cottage nestled between the other metropolitan buildings.

"Where are we going?" Nevada asked as he removed his helmet and looked around. "I thought we were having dinner."

"We are."

"This isn't Anna's."

I grabbed his hand and led him toward the front door. "We always go to Anna's. I wanted us to go someplace else."

"Here?" Nevada looked uncomfortable.

Mattéo's was a place that I'd overheard one of the female instructors bragging about. She'd gone on and on about how cozy and intimate it was, and I instantly knew it was just the atmosphere that I wanted to experience with Nevada. Anna's food was great, and the fact that she never charged us full price was nice, but every time we went, it just felt friendly, and I wanted us to be more than friends. What we needed was romance.

As we entered, that was exactly what I felt. The dining room was dimly lit by candles on each table. Soft violin music serenaded diners as they enjoyed their meals. The savory aroma of garlic instantly caused my stomach to growl.

"*Bon soir. Bienvenue à Matéo's. Avez-vous une réservacion?*" The maitre'd greeted us with a tight smile. I could tell that he was a little perturbed by us, and I wondered if it was because Nevada was black or that we looked too young to afford a place like that.

"*No, mais peut-on avoir une table pour deux, s'il vous plait?*" In impeccable French, I asked him for a table for two. I wanted him to understand that if he tried to say anything disrespectful, I would understand every word.

He gave us another tense smile and told us to wait there. We'd be seated momentarily.

"Isn't this nice?" I said as I cozied close to Nevada on a small bench in the entryway.

"Uh, yeah, it is." He shifted away from me slightly. "Natasha, I think we need to have a talk."

"A talk? About what?" I already didn't like where this seemed to be heading.

"About our friendship, and *this*." He glanced down at my hand that was now resting on his knee.

"What's wrong? You said that this was okay," I reminded him.

"What I said was I would walk you to class, grab food, and hang out sometimes." He sighed. "But I think it's gotten a little out of hand."

"Out of hand? What do you mean, Nevada?" I tried to remain calm. He sounded as if he no longer wanted to be my boyfriend, and I couldn't let that happen, for so many reasons. "You agreed that you would be my kayfabe boyfriend so I would stay safe. You know what the dean will do if I'm not with you."

"I know. And I thought it would work, but you've gotten to be a little . . . clingy, Natasha. The constant kissing and holding my arm . . ."

"Is that not what boyfriends and girlfriends do? We want people to believe us, right? If we don't show affection, then they will think it's not real," I said.

"It's not."

"No, Nevada, you have to keep me safe," I pleaded, fighting the tears that were forming.

"You will be. I promise. I'm not going to let that perv do anything to you." Nevada put his arm around my shoulder.

God, I hated it when the tears started to fall.

"Don't cry, Natasha."

"Is this because of Arielle?" I asked as I wiped my face.

"What?"

"Arielle. Is this because you like her? You want to be with her?" The questions rolled out so fast that I couldn't stop them.

"This doesn't have to do with anybody but us," he said. "You've gotta fall back. That's all I'm saying."

"Fine, but you'll still be my kayfabe boyfriend if I do that?" I held my breath as I waited for his answer.

"Yes, but you gotta stop with the kissing and being up on me all the time, Natasha, or I won't. We are really just friends, remember?" He stared intensely into my eyes until I gave him a small nod.

I was willing to say or do whatever I had to in order not to lose him. "I remember. Thank you."

"Good." Nevada sounded relieved.

"*Mademoiselle, monsieur, votre table est prête,*" the maitre'd, now carrying menus, came and announced to us.

We stood and followed him toward the rear of the restaurant. Suddenly, Nevada stopped.

"Mom?" His voice was tight and uncertain.

I turned toward the direction he was facing and saw what had him so bewildered.

"Nevada, sweetie." A beautiful woman of Latin descent stood, seemingly just as surprised to see him as he was her. "How are you, mi amor?"

She made her way to us and put her arms around him. Nevada hesitated for a moment, then finally embraced her. I watched them for a second, then turned my attention to the person still sitting at the table.

"Officer Picard," I spoke.

"Natasha." His response was short and simple. Maybe he was just uncomfortable being spotted on a date with a student's mother.

"What are you doing here?" Nevada asked his mother.

"Just a meeting."

Although I'd never met her, I could tell that she was nervous.

She quickly turned her attention from Nevada to me. "Is this your girlfriend?"

"She's my friend, Mom," Nevada answered quickly, then turned the tables back on her. "A meeting with the head of security at my school. Interesting."

"Yes, you know I've always met with your teachers."

"Except he's not a teacher," Nevada muttered. "How long have you been in town? Why didn't you call or say anything?"

"Well, I wanted to surprise you."

"This is definitely a surprise."

"I planned it a little different. But I don't want to keep you from being with your friend. You go ahead, and I'll come by the dorm and find you tomorrow morning and we will talk. Is that okay?" She grabbed Nevada's hand and held it to her smooth face.

The resemblance between her and Nevada was quite strong. I'd heard that he looked like his father, but from what I saw, he'd inherited his mother's long eyelashes, perfectly pouted lips, and beautiful smile.

"Okay." Nevada turned toward the table. "Good evening, sir."

"Good evening, Nevada. I hope you two enjoy your meal."

"I'll see you tomorrow, son." His mother kissed his cheek, leaving a smudge from her lipstick.

Nevada didn't say anything as we walked toward the maitre'd, who was waiting a few feet away. Seeing how bothered and uncomfortable he was, I grabbed his hand.

"You know, Nevada, I'm really not in the mood for Italian tonight, now that I think about it," I said.

"You're not?" He gave me an uncertain look.

"No, I'm not. Let's just go to Anna's and try this place another time." I pulled him toward the door, although he didn't really need to be convinced to leave.

"Sorry about that," he told me when we were outside.

"About what? There's nothing for you to apologize for. You did nothing wrong," I said. "You were just surprised to see your mother, that's all."

"You're right. I'm definitely surprised." He looked out into the distance as if he were deep in thought. "She's up to something."

"Why would you say that?"

"Because I haven't seen or talked to her in over a month, and instead of inviting us to dine with them, she rushes me off. I know my mother very well. She's not here to see me. She's here for something else," he said. "I just hope she's not planning something against my dad."

Nevada

38

"Ladies and gentlemen, this is the first defining moment you will have at the school this year as a team. I would say that I want a clean fight, but a part of me wants to see what each of your squads is truly capable of!"

The voice came from a small television that my squad and I were surrounding. Minister Farrah was live on the screen, talking to us as we huddled in our tower. I had tried my best to block out last night's chance meeting, but it was still at the forefront of my mind.

"In less than five minutes, the doors to your towers will open, and the match will begin. It will not be over until one of your flags is captured and successfully taken back to your tower. Good luck."

With that, the screen went blank. I turned to my friends, ready for battle. The site where we were located off campus had been used many times as a military training course. Behind us on a long table were all of the weapons we would need, which included exploding rubber paintball bullets, ten compressed-air paintball hand grenades, Demi's and Ivan's computers, and a drone.

"Okay, team, load up. And make sure to grab enough reloads," I said. "Remember the plan. It has the most coverage and least probability for any of Raheem's tricks or the headmaster's surprises."

"The most I'd say we may run into is some gas mines. Maybe a few trip wires," Clem said, looking slightly bummed out as he looked at the weapons on the table.

"What's wrong with you?" Demi asked him.

"I was hoping for some explosives. Really was looking forward to blowing some shit up."

"Yeah, and whose idea was it to make the Irish guy the weapons expert?" Richard joked.

Our laughter was cut short by the red lights flashing above the tower door. We quickly finished grabbing the things we would need for the match. It was go time.

"Is everybody ready to put Raheem and his squad of bozos to shame?" I asked.

"Been ready," Ivan said just as the door hummed and swung open.

"Then let's go."

We ran through the door, with Ivan in the front of the line. He knelt and aimed his gun in every direction. When he was sure it was clear, he motioned the rest of us forward.

Arielle and Richard got into their positions to protect the door, while Natasha went for the high ground. Demi launched the drone. Clem took point, and the rest of us followed around a series of cars and in between small buildings, crouching low and stepping carefully on the soft ground.

It was a little chilly, but my adrenaline pumping made it hard for me to feel it. We were passing another building when suddenly, Clem put his hand up to stop us abruptly. He put a finger to his mouth and made a gesture for us to get down behind the low brick wall nearby.

A few moments later, we heard footsteps not too far from us. I peeked around the edge of the brick wall and saw two members of Raheem's squad rushing toward our tower. They didn't see us, and we waited for a few more moments before we kept pushing forward.

I tapped my headset. "Natasha, you're about to have company."

"Copy that," was her response right before I heard two shots. "I have one down and the other pinned down behind a rock."

"That was close," Demi said, though she had spoken too soon.

From a structure near the building came a big black dude with an angry scowl on his face. He was another one of Raheem's, and he looked like he was out for blood. I knew him by name only, Kendrick. I didn't know who his parents were or what they did, but the way he had always kicked ass in training made those details unimportant at the moment.

"I got this," Ivan said, stepping forward and putting two shots in Kendrick's chest. Yellow paint splattered everywhere.

Out of nowhere, a colorfully dressed Brother Elijah jumped out and flagged him. "You are dead, Kendrick."

The disappointment on Kendrick's face was priceless as he clutched his chest. we were all wearing padded flak jackets and helmets, but those rubber exploding bullets were painful as hell. In our last match, they had knocked the wind out of both Richard and Demi. You did not want to get hit with one of them.

"Let's go. That shot gave away our position. If there was one of them, there have to be more." Clem walked carefully around Kendrick, whose face didn't reveal whether Clem's supposition was correct.

I stepped back and allowed my point man to lead us for a minute. We walked behind Clem in a straight line. Soon, we could see the enemy tower in the distance.

"Good job back there," I said to Ivan as we walked.

"It was nothing. I want to win for our team and for you to have confidence in me."

"I do," I said, then turned to Demi. "We're almost there. What do you see on the drone?

"Nothing. They're pretty well hidden," she replied.

"Are you ready to use your brain power? I'm sure Minister Farrah didn't give us an easy code to crack."

"I'm as ready as I'll ever be."

"Guys, you're going to have to make your move. Richard's down, and I'm taking on a lot of fire," Arielle shouted into the walkie-talkie.

"Copy that," I replied. I hadn't thought they would get to our tower and engage that quickly. "Natasha, Arielle could use all the help she can get."

"Copy."

"Clem and Ivan, if anybody is coming while Demi and I are working, use the grenades to take them out. And find the sniper with that drone."

"No problemo," Clem said, and Ivan nodded.

We checked the surrounding area and the rooftops, but the coast seemed clear. In the distance, we heard sound of nonstop gunfire. I knew we didn't have much time before Raheem's team captured our flag. Clem and Ivan took cover behind cars and pointed their weapons in opposite directions to watch our six.

I looked at Demi, and we nodded at each other before rushing quickly to the tower door. There was a keypad next to it, and above it were four sentences.

"A riddle?" Demi made a face.

"'I am three digits long. I hurt the most when lost, yet also when not had at all. I am a phrase used lightly, but still not enough. I can be given to many, or just one.'" I recited it out loud, hoping something would come to me. It didn't.

I thought the code to get into the tower might be an equation, but then again, Minister Farrah probably knew that would be too easy for me. A riddle required me to use a different part of my brain, and that made it the best choice. I recited it again in my head but still came up blank.

"Money? Maybe we're supposed to spell a word, like the way phones have letters on each number," Demi guessed.

I shook my head. "Then the word *money* wouldn't work. It's too long. The riddle says the code is only three digits." I continued to stare at the writing next to the keypad, and as I focused my attention, it was like the world around me faded. My mind dissected every sentence and every word, looking for meaning, until finally it hit me as gently as a feather falling into my lap. "I got it."

"Arielle is down!" I heard Natasha chirp. "They are at the keypad."

"Shit," I cursed. "Ivan, go get their asses."

"Copy that," the big man said.

"How the hell did they overwhelm us so easily?" Demi asked.

"Love," I said simply.

"Love?" Demi asked. "What are you talking about?"

"Well, I guess not *love*. The riddle says it's a phrase used lightly, but not enough. And the phrase is *I love you*. Try the number of letters in each word. One, four, three."

"Nevada, you're a genius," Demi said with a grin.

"Tell me that if it works."

Demi turned to input the number into the keypad, but a shot rang out, and Demi was splattered with paint. I jumped out of the way and ended up pinned down behind a car.

"Duncan!" It was Raheem.

I didn't know where his voice was coming from, but the next thing I knew, gunfire began raining down on us. The tower door was riddled with paint, and Brother Elijah was standing over Demi.

"You didn't think our team would really let you win, did you?" Raheem yelled out to me.

There were so many gunshots I couldn't tell if the weapon was automatic or if there was more than one person shooting. When there was a brief pause, Clem rushed up and crouched down next to me.

"He's on the roof!" Clem said. "Five o'clock."

"Where did you come from?"

"Thought you might need some company, mate." He laughed. "You figure out the code?"

"I've got it, but not that it's going to do us much good."

We heard more gunshots hit the car.

"That's Raheem. They sent everything but the kitchen sink at our tower and left him, their best shot, to protect their tower. They figured even if we get the code, he can keep us pinned down and hold us here."

"Which he has," I said with a sense of urgency. "Any ideas? I don't think our people can hold out much longer."

"Yeah, but it's a suicide mission for me. I'm gonna rush his position and draw his fire. He'll probably hit me with those damn rubber bullets about ten times, but I figure you'll have three or four seconds to put the code in."

"Clem, you're one hell of a teammate."

"Remind me of that when you're rubbing liniment on my big-ass purple bruises." He lifted his fist and I fist bumped him. "On three."

I did a countdown with my fingers, and Clem shot out from behind the car, screaming and shooting. He zig-zagged his way in the direction where the bullets were coming from while, at the same time, I bolted to the keypad.

Marie

39

"Twinkle, twinkle, little star. How I wonder . . ." I sang as I leaned out the small steeple window, smoking a cigarette as I watched some students playing capture the flag. From where I was, I could see just about anything going on around the campus without being seen myself, which was why I had chosen to stay in the five-by-five attic-like structure in the first place. Using the underground tunnels, I'd already stolen enough food from the dining hall to last me and the rats a month, so eating wasn't a problem, but I was going to have to go to town soon, because I was on my last pack of smokes.

"Get down! Get down!" I heard someone yell, and then I heard shots.

I froze for a moment, then realized the orders weren't directed at me. I scanned the legion of bodies running back and forth across the huge makeshift field that was a combination of wooded areas, small buildings, abandoned cars, and two small towers on the south side of campus.

"Calm down, Marie." I laughed. "They're just playing war games."

I scanned the area, and sure enough, I recognized Nevada, even though he wore goggles and a mask. He had his dad's humble cockiness about him.

"That's him," I whispered, relieved that he was safe. I watched him as he maneuvered his way to a makeshift bunker for cover. "Go, Nevada, go."

I became engrossed in the faux battle, silently cheering for Vegas's son. It was intense, and the grit and tenacity of the teams was apparent. Nevada arrived at the bunker and joined a girl and another guy just as I heard more shots. That's when I saw a black boy on top of a building dressed similarly but in a different color. He had them pinned down pretty good, but Nevada and his people fought back until the girl was shot and her outfit was covered with yellow paint.

"Damn," I said to myself, though it wasn't over yet. Nevada and his teammate still had a chance. Or did they? From the corner of my eyes I spotted something strange on the castle wall. It wasn't so much that a man walking on the wall was strange as it was that he seemed to be carrying—Shit. It was a sniper's rifle case! What the fuck was he going to do with a sniper rifle?

He's going to shoot someone, you fucking idiot!

I watched him kneel and begin to unzip the bag, looking in the direction of Nevada's war games match. That's when I realized the bastard had red hair, and my stomach tightened up like a knot.

He's one of them, and he's going to shoot Nevada! Don't just stand there, Marie. Do something! the little voice in my head screamed.

I was frozen in place. That man would kill me if I revealed my location.

If you don't, he'll kill Nevada, and Kia will never forgive you!

I ran toward the steeple access door on the floor, flipping it open and quickly climbing down the narrow tower until I was right above the level of the castle wall. I opened the window and looked over at the redhead. He now had the rifle out of the case and was assembling the scope.

Do something, Marie!

I was trying, dammit, but I was scared! I looked down at the castle floor, which was about an eight-foot drop. If I survived this, that kid had better visit me in the old folks home, I thought.

I took a breath and jumped, landing hard on the castle wall. It took me a moment, but I was okay. Nothing was broken or sprained, and the redhead hadn't even noticed me because he was concentrating so hard on the field as he put his weapon together.

Bitch, snap out of it! He's going to shoot Nevada!

The voice was right. The sniper was now taking position. I had to do something, so I just started to run.

Faster, dammit! Faster!

I was going as fast as I could. By the time I reached him, he was prepared to shoot, so all I could do was run into him as fast as I could.

"Nevada's got the flag?" I heard someone yell.

Pow! Pow!

A series of loud shots rang out as the both of us went over the side of the wall. All I can remember is thinking, *God, please don't let him have shot Nevada and made my sacrifice in vain.* I braced myself for impact and my most certain death, but the landing wasn't that bad. In fact, I hit the water in the moat, not land.

I didn't know how deep it was, and I didn't care as I made my way to the surface. The sniper was in the water with me. When he looked my way, I submerged myself underwater, swimming until I was under the drawbridge and out of sight.

Vegas

40

"Go, Nevada, go!" I had promised myself I would never be one of those overzealous parents that screamed like a maniac on the sidelines, but as I watched my son move at the speed of light toward his home base with his opponents' flag in his hand, I couldn't help myself. I literally forgot any sense of decorum and cheered him on. He wove his way down the field, dodging paintball bullets and the guy right on his heels simultaneously.

"Jeez, your boy is fast as hell," Security Chief Picard complimented.

"What he lacks in brawn, he makes up for in speed. Much like his father at that age." Minister Farrah commented with a nod toward me.

"I don't think I was ever that fast." I smiled, watching Nevada.

Pow! Pow!

I turned to Minister Farrah. "Did you hear that? Sounded like a gunshot."

"Probably some of the younger students at the gun range with Professor Grant," Picard said.

"Yeah, I guess," I replied, but my senses told me to be alert. I glanced at the castle wall and saw just the slightest puff of smoke.

Minister Farrah seemed unconcerned. He pointed my attention back to the competition. "Looks like your son is securing his victory."

Nevada had just arrived at the bunker with the flag. His teammates surrounded him, all jumping and screaming.

I was a proud father, for sure. However, instead of rushing to join the victors, I ventured to the far edge of the field near the castle wall. If my instincts were correct, which they usually were, this would be the most reasonable place for a gunman to position himself.

I searched the ground quickly for shell casings but came up empty. I was about to call myself paranoid when I spotted a shiny black object in the grass near the concrete barrier. I leaned down and picked it up. It was the scope of a rifle. Damn it, someone had taken a shot. What the hell was going on? And who took that shot?

I turned and saw Minister Farrah and Picard looking toward me, so I slipped the scope into my pocket and strolled back toward them. Nevada ran to meet me before I made it back to the field.

"Dad, we won!"

"I saw. I could tell everyone on your team knew what they were doing. That lets me know y'all had a strategy." I put my arm around his neck.

"It was more Clem than anyone. He sacrificed himself so that we could win." Nevada looked up at me. "I did what you said. I didn't choose a squad based on who would do well in competition. I picked the best individuals I knew I could count on no matter what. Today, I could count on them all."

"That's what's up. Nice to know you listen to your old man."

We shared our secret handshake.

"I do. By the way, I called you last night to give you a heads up, but you didn't answer."

"Heads up about what?" I asked.

"Mom is here."

"Here? As in France?" I frowned.

"Yeah, here in town. I saw her last night in a restaurant with Officer Picard. She's definitely up to something," he explained.

Goddamn, Consuela was such a nuisance. No doubt she was plotting some way to use Nevada to get back at me. "We'll talk about her later. In the meantime, any update on the pin situation?"

"Not yet, but I got somebody working on it, so it won't be long. I'm sure I'll have the information for you soon."

"Good to hear," I said.

"I gotta get back to my squad."

"That's fine. I have somebody I need to go find myself. I'll call you later." I hugged him again. "Good job, Nevada. I'm proud of you."

As he ran back across the field, I reached into my pocket and touched the object inside. I hated to think that the person it belonged to had put my son in danger. I damn sure was about to find out who it was.

Vegas

41

"Nice place you have here, Demetri," I said as I stepped inside the quaint, cottage-style home. I could smell the liquor on him, but he wasn't totally inebriated. He led me to the living room, where I made myself comfortable.

"It's one of the few perks of working at the school. But I know it's nothing like the mansions you've lived in, Duncan," he replied in his thick Ukrainian accent.

"You're right. It's nothing like it. It's quiet here, something I've learned to appreciate over the years. But enough of the small talk," I said, then got right to my point. "I've been doing a lot of thinking about what we talked about on the ride over. You said you have proof of Stark's murder. I'd like to see it."

"All of a sudden you believe me?" He laughed, pouring himself a drink. There was a glass next to his, but he did not offer me one.

"Let's just say I've heard crazier things in relation to this school as of late, and I'm determined not to be closed-minded until I get to the bottom of things. So, what you got?"

"Do you remember how I mentioned the perks of working at the school?"

"Yeah, that was like two seconds ago."

"Don't patronize me, Duncan. I told you about one perk. The other is having access to all the security footage of the grounds at the school. It helps me keep an eye on misbehaving students, vandals, and my grounds crew." He paused and stared at me as if he weren't sure if I could be trusted. Then, after gulping down his drink for courage, he relinquished. "After Starks' death, I took the liberty to play back the week's footage around the headmaster's house."

"Why? How was that going to help . . ." Then I stopped myself. I'd answered my own question, but I let Demetri spell it out in his own words.

"Because his death had the whole campus on fourteen-day quarantine, and we were only four days in. I'd just finished my last bottle, and I needed a drink. I figured in my own warped way that if I could prove Starks didn't have COVID, they'd let me go to town and buy a few bottles."

"And what did you find?"

Once again, he poured a drink and gulped it down. "Something I wish I could get out of my head."

That statement got my attention, because Demetri was not a soft man at all. "What happened?"

"Three men approached Starks' home that night, and when he opened the door, they slit his throat and dragged him inside the house."

Slit his throat? Where had I heard that before?

"Shit! What did you do after that?"

"I called the head of security and explained what I saw. Picard had me meet him at the house, which I did. I thought for sure there would be some kind of evidence with a butchery like that, but there was nothing."

"Nothing at all? No trace, no nothing?" This wasn't making sense.

"That's exactly what Picard said to me when he arrived."

"Did you take him back to your place and show him the footage? Sounds like a problem solved to me."

"I offered to, but that's when he said he smelled alcohol on my breath, which I'm sure he did."

"Oh, shit." I lowered my head.

"Oh, shit is right. He asked me to take a Breathalyzer. When I refused, he and his rent-a-cops tried to force me to take it."

"I take it that didn't go so well?" I sat up in my chair.

"Not well at all." He paused to finish his drink. "I think I broke two of their arms and knocked out at least ten of their teeth before they finally put me down. I was surprised they didn't take me to the local constable, but instead, they threw me in the brig for two weeks."

That wasn't too surprising. "The school likes to take care of school business internally. The less outside interference the better. It's been like that for almost a century. You know that."

"Perhaps, but it was a very short sentence, and I was not taken in front of the board, just released. The whole thing was swept under the rug."

Now, that was interesting.

"So, nobody ever saw the footage?" I asked.

"By the time I was finally released from the brig, someone had professionally wiped the footage clean from both my computer at home and the server."

My eyes widened in disbelief. "Which means whoever killed Stark had help from within the school."

"Exactly. I think you are beginning to see the big picture," he replied.

"You called me over here to tell me something like this, and all of the proof is gone?"

He grinned. "I never said that."

"You just said the footage was wiped clean."

"It was." Demetri pulled a jump drive from his pocket. "But I made a copy before I left my house. I don't trust anybody. It is grainy and low res, but now you can see what I have seen."

He popped the drive into a laptop and handed it to me. I opened the file and watched the screen in silence. It was dark, but I could make out Stark's face clearly. The three men's backs were facing the camera, and when they turned, I could see black N95 masks that concealed their faces.

Demetri was not wrong. They took Starks out quick. They were relentless, sticking their long knives in him from all angles before finally putting him down and slitting his throat. It was brutal, but I watched it again, trying to zoom in on the men's faces. The combination of darkness, a low-res picture, and those damn masks made it impossible to identify any of them.

"You recognize any of these guys?" I asked Demetri.

"No. That's why I need your help." He took the laptop back.

"Demetri, my friend, I think we need to help each other." I reached over and lifted the bottle, pouring myself a drink. "I think it's time for me to tell you a story, a dark story about twelve gruesome murders."

Richard

42

My first week at the alumni office had gone by quicker than expected, maybe because I knew so much was riding on the information I was hoping to provide to Nevada and his father. For all I knew, the person they were looking for might not exist, but for the sake of his sanity and my future with the squad, I sure hoped they did. So far, only five people had come in for replacement pins, and two had called.

"Can I help you, sir?" I asked in the same pleasant tone I'd been using all evening.

"I hope you can." A tall, rugged-looking man with dark brown hair approached the counter. He had a British accent, and his hands were ten times the size of mine. "My name is Vincent Chest, and I seem to have misplaced my pin. I'd like to replace it."

"Of course, Mr. Chest." I handed him a piece of paper. "I'm just going to need you to fill out this request form. I'm also going to need to know your method of payment, and we will get that taken care of."

"Method of payment?" He looked at me like I was out of my mind.

"Yes, sir. A replacement pin costs—"

"I know how much the bloody pin costs, but what I don't know is why I have to pay it!" His face was starting to become very red. "As much money as I donate to this bloody school?"

"I'm sorry, sir. It's just protocol. I was under the impression that all alumni knew there would be a fee to replace a missing pin."

"Protocol? Fuck protocol! You little she-man, do you know who I am?" He placed his large hands down on the counter.

"From what you've told me, your name is Mr. Chest," I replied. I knew I was being a smart-ass, but only lovers and friends could call me a she-man.

"Just shut your trap and go back to the damn safe and get me my fucking pin, or I'll bloody come across the counter and get it myself!" The fire in his eyes let me know he probably would make good on that threat.

Luckily for me, Mr. English came out of nowhere and stepped beside me.

"You will do nothing of the kind, Vinny," Mr. English said, pointing a shotgun at the man's chest. "Now, what's the problem? Did you lose your pin again?"

Mr. Chest didn't lose any of his attitude. "Yes, I lost the fucking pin, and I want a new one." The guy had balls. Even with a shotgun pointed at him, he was still belligerent.

"I'll gladly to go to the back and grab you another pin as soon as you pay for it," Mr. English said, not backing down.

"Fine! I'll pay for the damned thing," Mr. Chest grumbled and pulled a checkbook from his pocket. He scribbled on one of the checks and slammed it on the counter. Mr. English examined it, and when he was satisfied, he lowered the shotgun and stepped away from the counter briefly. When he returned, he had a small maroon box in his hands.

"Here you are," he said, handing Mr. Chest the box. "Maybe this time you'll be more responsible with it."

"Fuck you, English." Mr. Chest stormed out of the office.

"I'm sorry about that," Mr. English said to me, his eyes full of concern. "Are you all right?"

"Yeah, I'm fine. He was just very rude."

"He's just a drunk. This is the third pin he's lost, and I have a pretty good idea why," Mr. English said and reached to tuck a piece of hair behind my ear. "But don't you worry. I'll be right here to set anyone straight for you."

"Uh, thank you?"

I was relieved when another alumnus walked in and interrupted the awkward moment. All week, Mr. English had used every opportunity he could to flirt with me. That day, he'd even combed and gelled his hair and sprayed some cologne over a nice collared shirt. Normally he dressed casually, and I didn't remember ever noticing cologne on him. I hoped he hadn't gone through all of the trouble for me, but a part of me knew he had. On the other hand, I wore tight jeans and a tight-fitting shirt along with a sports coat because I knew Mr. English liked to see my body. I was doing my part for the team, but I sure hoped I wouldn't have to do it for much longer. His attention was kind of funny at first, but now it was giving me the creeps.

"Can I get some help?" I heard a man ask,

I looked up and froze for a second. It was Demi's dad. I hadn't seen him since move-in day, but he was unforgettable. His gaze was electrifying, and not in a good way. His high cheekbones made his face look tight and angry, and he didn't seem so happy to see me now.

"What can I assist you with?" I asked.

"Isn't it obvious?" He pointed to the fabric on his shirt. "I lost my pin."

"Okay, I can help. Just fill this out and tell us how you'll be paying."

"I have a check," he said, pulling it out of his pocket. "Just take it and give me the pin, please."

"Unfortunately, you still have to fill out the form for our records, sir."

"Fine. Fine! Here."

What was it with these alumni and their demanding bull-shit? I swore I would never act that way toward students when I came back to campus after graduation.

Demi's dad hastily filled out the form and handed it back to me with his check. I went to give the paperwork to Mr. English. He scrutinized it for a minute, peered at Demi's dad, then went into the back. It didn't take him long to come back out and hand me a box, no more than five minutes, but when I got back to the front desk, Demi's dad had the most anxious look on his face. He seemed . . . antsy. He kept looking over his shoulder like he didn't want anybody to know he was there. When I finally handed him the pin, he grabbed it, ducked his head down, and left the office. Strange. I made a mental note to tell Nevada about it.

"All right, we're done for the evening," Mr. English said to me a few hours later. "How about a cup of coffee?"

"Sorry, Mr. English. No can do. I have to meet with my squad," I said, turning away to grab my bag so he wouldn't see the face I made.

"Maybe next time." I could hear his disappointment.

We were about to leave when the door to the office swung open. A man bounded inside, breathless, like he had just run a marathon.

"Did I make it? I'm not too late, am I?" he asked with a heavy Irish accent.

"That all depends. How can we help you?" Mr. English asked.

"I called earlier. I'm embarrassed to say, I lost my pin," he said humbly. "I filled out the paperwork online. I just wanted to give you a check and pick up a new one."

"Yes. You're Patrick McCloud's son Michael. We talked on the phone?"

"Yes, sir, we did."

"Let me go back and get your pin." He turned to me. "Richard, why don't you take care of his payment so we can all get out of here? Michael has a long drive back."

Mr. English went back to where the safe was kept.

"I know your brother Clem. He's on my squad," I said as McCloud handed me a check.

"Yeah, I heard about this squad of yours. On the school's website, they call you guys The Baby Terminators." He chuckled. "I hear you guys refuse to lose."

"We're pretty good," I replied, trying to stay unpretentious. "You coming by the dorms to see your brother?"

"My da's there now, telling him about our brother who passed."

"Oh, wow. Sorry to hear that. What happened?"

"He was hit by a truck."

Jesus, poor Clem, I thought.

Consuela

43

I checked my lipstick and put on my sunglasses as we pulled up to the entrance of the school. The text I had sent Nevada before leaving my hotel had gone unanswered, but I figured it was because he was in class. Seeing him at the restaurant had been unexpected and uncomfortable for everyone. My plan was to surprise him, but I'd had some important business to discuss with the head of security. Now that it had been taken care of, I could spend time with my son.

"I'm here to see Nevada Duncan," I told the receptionist who was seated at a small desk in front of the gate.

"Do you have identification? This is a secure facility." The woman looked more like one of the students than an employee.

I handed her my almost-full passport. As she typed into the computer in front of her, I glanced around at the students walking past, all wearing the same uniform. It was still unbelievable to me that Nevada had chosen this overpriced boarding school over Harvard. He wanted to be so much like his father.

"Madame, it appears that you are not on Nevada Duncan's visitation list, and he is not presently in his dorm."

I stepped out of the car and approached her, trying to see the computer screen over her shoulder. "What do you mean? I'm his mother, for God's sake. Why would I not be on there?"

"I'm not sure, but I cannot allow you beyond this point, because you have not been granted access," she explained.

"I don't need to be on a list in order to have access to my son. Never mind. I'll find him myself." I moved to walk past her, but a security officer appeared out of nowhere and stopped me.

"Madame, I'm going to have to ask you to leave the premises," he said.

"I'm not leaving anywhere without seeing my son."

He was so tall that I had to crane my neck and look up at him, but neither his height nor his dominating demeanor intimidated me. I'd dealt with far more brutes who'd been taller, bigger, and way more dangerous. If necessary, I would have no problem showing him my defense skills.

"Madame, please, we do not want to cause a disruption in front of our students," the receptionist said from behind her desk.

"Then both of you get the hell out of my way and there won't be a disruption!" I yelled, causing several students to stop and look.

The security guard reached for my arm, and I stepped back before he could grab me.

"I'll have you know I'm a close personal friend of Minister Farrah. I can have your jobs for this," I threatened them.

"Then I suggest you call him," the nasty lady guard said.

I heard a familiar voice over my shoulder asking, "What the hell are you doing?" I stopped struggling with the guard and turned around. The look on my face had to be identical to the one Nevada had worn when he saw me at the restaurant. I was just as shocked.

"What are *you* doing here?" I stared at Vegas, who was standing a few feet away. "I'm here to see my son," I told him.

"What the hell are you up to, Consuela?"

"Like I said, I'm here to see my son. But for some reason, I'm not on his visitation list. Undoubtedly, that was your doing."

"Had you been a decent mother and been here when we brought him, your name would be on that list," Vegas shot back at me.

"You bastard. How dare you speak to me that way?"

"I speak to you the way you deserve to be—"

"Stop it!" Nevada rushed over and jumped between us.

I looked at him, then looked around, realizing that we now had a crowd watching. We had not only embarrassed ourselves, but our son as well.

"What's going on?" he asked us.

"I came to see you, but they wouldn't allow me." I tried to explain before Vegas could convolute the situation like he always did. "I think it's your father's doing."

"She's with me," Nevada told the security guards. "You can put her on my list."

The guard nodded and stuck out her hand. "Madame, your passport."

I snatched my property from her and put it into my purse. Nevada motioned for us to follow through the gate. I ignored Vegas, who was rolling his eyes at me as he held the door. I felt a bristle of electricity as I passed by his body. As much as I disliked him in that moment, I couldn't deny the fact that I was still attracted to him.

"Can someone please tell me what's going on?" Nevada asked when we were far enough away that others couldn't hear our conversation.

"When I got here, she was being hauled out, son." Vegas smirked.

"Hauled out? You're lying, as usual." I glared at him, then turned to Nevada. "That's not true, mi amor."

Nevada sighed. "Mom, why are you here?"

"I came to see you. I told you the other night I was coming to see you, honey."

"That was a week ago." He did not sound happy.

"I know, but I got caught up in a few things in Paris. I—"

The ringing of Vegas's phone interrupted me. Surprisingly, he didn't even bother looking at it before he pushed the button to turn it off. *It must be one of his other whores*, I thought. *At least he has the decency to ignore their calls when he's with me.*

"Yeah, that's another question I have. If you came to see Nevada, why were you on a date with the head of campus security instead of here?"

I smirked at his invasive question. "Date? Is that what you think I was on? Not that it's any of your business, Vegas, but that wasn't a date. That was a business meeting."

"A business meeting in the back corner of a candlelit restaurant? Tell that bullshit to someone else, Consuela," he snapped.

"You sound like you're jealous." I laughed. "Just because I had a dinner meeting doesn't change the fact that I came to visit my son. Despite what you may think, I am a good mother, and Nevada knows that."

"I wonder if he'll feel the same way after I show him what I found in your safe."

I gasped. "You wouldn't fucking dare!"

"Oh, trust me, I would."

Now Nevada's phone interrupted the conversation. Unlike his father, he looked down at the screen before answering. "Grandpa?" He stepped away to take the call.

"Why do you insist on being like this, Vegas?" I lowered my voice. "You know I love you."

"Because you're up to something, and whatever it is, it isn't good. I'm not gonna allow you to get my son caught up in your bullshit."

"Your son? He's my son too, and I think you sometimes forget that," I told him.

"Dad. Dad!" Nevada had to yell a few times before we heard him over our arguing.

"Grandpa tried to call you. He wanted you to know that the DNA isn't a match," Nevada said to his father.

"Don't tell me you had a paternity scare, Vegas. Shouldn't you be more careful than that?" I raised an eyebrow.

"Go to hell, Consuela." Vegas turned away from me and spoke to Nevada. "The DNA from the Hellfire Club. One of the orderlies ended up dead at the hospital where Marie was."

"Marie killed someone?" Nevada sounded alarmed.

"That doesn't surprise me one bit." I shook my head in disgust. "That woman—"

Nevada held up a hand to stop me. "Mom, please, not now." Then he asked Vegas, "What's that mean for us?"

"It means we're still looking for a redhead, son." He took a step away from us. "Look, I gotta go take care of something. I'll be back later so we can talk." Vegas glanced at me, then added, "Alone."

"Okay, Dad." Nevada hugged his father.

When Vegas walked away, he said, "Mom, wait here. I gotta go grab my bag and then we can go somewhere and chat."

"I'd like that, mi amor."

As Nevada walked away, I turned around and noticed Vegas now engaged in what looked like a serious conversation with one of the groundskeepers. From the expressions on the man's face, I could tell he was quite upset. Vegas might have been wondering what I had going on, but now, I was wondering the same thing about him.

Nevada

44

Our squad had reassembled back in the lounge at my dorm. Everyone was there, camped out in their respective corners, except Richard, who had been working in the alumni office, and Clem, who had just left for Ireland to bury his brother. Although we didn't know him, Clem's brother's death hit us all hard because it hit Clem hard.

"One of us should have gone with him," Demi said from the kitchen table, breaking our silence.

"When I came back from town with my mom, I asked if he wanted me to go, but one glance from his father put an end to that," I explained, checking my watch and glancing at the door.

"Okay, why in the bloody hell do you keep looking at the door as if you're waiting for someone to come through at any second?" Arielle asked. "Do you have a hot date?"

Natasha, who was seated near me, whipped her head in my direction and gave me a piercing gaze. I was really starting to think that she had forgotten that we weren't really a thing. Glancing at the door again, I didn't want to jump the gun and tell them exactly what I was waiting on, but when Richard came bursting in, out of breath, I didn't have to.

"It's about time. You were supposed to be here an hour ago!" I snapped at Richard.

"My bad. I had a last-minute pin replacement to do. One you might be interested in," Richard said as he plopped his knapsack down on the kitchen table by Ivan and Demi. "Did you guys hear about Clem's brother?"

"Yes," Natasha said. "To be mauled by your own dog. That's a horrible way to go."

"Mauled? I thought he was hit by a truck." Richard looked confused.

"That's not what Clem told us when he left," Demi said.

Richard shrugged. "Maybe I'm mistaken."

"Sounds like you were," Natasha said.

I got up from my seat and headed toward my room.

"Richard, can I speak to you for a minute?"

"Sure thing."

I entered my room, and he followed.

"What do you got? My dad's been asking."

Richard pulled a small piece of paper out from one of the pockets of his bag and handed it to me. It was a list of names and addresses of people who had lost their pins. I felt Richard's eyes on me as I went down the list. Most of them, I had no clue about, but my teeth clenched slightly when I saw the name Michael McCloud.

"Michael McCloud." I turned and stared at him. "Is he related—"

"Uh-huh, sure is."

Fuck! I sat on my bed somberly. "He's Clem's brother?"

"Yep."

"Does he have red hair too?"

"He sure does."

"Thanks. You did good." I gave Richard a pat on the shoulder. "But let's keep this between us until we're sure."

"Sure about what? You haven't told me anything."

"I will, sooner than later," I said. "Do me a favor. Ask Ivan and Demi to come in here."

"You think Clem's family is involved in whatever the hell you and your father are trying to figure out?" he asked.

"I hope not," I said seriously as I stared at the list, hoping I'd discover that some of the others on the list had red hair, so we could rule out Clem's brother. "Because I'd hate to have to kill my best friend."

I could feel the intense look Richard gave me before he walked out of the room.

Vegas

45

The urgency of the situation showed in the way I knocked on the minister's door. It was the second time I'd dropped in on him unannounced, and just like the last time, I was preparing to tell him something that he wouldn't want to hear. I kind of wished I had come a few days earlier, but convincing Demetri of Minister Farrah's trustworthiness had not been easy. We were now on the same page, and I was determined to have the minister on that same page as well. What I wasn't prepared for was his right hand man, Brother Elijah, answering the door.

"Vegas." Brother Elijah greeted me with a smile. "Good morning."

"Morning. I need to see the minister," I said.

He looked past me toward Demetri with worried eyes. I'm sure he would have allowed me in if I were alone, but from his demeanor, I knew that Demetri concerned him.

"Let me see if he's available." He stepped away from the door, and a few moments later, the minister was standing before us.

"Vegas, is everything all right?" he inquired.

"Can we come in, Minister?" I asked.

The minster looked to my left and took notice of Demetri standing there. "I see you've brought our friend Demetri with you. Yes, yes. Please, come in."

"Thank you," we said.

He took us to the dining room and poured us some hot tea his wife brought out. Brother Elijah stood off to the side. I didn't want any, but I sipped the tea out of respect. Demetri, on the other hand, took the tea gladly, although he pulled out a flask and poured something in it before he drank it.

"From the serious looks on your faces, I'm going to skip the pleasantries and just ask why the two of you are here."

"We come with news about Headmaster Stark's death, Minister," I said.

"His death?" Minister Farrah looked genuinely confused. "He's been dead for months now. He died of COVID."

"No, he didn't. He was murdered," Demetri said loudly.

Brother Minister glanced at Brother Elijah, who remained pokerfaced.

"I'm well aware of your theory, Demetri. Security Chief Picard has informed me of your accusations and your tenure in the brig."

"He was murdered," Demetri repeated, ignoring the minister's condescending tone.

"If this is true, why would the doctors say it was COVID?" Minister Farrah asked, unconvinced.

"Everyone has a price, even to do the most unholy things, like cover up a murder," Demetri said.

"And COVID was one of those things that nobody wanted to get close to. It was like carrying a poisonous viper around at all times. It worked in their favor," I added.

"Whose favor?" Minister Farrah looked at me as if I were the drunk one.

"The killers."

Minister Farrah scoffed. "Vegas, I am sorry, but this is just something I don't believe. Who would want to kill Starks?" He put a hand up to silence Demetri, who had opened his mouth to interject.

"Vegas," the minister continued, "I can tell by your body language and the way that you have been staring at that teacup like it has poison in it that you don't trust me."

"It did happen, and if you didn't do it, someone else did," Demetri said firmly.

Minister Farrah turned slowly toward Demetri. "What exactly are you accusing me of?"

"I saw it for myself," Demetri insisted. "Starks was murdered!"

"Saw it?" the minister asked, crinkling his forehead. "How?"

"I have it stored on a jump drive. There is no other footage anywhere else. It was wiped clean. Whoever did this, they covered the hell out of their tracks."

Minister Farrah's body language was hard to read, but he did appear to be surprised by this news.

"If what you say is true, we may have a fox in the hen house." Minister Farrah glanced over at Brother Elijah, and then he looked back at us.

"I must see this recording," he said.

"It's not with us, but it is real. I can promise you that," Demetri said.

"And if my word means anything to you, Minister, believe him," I said, looking him in the eyes. "Believe him and help us."

There was a long beat of silence before Minister Farrah gave us a small nod. "Fine," he said. "I'll call a meeting of the board, and you can present your case. But don't make me look like a fool. Bring the drive that I'm hoping exists. We have some of the best forensics people in the world working for us. Perhaps we can have the body exhumed and get to the bottom of this."

"Thank you, Minister. Thank you," I said.

Demetri and I stood up to leave, but not before he finished his tea in one long gulp.

"Come on, Demetri. We have work to do."

"Vegas, why didn't you mention the scope you found and the connection to the murders in New York?" Demetri asked as we walked toward the castle.

"Because until we actually get a meeting with the board and present our evidence, I don't fully trust the minister or his flunky."

Vegas

46

There was a knock at the door as I lay across the bed in room 602 of the castle. I got up and let Demetri in, then sat back down on the bed. Instead of taking a seat, Demetri hovered over me like the Incredible Hulk with a grim expression on his unshaven face.

"You were correct. There was a sniper on the castle wall, and he was targeting one of the children, most likely your son."

I'd had a feeling he was going to say that when I asked him to search on the security cameras for the day of the war games match. I specifically asked him to check the northeast wall to see if we could find a sniper.

"I can also tell you that whoever it is, they have intimate knowledge of the castle's surveillance system."

"Why do you say that?"

"Because they chose the one spot on the wall where the closest camera is almost three hundred meters and at a very bad angle."

"In other words, you could not make out his face," I said. We had hit a dead end.

"As always, you are very astute. There is, however, one interesting bit of news. The sniper was unsuccessful—not because he was a bad shot, but because it appears we have a friend."

"A friend?" I sat up quickly. "What are you talking about?"

"I was unable to determine where she came from because of the camera angle, but a bald, weaponless woman attacked the sniper before he could get a good shot off. She knocked them both into the moat. Very courageous, but otherwise insane."

"Did you say she was bald?"

"Yes."

"Marie," I said with a smile on my face and admiration in my voice. "Son of a bitch, she actually made it."

There was a knock on the door. Demetri looked at me, and I nodded to let him know it was okay to open it.

Nevada and Ivan came into the room wearing sweatsuits with the school emblem on the front. Seeing the two of them was like looking in a way-back machine at me and Demetri when we were students.

"Hey, Dad." Nevada walked over and threw his arms around me. It felt good to hug my son, considering everything that had happened over the last few months, and especially the last few days. There was no way I was going to chance putting him in harm's way anymore.

"Hey, son."

"What's going on?" Ivan mumbled, flopping down on the sofa. There was definitely more tension than affection between him and his father.

"Why would you drop on the couch like that, you big loaf? Dontcha care if ya break it?" Demetri yelled at him.

Ivan's face turned beet red. "Sorry. I was just sitting down."

I watched as Nevada made sure to carefully sit beside his friend.

"Son," I said, "there are a lot of things going on right now, most of them I don't understand, and things are quite dangerous. So, I think you should go underground for a while."

Not surprisingly, Nevada protested. "We already agreed that my being here made sense and you trusted—"

"That was before I found out there was a sniper out there the other day who had a bullet with your name on it. You're lucky to be sitting here having this conversation."

"A sniper? What are you talking about? When?"

I turned to Demetri for help. "During the war games, there was a sniper perched on the northeast wall," he explained. "He most likely planned to use the gunfire from the games to disguise his shot. I saw the footage myself."

Nevada took his time to process what he was being told, looking from me to Demetri to his friend.

"Are you sure they're after me?" he asked.

"I can't be sure of anything right now, but I can't take a chance on being wrong."

Nevada shook his head in frustration. "Where am I supposed to go, Dad? You said yourself we don't know who's behind all of this, but whoever it is, they're powerful. Sending me home isn't going to help. That's the first place they'll look."

"I wasn't planning on sending you home. Just to a safe house until we figure this thing out."

"But I'm squad leader. I can't leave my team. They may be in danger too," Nevada said.

Ivan spoke up. "I'll go with you. The whole squad will go. Who better to keep you safe?"

Nevada looked just as surprised as Demetri and I did. "Are you serious?"

I looked at Demetri to see if he had anything to say to his son, but he stayed tight-lipped. My heart went out to Ivan. He was trying to step up and be a man, and his father seemed to have no opinion on the matter.

"I appreciate the offer, Ivan, but I don't think that can happen," I said.

"Why not?" Nevada asked. "They should be allowed to come if they want. One of the most valuable lessons we've learned here at the school is loyalty. They put us in squads because they want us to learn teamwork."

"There is no *I* in team," Ivan added, sticking his hand out for Nevada to fist bump.

I thought about how my own squad had banded together back in the day. We stood by one another whenever we were facing adversity. As much as I wanted to protect Nevada, I couldn't deny that soon enough, he would become a man, and I would no longer be able to shield him. He appeared to be ready for that a lot sooner than I was. Maybe I needed to let my son make this decision for himself. He had already shown me so much growth in the short time he'd been at Chi's.

"Okay," I relented. "If they want to go, I'll talk to the headmaster."

"They're gonna say yes. Trust me," Ivan said confidently. "We're a team."

"Let's go," I said, and we headed for the door.

To my surprise, Demetri finally offered his voice to the conversation. He stop Ivan with a hand on his shoulder.

"Bravery begins in the heart and extends to the mind. It's not anything you can think about. You have to feel it. I am very proud of you, Ivan." He hugged his son, quite possibly for the first time.

The lesson Demetri imparted was one of the first ones we learned from Minister Farrah when we were students, and they were words I'd come to live by. That didn't mean I wasn't still concerned about our sons. They had demonstrated bravery, and I knew it was in their hearts, but I also had to be smart and think about the best way to keep them safe.

"Gather up your people and meet me at Demetri's," I told them. "We'll leave from there in the morning. See you in a couple of hours." I hugged my son again.

Nevada asked, "Where are you going?"

"To see the minister and find out when the hell he's planning on having this board meeting."

Nevada

47

"Find Richard and the girls. They're probably still in my room. I'll go get Natasha," I instructed Ivan as we rushed back to campus. As much as I hated the thought of leaving school, having my squad with me made it a little easier to accept this time. There was also the fact that if someone really was after me, there was a chance that my team was in danger as well. Being together meant that we could look out for one another.

I went to Natasha's room first. It took a little longer than usual for her to answer the door. As I was about to knock a fifth time, I heard her yell, "Who is it?"

"It's me."

The door cracked open.

"Sorry. I know it's late, but I need to talk to you."

Natasha grabbed my hand and gently tried to pull me inside her room, smiling seductively. "My roommate's gone with her squad. You come in and we can talk here."

I pulled away. "No, we don't have time."

"Why can't we just talk here?" Natasha pouted. "Is this about kayfabe?"

"Natasha, not everything is about you. Now come on. This is an emergency."

"What's wrong?" Her eyes became serious.

"I'll explain in a bit. Just get dressed and pack an overnight bag, then meet me at my room. And hurry." No longer having the time or patience to reason with her, I turned to walk away. By the time I made it to my room, Demi and Arielle were both ready to go.

"Ivan gave us a head's up. He went to get Richard," Demi said.

"We got your back, Nevada. Whatever you need," Arielle added, pointing to the duffle bags sitting by the doorway.

"I appreciate that. I really do," I told them. "But let's talk to my dad first and see what the plan is."

The three of us headed out and met Natasha in the hall. I could tell by the look on her face as we approached that she wasn't pleased. Frankly, with everything going on, I didn't give a shit.

"I thought you said you wanted to talk," she said, arms folded. "Why are they here?"

"Because they need to be, just like you. Now, lose the attitude. This is life and death." I snapped.

She stepped back to let me pass.

"There's something going on, and it involves everyone. My dad needs to talk with all of us," I continued.

We met up with Ivan and Richard out front, then headed to Demetri's cottage. As we got close to the house, Ivan stopped us.

"Do you guys see those shadows?" Ivan whispered, pointing to one of the windows.

Something was wrong. Very wrong. The blinds were closed, but the lights were on inside, and I was able to make out the silhouettes of two, maybe three men.

"That's not my dad," Ivan said.

"That's not my dad either," I replied.

"Could he possibly have friends visiting?" Arielle asked.

"The only friend my dad has is in a bottle," Ivan said suspiciously. "I am going to go see what's going on. You guys stay back."

"Not a chance in hell," Demi said, placing a hand on her hip. "I'm not going to let you walk into that mess by yourself."

"Maybe if they see all of us, they'll be less likely to act up," Natasha said.

"When you say all of us, do you mean, like, *all of us* all of us? Richard asked.

"Cut it out, Richard. We all go," I commanded and waved everyone on. "Ivan will go in first. I'm behind him, and then the rest of you follow."

Ivan and I got close to the door, and we heard yelling and thumping like a scuffle was happening.

"Where the fuck is it, you drunk piece of shit?" A voice came from inside the house. Then we heard a thud and someone groaning.

"Dad!" Ivan burst through the doors. The four of us were right behind him.

Ivan's father was doubled over on the ground with blood covering his face. He'd been beaten pretty badly. Standing over him were three men in ski masks, each with some sort of weapon in his hands.

"I–Ivan, get out of here, son."

"No!" Ivan ran over to his father. He looked up at the three big assailants with hatred in his eyes. "Why did you do this to him?"

"Your father has something that belongs to us and is trying to show it around," one of them said, flexing the hand that held a set of brass knuckles. "We want it, and we want it now. You can either talk him into getting it for us or get hurt too."

"We're not scared of you!" Arielle spoke up. "Are you even supposed to be on campus? Because you don't look like you belong here."

"How about you go back to your room and play with your dolls, you little bitch?" One of the other men said. He was holding a thick black club.

"Or I can just call campus security to take care of you." Natasha held up her phone.

"I can do better than that. Smile, you bastard. You're on Instagram live," Richard yelled.

As the assailants realized they were being filmed, their energy instantly shifted. I was prepared to fight, and Ivan's stance indicated that he was too. Instead of attacking us, they rushed toward the back door to leave. They left Demetri with one last threat.

"Next time, you won't have any brats to save you. Remember that."

Arielle slammed the door shut before they could say anything else. I helped Ivan get his father off the floor and onto one of the couches in the living room. He was badly injured and would need medical attention.

"Dad? Who were those guys?" Ivan asked, but Demetri focused his eyes on me.

"Tell your father that they're trying to kill us all," he said.

"Who is trying to kill us?" I asked.

"He'll know what I'm talking about," he said weakly before he passed out.

Vegas

48

"So, what exactly does that mean?" I was standing across from Brother Elijah, a man I had history with. He had turned his back on his father figure, Brother X, to protect my cousin and my family. He wasn't my favorite person in the world, but I knew he was a man of his word.

"It means we're behind you, both the minister and I. He is presently speaking to a key member of the board and has secured support from quite a few others. Tomorrow, they will launch an inquiry into Headmaster Starks' death, giving you and Demetri Igor the chance to present your case. You have won, Vegas Duncan," he said.

"I wouldn't say I won anything. Winning is a happy occasion. What may come to light is not something I feel happy about," I replied.

"I understand your mindset. Let's just say things are going in the right direction."

"Fine. So what about the children? Is it okay if they leave the school for a week or so while we wrap this up?"

"Yes, of course. We'll call it a field trip training exercise. They can access their assignments via the internet."

"Good. I'll be in touch in the morning." I shook brother Elijah's hand, then exited Minister Farrah's house, headed toward Demetri's cottage.

My plan was to find the most secure place for Nevada and his friends to go. Then I was going to take down whoever was behind the events at the Hellfire Club and at Chi's.

I was going to need some bona fide help. Demetri was a good ally, but his drinking made him unreliable, and he lacked resources. I pulled out my phone and made a call to the only people I could always rely on no matter what—my family.

"Hey, son. I'm glad you called. I was—"

"Pop, Nevada and I need your help." I cut him off before he could finish his sentence. I'm sure he could hear the urgency in my voice.

"You don't even have to ask. What do you need?"

"I need you to get everyone and head over here. And I mean everyone. Paris, Sasha, Junior, Orlando, the twins, DJ, Big Mike. Everybody, Pop." My voice may have sounded like I was making a demand, but I was pleading.

"You got it. We're experiencing some unusually heavy thunderstorms, but as soon as they pass, we're in the air," he replied. "Now, can you calm down enough to tell me what's going on?"

"I don't have a lot of time to explain, but someone tried to kill my son." I braced myself for my father's reaction that I knew was going to be legendary. He loved Nevada as much as I did, and they shared a bond almost as close as the one we had.

"What? Is he all right? Where is he now?" Pop was usually very cool, calm, and collected, but he sounded like he was about to explode.

"He's safe, Pop. As soon as you get here, I'm going to have Paris and Sasha take him to our safe house in Milan." We didn't really have a safe house in Milan. Our European safe house was a yacht we had moored in Nice, but just in case someone was picking up our signal, I wanted them to think we were headed to Italy.

"Understood. I'll make sure it's secured. I'll see you in about nine hours. You be safe and lay low until we get there."

"I'll try," I replied. "Oh, and Pop, can you reach out to Daryl? I've been trying to reach him for the past two days."

There was a silence on the line that told me something was wrong.

"Pop?"

My father sighed. "Darryl was shot earlier today."

My heart dropped. I knew it was odd that my best friend wasn't responding to my texts or calls, but I hadn't expected news like this.

"Is he okay?" I asked tentatively.

"He's okay, Vegas. Lucky for him, the bullet just missed his heart and went through. He's in a lot of pain, but he'll be good as new."

I exhaled. "Thank God."

"You okay?"

"Yeah, yeah, I'll be okay. It's just a lot going on at once."

"I can imagine. Just sit tight. We're on our way as soon as these thunderstorms pass. Be careful until we get there."

"I will. You have my word." I ended the call.

As I walked toward Demetri's cottage, I got the sense that someone was following me. I wasn't sure who or how many, but the last thing I wanted to do was lead them to the kids, so I headed in the opposite direction.

Nevada

49

It was almost two o'clock in the morning, and my dad still hadn't showed up. We'd placed Ivan's dad in his bed, and Arielle and Natasha were taking care of him the best they could. There was no doubt in my mind he had a concussion, but we didn't dare to take him anywhere until my dad got there.

I dug my phone out of my pocket and checked the screen. There had been no messages since he sent a text to say that my family would be in Paris in the morning. That was at least an hour ago, and nothing had come in since.

I hit the call button by his name and listened to the phone ring all the way through to voicemail. I repeated that two more times, but still no answer. Where the hell was he? Why wasn't he answering his phone? I *never* had to call him that many times to get a hold of him.

I thought about what had happened to Ivan's dad. Did the assailants leave Demetri's place and meet up with my dad? That was only a passing thought, though. My dad was always on alert. He was strong as hell and a gifted fighter. Nobody would be able to do that to Vegas Duncan. Not unless there were a hell of a lot of them.

"Nevada?" I heard someone call my name, but I was busy trying to dial my dad for the fourth time. "Nevada!"

"What!" I whipped my head around and found myself face to face with Ivan, who was taken aback by my outburst. As fast as I could, I steadied my breathing and tried to calm my face. As squad leader, I needed them to trust me, and I needed to show that, no matter what, I was in control.

"Sorry, man. How's your dad?' I asked.

"He's still unconscious, but Arielle says he's stable, and she's been through all the Grail medic training."

"Yeah, she knows her stuff. But if you wanna take your dad to the infirmary or into town to the hospital, you can. I'll have Natasha drive you in the jeep."

"No, my dad hates hospitals, and it's not safe. At least here we have his two guns." He patted the .44-caliber pistol tucked in his waist. "We gotta stick together."

I nodded.

"You okay?" Ivan asked.

"Yeah, I was just—" I looked down at the phone in my hand before I put it away. "Ivan, I can't lie to you. I'm worried about my dad. I'm thinking about going to the minister's to see if I can find him."

Ivan stared at me for a moment, then nodded his head. He reached into his waistband, pulling out the large .44. "Take this for protection."

"No, I'm good. That thing's too bulky to be running around campus with, and you guys may need it." I walked over to my bag and removed a cloth pouch. I emptied it on the coffee table, revealing four razor-sharp throwing stars my aunt Paris had given me. "These will work."

Ivan raised a skeptical eyebrow, until I threw one at the front door, embedding it an inch into the thick wood. I slipped the other three stars into my sweatshirt pocket.

"Be careful," he said.

"I will, but if I'm not back in forty minutes, you pack everybody, including your father, into the jeep, and you head straight to the Paris-Orly Airport. My family will be landing there sometime around eight or nine. You'll know them because they'll be the bad-ass black family nobody wants to mess with."

"Come back," he said.

"That's the plan." I slipped out the back door so none of the squad would know I was leaving and headed straight across campus to the minister's cottage. I hadn't gotten very far before I began to get the unnerving feeling that someone was watching me. Then I saw a figure out of the corner of my eye, and there was no doubt it was headed toward me.

"Shit." I picked up my pace from a brisk walk to a run. I held one of the throwing stars in my hand, preparing to inflict major damage.

"Nevada!" The figure was calling my name. I had no intention of slowing my pace; however, I turned my head in the direction the voice had come from.

"Nevada, slow down!"

"Clem?"

It sure sounded like Clem. I slipped the throwing star back in my pocket and came to a halt. God, I hoped it was Clem.

"Damn, mate, why the hell did you have to run so fast?" Clem asked. I was so happy when he came into focus and appeared at my side. "I could barely keep up. It's good to see you."

"Good to see you too." We hugged. It was good to have my boy back. "How's the family? When'd you get back?"

"Da brought me back about an hour ago. I been looking all over campus for you guys. Where's the squad?"

"At Ivan's house."

"Ivan's house? What're they doing there?" he asked, obviously confused. Clem still did not one hundred percent trust Ivan like I did.

"It's a long story," I said. "Come on. I gotta get to the headmaster's cottage."

Clem gave me a weird look, then shrugged. When we got close enough to the headmaster's cottage we could see the flashing blue lights. Parked in front were three local police cars, alongside two campus security cars.

"What the bloody hell is going on here?" Clem asked.

"I don't know, but it doesn't look good," I replied, waving him on.

We got a partial answer when the front door of the cottage swung open and Minister Farrah and Brother Elijah were escorted out of the house, shadowed by Mrs. Farrah, who was weeping loudly. I was baffled by the presence of the police officers, but I was completely puzzled when I saw that they had the minister and Brother Elijah in handcuffs. I didn't usually curse, but *what the fuck*?

"Teacher, what's going on?" I asked, hurrying over to him.

He looked surprised to see us, but he remained dignified.

"Nevada, listen very carefully to me. Find your father," he said as the officer holding him jerked him away. "Tell him we've been arrested and that the fox is definitely in the hen house."

"I'll tell him. But why have you been arrested?"

"Murder!"

I heard a voice yelling from the steps. It was Security Chief Picard. He had not been my favorite person ever since I caught him with my mother at the restaurant. Jesus, was she involved with this?

I looked up at Picard and asked, "Who did he murder?"

"Headmaster Starks."

"Oh, shit!" Clem and I said in unison.

They put the two of them in separate cars, and before I even had time to fully process what was going on, they were gone. I pulled out my phone and called my father, forgetting that he hadn't even returned my other calls. He still didn't answer. Why wasn't he answering? I was so stressed, and at this point, with the minister in handcuffs and my father AWOL, I wasn't sure who I could turn to. With no definite plan in mind, I started to walk back to Demetri's place.

Marie

50

From my perch in the castle turret, I was able to keep a careful eye on both Nevada and Vegas for most of the day. However, once night fell, I officially turned into a stalker, using the tunnels throughout the school grounds to keep tabs on them. I wasn't ready to speak to either of them yet, especially Vegas. I just wanted to make sure that they were safe. Vegas was there to protect Nevada, and I was there to protect both of them. Today, I was especially concerned because of the congregation of cars I'd spotted about halfway down the road from the bridge.

A little after dark, I'd picked up Vegas's trail when he left the castle and headed toward the headmaster's cottage, where he stayed for almost two hours. From there, he walked across campus and entered a wooded area. There weren't any other buildings or any other reasons I could think of for him to be in there, so I left the confines of the tunnels to follow. He had to be meeting someone. *But this late? Who?*

"Shit, where is he?" I whispered when I emerged. Crouching low to the ground, I scanned the area around me, listening for anything that would reveal his location. If I couldn't see him, maybe I could hear his footsteps. I had to find him quickly.

I heard a deep muffled voice. It was him. I scrambled as quietly as I could toward the direction it had come from. Then, I waited and listened. It was so quiet that I thought I'd been mistaken. Vegas was nowhere in sight. There was a rustling in the trees before something fell in front of me. I gasped, prepared to run off.

"Marie."

I froze. The voice caused what little hair I had on the back of my neck to stand up. My voice was nowhere to be found.

"Marie, what are you doing, baby?" He approached me.

"I . . . I'm . . . trying to find you."

"Well, I'd say you found me a while ago, considering you've been following me half the night." He pulled me into his arms.

For a few seconds, I let myself relax into his embrace. It felt amazing being comforted by him. I wanted him to hold me forever. But we couldn't afford to relax right now, so I pulled away from him.

"Vegas, you have to get away from here. They're after you," I hissed desperately.

"Marie, it's okay. Backup is on the way. Pop and the family are on their way. We're gonna be okay. I promise. You're gonna be safe." He stroked my cheek gently, but I couldn't relax into his touch this time.

"No, Vegas. It's too late. Your family isn't gonna get here in time. They're here! Carloads of them," I warned him as my heart began racing.

"Marie—"

"Oh, shit! Vegas, run! Run, baby, run!" I screamed and took off into the darkness, running as fast and far as I could until I had no choice but to stop to catch my breath.

"You okay, baby? Baby, are you okay? Baby!"

I waited for Vegas to answer, but I heard nothing.

You fucked up. They got him.

"No, they couldn't have him," I answered the voice in my head. "He was right behind me."

No, he's not.

"Vegas? Baby, where are you?" I turned around, praying that he would be standing there. The only thing I saw was darkness. "Shit!"

You're pathetic. First the girls, and now Vegas. You might as well go get Nevada and hand him to them.

"No. This cannot be happening."

Oh, it's happening!

"Calm down, Marie." I quickly yet cautiously returned to the spot where we'd stood. There was no sign of him anywhere. I continued into the thick trees, fighting tears while I searched.

Then, I saw them. There had to be at least ten of them, gathered together, looking like a cluster of carrot-top thugs. Two of them carried Vegas's limp body. My heart pounded in my chest as I realized that the bastard giving the orders was the one from Bobby's apartment, the one who killed my girls.

Now what the fuck are you going to do? They're taking him to who knows where, to do who knows what.

I could charge them, I thought. It had worked with the sniper on the wall.

Are you fucking nuts? That was when there was only one of those redhead bastards. There's damn near a dozen of them now!

The odds were stacked against me, but I couldn't just let them take him. Not without a fight.

To go up against them, you're going to need a whole team of motherfuckers! The voice reminded me.

"Or a squad," I replied.

Nevada

51

Despite my return to the cottage without my father, the entire squad was stoked about Clem's return, and there was a round of hugging and cheering throughout the room. Natasha even offered him the first piece of the strudel she'd baked in Demetri's kitchen, an act that had always been reserved for me. Not that I complained. Far be it for me to get bent out of shape about anything that girl might misconstrue.

While the others had their homecoming with Clem, I slipped into the bedroom. Arielle was tending to Demetri, while Ivan sat beside the bed.

"How is he?" I asked Arielle.

"Still unconscious. They beat him up pretty good. I think he has a bad concussion. We probably should take him to a hospital."

"No, no hospital. I need you to give me your word, Nevada." Ivan's eyes were fixated on me. "He hates hospitals."

"Okay, but if he's not better by the time my family gets here, we don't take any more chances. Fair enough?"

Ivan nodded. "Where is your father anyway?"

"I don't know. He's not answering my calls."

"He was not at the headmaster's cottage?"

"No. Minister Farrah and Brother Elijah are now in police custody for the murder of Headmaster Starks," I told them, still barely able to believe it myself.

"Shut up!" Arielle gasped.

"Do you believe that?" Ivan asked. I could see from his face that he was skeptical.

"No, I don't. I believe he was set up."

"This place is getting out of control," Arielle groaned.

"Tell me about it," I replied.

"What do we do now?" Ivan asked. "You are our leader."

I sighed. "I hate to admit it, but I don't know. I'm open to suggestions."

"I've been thinking about what happened to my dad and why those guys were there. They were looking for something, and they really wanted it bad," Ivan said as the rest of the squad entered the room.

"Yeah, but whatever it was, they didn't find it. That's why they tried to kill your old man," I said.

"Maybe they just didn't know where to look," Ivan said.

"What are you talking about?"

"Ever since I was a kid, my dad was always private. Really private. Nobody would be able to find anything of my dad's if they didn't know where to look, even if it was in plain sight. Well, nobody except me."

"Are you saying that you might know what they were looking for?"

"Maybe."

Ivan walked past us and went to a far corner in the living room. Kneeling down, he felt along the corner where the wall met the floor. The common observer would have missed it, but not somebody who knew his father. When his hand got to a point where it was loose, he gently pulled it away from the wall and grabbed something small.

"A jump drive?" I asked.

"They didn't get it. Assuming this is what they came for." Ivan held up the little black device. "I saw my dad messing with that spot a few weeks ago. I knew it could only be for one reason—to hide something. I didn't think about it until the other day."

"We need to see what's on it," I said.

"I guess it's a good thing that those blokes didn't destroy your father's laptop," Richard said, pulling it from underneath a pile of rubbish.

Ivan took the laptop from Richard, turned it on, and pushed the drive in the USB port. We gathered around him as he double-clicked the only file on the device. A surveillance video from the headmaster's cottage popped up, and we all watched in horror at the events taking place on the screen.

"Holy shit," Richard cursed. "Are guys seeing what I'm seeing?

"Yep. Starks was definitely murdered, but not by Minister Farrah or Brother Elijah."

Marie

52

I lifted the cover to the access tunnel about eight inches off the ground, just enough to give me a line of sight to the cottage. I had been watching it for at least two hours, moving from access cover to access cover to see if I could catch a glimpse of Nevada, but all I could see were silhouettes.

Go knock on the door. He's in there.

"What if he isn't?"

Are you forgetting that those carrot-top motherfuckers have Vegas?

"No. But what if he's not there?"

Then ask them where the fuck he is. Time's running out.

"Okay, okay. You don't have to be so nasty about it." I might have been in a mental facility, but those damn doctors were useless. They hadn't done a damn thing to help me get rid of these voices in my head.

You're the one scared of a bunch of damn kids.

I shook my head to empty it of all thoughts, pushed the access cover up, and climbed out of the tunnel. I placed it back down so nobody would know I had been there. Then I did my best to straighten out my clothes so I would look presentable before walking up to the door.

There was a lot of commotion on the other side of the door, but no answer when I knocked.

What the fuck are they doing? Knock again. The voice was back, bossing me around again.

I knocked three more times. I heard a lot of commotion and hushed voices, and then the door opened.

Holy shit! These kids ain't playing.

Standing in front of me like the cover of a comic book was Nevada's squad, geared up with everything from handguns to a couple of knives, a hammer, throwing stars, and a baseball bat. If they weren't so cute, they might have been intimidating.

Say something before that tall bitch shoots us. She looks like she's got a hairpin trigger.

"Nevada, they have your father," I said.

"Ms. Marie?" Nevada stepped up for a better look. His dazed expression let me know he didn't comprehend what I was saying. I didn't want to believe it either.

"They have your father," I repeated, taking his hands in mine. "They have him right now."

"It's all right guys. I know her." Nevada looked back at the young people behind him. They were staring warily at us, no doubt wondering what Nevada was doing talking to the bald woman at the door.

He turned back to me. "Come on, Ms. Marie. It might not be a good idea to be out in the open like this."

His friends parted, letting him lead me inside the house. I could feel all of the suspicious eyes on me, but all that mattered to me was Nevada. The others sat down in various places, but Nevada and I stood. His concerned expression made him look like a grown man with the weight of the world on his shoulders. I hated to lay such a burden on him, but there was nobody else.

"How do you know someone took him?" Nevada asked.

"I saw them."

"Who?" one of the other kids asked. I turned in their direction and focused on them for the first time. The sight of one of them in particular made my heart skip a beat.

"They all looked like him." I snatched the gun from the tall bitch and pointed it at the redheaded kid sitting at the counter, eating cake. "Where the fuck did you take him, you crimson bastard?"

"Aw, fuck," the little redhead bastard squealed. "Somebody stop this crazy bitch!"

Shoot him! Shoot him, Marie! What are you waiting for? He's one of them.

I was two seconds away from pulling the trigger when Nevada jumped in front of me in a panic, blocking my shot. "No! No! He's been with me. The fact that the killers are redheaded and so is Clem is just coincidence. He's my best friend."

The others stood around muttering to each other, looking like the kids that they were. Maybe I had been wrong to think this squad would be of any use to me.

"Then you need to pick better friends. Now get out of the way," I demanded.

"I can't do that." He pumped his chest like his father, standing his ground.

"Nevada, he's responsible for Kia's death. Get out the way!" My eyes were starting to tear. I was becoming too emotional.

"No," he said defiantly. "Now, do you know where they took my dad?"

"I was hoping you could help me find out." I stared past him at the redhead. "But I guess I was wrong."

I kept the gun pointed at anyone who moved as I backed up toward the door, opened it, and slipped out running into the night.

Nevada

53

"Jesus Christ, who the fuck was that crazy bitch?" Clem's face was still pasty white, and his forehead was shiny with sweat. Ms. Marie had scared the shit out of him. Hell, she'd scared the shit out of me as well.

"She's my father's girlfriend, and she's not a bitch. She's just troubled." I turned away from the door and faced Clem. "Speaking of troubled, I don't have time to be playing games, so I'm only going to ask you this one time, Clem. Did you or your people have anything to do with my girlfriend's death or my father's disappearance?"

"No," Clem replied adamantly. "I swear on my mum. I have nothing to do with it. How could you ever think that?"

I studied his face for a second. If Ms. Marie was right, we were fucked, but I knew Clem. Other than to play a practical joke on me, he'd never lied and always had my back. My dad had always said go with your gut; your gut will never lie to you. So, I was going with my gut. I had to trust him. "That's good enough for me. Anybody else wanna chime in?"

"He's one of us," Ivan added.

"Clem's okay," Demi said.

"We're a team. Clem's part of the team," Richard said with finality.

"Your father's girlfriend, on the other hand, took one of our guns," Ivan reminded me. He shot a look at Natasha, who had not been able to stop Marie from snatching the gun from her.

"What did you expect me to do?" Natasha asked, looking like she wanted to cry.

"Now what do we do?" Arielle asked.

The entire team looked deflated.

I glanced at my watch then reached over and took the gun sitting in Ivan's waistband. "You guys are going to get Demetri into the jeep and take him with you to the airport and meet my family. I'm going to go get my dad."

"I don't know, Nevada. I think this may be more than we can handle," Natasha said. "Maybe you should call the police."

This surprised me because she was highly skilled and, I thought, fearless. But I was beginning to understand what our professors had been trying to show us for a while now. We might be Elite students, but we still had a lot to learn from Chi's before we'd all be ready to handle real-life situations like this one. Still, I wasn't ready to give up yet.

"By the time the police get there, they might have killed my dad. I have to get him."

"Isn't that too dangerous?" Demi asked. "I mean, your dad is supposed to be a tough guy. If they got him, how do you think you'll be able to save him?"

"I have to try, Demi. He's my dad!"

"I'll come with you," Clem said.

"Where Nevada goes, I go," Ivan replied. "You helped me save my dad, so I'll help you save yours."

"Thank you, Ivan, but I can't ask you to put your life on the line. I can't ask any of you to do that."

"You don't have to ask. I am coming," Ivan told me firmly.

"Me too!" Arielle said.

"If Arielle is going, I am too," Demi said. "It's dangerous, but you'll need us to watch your back."

When the other girls stepped up like that, Natasha suddenly found her courage. "And it is no question that I will be there with my Nevada."

"Like Demi said, it's too dangerous," I told them.

"What have we been in Elite training for if we bow out of real situations?" Richard finally spoke. "Kicking some ass will give me a reason to go get a fresh manicure and see Belmont."

"You guys sure about this?"

"Yes," they all said unison.

"Okay," I finally said, giving in. "But if these guys are as much of a problem as I think, then we're going to need to get our hands on some more weapons. One handgun isn't going to do it."

"Why don't we just break into the armory?" Arielle asked. "If Brother Elijah is locked up, it can't be but so hard."

It sounded like it could be a joke, but we all stared at her as if she'd said the most brilliant thing.

"Okay, then let's break into the armory," I stated, and Arielle's eyes grew wide.

"I–I was just kidding."

"Well, it's a damn good idea," I said. "I'm going to need you, Clem, and Natasha to do that while Demi, Ivan, and I, with a little luck, will figure out just where my dad is."

"Uh, did you forget about me?" Richard chimed in.

I ignored his attitude because I didn't have time for it. "You stay here with us and find some way to make yourself useful."

Nevada

54

"Nevada, I got him!" Demi shouted, high-fiving Ivan.

I ran over to the kitchen table. The two of them separated so I could see what they had come up with. Half an hour earlier, I had given them the watch that my dad had given me. He wore a similar watch, so they'd been trying to locate his signal. It appeared they'd done just that.

"He's somewhere in this area right here." Demi pointed at the screen. "If you give us another fifteen minutes, we can pinpoint it."

"I can give you ten."

"We'll do our best."

I stepped away and walked into the living room, where Richard was intensely focused on something on his iPad.

"The first articles on the headmaster's arrest have started to come out. They are trying to paint him as some deranged religious zealot with an axe to grind. No way this story wasn't prewritten."

"Yeah, he said the fox was in the henhouse."

"Any word from the rest of the squad?"

I checked my phone for the fifth time and pumped my fist in the air when I saw the text from Clem. His thumbs up emoji let me know that they had successfully broken into the armory.

His second text read: Be back in ten minutes.

"Go tell Demi and Ivan that they're on the way," I said to Richard. He stood up from the sofa. "And get Demetri ready to move. We're outta here in fifteen minutes."

Richard left the living room, and I became caught up in my thoughts. *Hold on, Dad. We're coming.* I tried to shove aside the doubts that still lingered about how we would do that.

The ringing of my cell phone snapped me out of my thoughts, and the name on my caller ID actually brought a smile to face.

"Grandpa. You guys on the ground already?" A huge sense of relief washed over me.

"No. That's why I'm calling. I tried to reach your dad, but he didn't pick up. We ran into some bad weather and had to put down in Bermuda." I could hear the stress in his voice. My grandpa hated to let anyone down. I guess that's where I got it from. "It's going to be at least three hours before we get back off the ground, and another four or five hours in the air. Tell your dad we will be there. We're on our way," Grandpa said.

"Okay, I'll let him know as soon as I see him."

I didn't want to worry my grandfather any more than I could tell he already was, so I decided not to tell him what had happened. That was a conversation that needed to happen face to face. It could wait until he arrived. There was nothing he could do until then anyway.

"Good. Now, I have some information I need you to relay as well."

"Sure." I tried to keep my voice calm, but I could feel the tension rising throughout my body.

"They stole the body from the morgue, but—"

"Body? What body?"

"The body of the guy Marie killed," Grandpa said. "But the cops managed to get a DNA sample and compare it to the sample from the Hellfire Club. Not only did both men have red hair, but they're related. It looks like it's a family of these fuckers."

Grandpa didn't usually curse in front of me like that. His choice of words surprised me, but his news sent my mind reeling.

"I'll let him know," I said, trying to remain calm.

"We're gonna get there as soon as we can. You and your dad hold tight."

Related. The word echoed in my mind after I ended the call. *Both men had red hair. One of them was dead. The Chi pin. They were related.*

The pieces of the puzzle were beginning to come together, and I didn't like the picture that was forming.

Rage. Pure rage. It was coursing through my body as the jeep pulled up. When the squad saw me coming, I was greeted with smiles, but all I could see was Clem's fucking red hair. I had been deceived in the worst way, and even more horrifying was the reality that my gut had lied to me. Clem McCloud, my roommate, my wingman, and someone I had once called my best friend, was a lying, murdering bastard.

"Aye, mate, we did it!" Clem strode toward me from the jeep like a superhero, holding a hand out to me. He was met by a fist to the head.

"You son of a bitch!" I punched him again. "You lied to my face! It's been you this whole time!"

"What the hell are you talking about?" Clem asked, his hand rubbing the spot where I'd punched him.

"You know what I'm talking about!" I tried to hit him again, but Natasha grabbed my arm.

"Let go of me! Let go!" I roared at her.

"Whoa, whoa, Nevada. Take a chill pill," Richard said, grabbing my other arm. "Tell us what you're talking about."

"The murders! Marie! Kia! And now you're after my family!" My rage was too much for them, and I broke free, pounding him again and again until Ivan, the only one strong enough, pulled me off. "You killed her, you bastard!"

"Get them both inside," Ivan commanded, dragging me kicking and screaming into the cottage. "Calm down, Nevada. You are going to bring too much attention to us, and we still have to rescue your father."

Ivan's words about my dad were the only thing that could remotely calm me down, although my eyes never left Clem's, and I kept thinking of ways to get out of Ivan's grip and get to him. Clem just stood there wiping blood from his lip.

"What happened?" Demi asked.

I could feel everyone's attention on me. They were surprised by my actions. I still wanted to kill Clem, but some small part of me remembered that a squad leader had to maintain control over his emotions. I would deal with Clem when the time was right.

I lowered my voice to a more normal decibel. "He did it. Him and his family of redheads. Ms. Marie was right. He lied to our faces about everything. His brother wasn't killed by a truck or a dog. Ms. Marie killed him in New York."

"That's a lie!" Clem shouted.

"Is it a lie that your brother Michael lost his pin?"

"My brother didn't lose his pin. My dad did."

The room went silent for a moment.

"That's why your brother paid with your father's check, isn't it?" Richard asked.

"I don't know," Clem replied in a shaky voice.

"I do," I said to the group. "Because they didn't want anyone to know his father lost his pin in New York, so they covered their asses by saying Michael had lost his pin in Ireland."

"Can you say cover-up?" Richard mumbled.

"You guys don't believe that, do you?" Clem looked around for support but got none. No one would even make eye contact with him at this point.

"Get the fuck outta here, Clem, before I kill you."

"I don't—" Clem tried to defy me again, but Ivan stood up and towered over him.

"Did you know those men who hurt my father?" Ivan got in his face.

"I was talking to Nevada." Clem glared at him.

"You are not answering my question," Ivan growled. "You are a liability, and until further notice, the enemy."

"You're letting them do this?" Clem asked the rest of our friends.

"I'm sorry, Clem, but I think they're right. You should go," Arielle told him. "Staying might not be good for you."

He looked to the others, but no one spoke up in his defense. Clem's face went bright red, and he turned his attention back to me. If he were a cartoon character, steam would have been coming from his ears. But even still, his anger didn't come close to mine.

"You'll regret this," he said, pushing past Ivan.

"We already do," Richard said.

It wasn't until he was gone that I relaxed my fists. I couldn't believe all that time I'd had a rat sleeping across the hall from me. I still had to deal with the fact that my father was missing, and the weather was now preventing the help I needed most from coming.

Vegas

55

I felt like I'd been hit by a ton of bricks. The back of my head throbbed, and my neck ached. I didn't know how long I'd been unconscious, but it was still dark when I came to, and I was tied to a chair in the middle of a room.

"I was paid a lot of money to do this." The Irish accent was thick and gruff. "But I would have done it for free after your bitch killed my son."

I opened my eyes and focused on the figure standing in front of me. It had been years since I'd seen him, but nothing had changed about Patrick McCloud, other than the red clump of hair on his head was now sprinkled with gray and his pasty skin was more wrinkled.

"She just did what she had to, Patrick." I winced from the pain that coursed through my jaw as I spoke. "Besides, your son was a pussy."

"Yeah, maybe you're right, but he's still my son, and my honor says I have only one thing to do," he said.

"What's that?"

He stepped closer and gave me a wicked grin. "Make you suffer."

"You've got it backwards. Your son's death was retaliation for the pain your family had already inflicted. You killed all of Marie's girls. You killed my son's girl. Did you think there would be no repercussions?"

"Your son's pain is of no concern to me," he said.

"I know it was your people who shot Daryl and murdered Starks." As I spoke, I glanced around the room, trying to figure out how I was going to get out of this situation.

"Hmmm, perhaps, but you don't seem to be in a position to do anything about that." Patrick smirked at me. "And to think I didn't even have to do anything to Demetri. He did it to himself."

I glared at him. "Fuck you, Patrick. Demetri's a lot stronger than you think."

"Demetri's a pathetic drunk, and his son will turn out just like him. Fat ass can't even finish the school." Patrick leaned down close and hissed in my face, "But you, you're gonna get it the worst."

I tensed up, fearing what he was implying. Then, he confirmed that fear.

"You're gonna watch your son die." Patrick snatched me up out of the chair and began dragging me out of the room. I felt the cold blade in his hand pressed against the back of my neck.

The tight handcuffs and his vise grip on my arm made escape impossible. "You son of a bitch! You better not even look in my son's direction or I swear to God, I will slit your ass up and down and it'll *be nothing* compared to what you did to Marie's girls."

"Don't worry, Vegas. I'll make sure you get a good view." He taunted me as we continued out into the darkness.

The more I struggled, the harder Patrick pressed the blade into my skin. I could feel blood running down my neck from the wound. He was laughing maniacally as he dragged me to wherever we were going. My frustration was his entertainment.

"Leave him alone! You wanna kill someone, kill me!" Sweat was pouring down the side of my face, burning the open wounds left there when they had beat me unconscious. I was full of rage but powerless to do anything about it. My only hope was that Pop and the rest of the family had arrived and Nevada was safe.

"Oh, I'm gonna kill you, but you're going to have to watch your boy die first."

Marie

56

"Twinkle, twinkle, little star. How I wonder . . ." I'd been running around those tunnels, popping my head up above ground like a prairie dog when I spotted the little redhead bastard walking along the path like a lost puppy. The rest of the squad was nowhere in sight. I puffed on my cigarette, watching him sulk.

It's him! the voice in the back of my head shouted. *It's him! Here's your chance.*

He may have had Nevada to save him last time, but he would not be so lucky this time. I put out my cigarette and wrapped my fingers around the barrel of the pistol I'd taken from the girl, then moved down to the next tunnel access point.

Hurry up! He's going to get away!

I was moving as fast as I could. I was not going to let him get away.

At the next access point, I popped up my head and saw him. He was still walking in the same direction. If I went down two more access points, he'd walk right into me, and surprise! That redhead motherfucker would be dead.

Great plan. Now fucking execute!

I moved as fast as I could through that tunnel until I was right where I needed to be. Moving the access cover out of the way, I positioned half of my body above ground, then aimed the gun so that when that bastard turned the bend, he'd be directly in my sights.

You better not miss! the voice warned.

"I'm not going to miss. A blind man could make this shot."

I don't give a fuck about what a blind man can do. I'm worried about what a bald woman can do.

"Ms. Marie! Ms. Marie! Come back! Please!"

I heard a voice calling my name in the distance. Nobody called me Ms. Marie but Nevada. His voice was coming from the direction of the cottage where'd I'd last seen him. Something in his voice tugged at me. Was something wrong? Was he hurt? I had to get over there and see. I lowered my body back underground and closed the access point.

What the fuck are you doing? That bastard is like thirty seconds away.

That was thirty seconds Nevada might need me. We could always get this kid. We knew which dorm he lived in.

Well, now that you put it that way, hurry the fuck up! If something happens to Nevada, Kia will never forgive you.

I scrambled down the tunnel, headed in the direction of the cottage, popping my head up every so often to see what was going on. I finally reached the access point by the cottage and removed the cover to look around.

"Ms. Marie! Ms. Marie!" Nevada was standing by a jeep with the rest of his squad inside. "I know you're out there somewhere!" he yelled. "I'm sorry! You were right, Ms Marie. He's gone."

Was he talking about the redhead kid?

Well, he's not talking about Donald Trump. Who the fuck else would he be talking about?

What should I do?

You came all this way. Go see what the fuck he wants.

I climbed out of the tunnel. "Nevada."

"Ms. Marie!" He came running toward me and scooped me up in a hug. "I'm sorry. I should have listened to you."

Damn right! He should have let you kill that redhead bastard.

"It's okay," I told Nevada.

"We're going to find my dad." Demi had pinpointed the location of the signal from Dad's watch. "Come along. Be a part of our squad?"

I looked over at his people, who all gave me encouraging smiles. Without the redhead there, it felt like the evil had left the group.

"Let's go get my man," I said, then hopped in the jeep behind the driver. "And can I get a better gun?"

Nevada

57

"Excuse me?" Demi said sweetly as she pranced in front of a heavily guarded door. The building looked like a warehouse. It was deep in the woods, a perfect place to hide out. If you didn't know it was there, then you would never be able to find it—which was probably why the two McCloud men looked so surprised when Demi came out of nowhere.

"Who the hell are you?" One of them asked in a gruff Irish accent that sounded exactly like Clem's. "You shouldn't be here."

"I'm sorry, but my car broke down up on the road. I've been walking for forever. Please help me." She stuck out her bottom lip, but they weren't moved.

"Get the fuck out of here!" He pointed his gun at her head.

"Damn, a girl can't get any help?" She switched it up a little. Since innocent wasn't working, she went with promiscuous. "Well, what if I give you something in return?" She unbuttoned her blouse. The men's eyes fell on her chest like she had hypnotized them.

"Nobody's around," she said. "How about you all come have some fun, and *then* help me with my car?"

They looked at each other, having a silent conversation about what they should do. The moment I saw their fingers relax on their triggers and they lowered their guns slightly, I gave my order.

"Now!" I shouted, then watched three men drop instantly from the silenced bullets Natasha and Ms. Marie sent out. "Watch my back!"

I ran to join Demi and broke one of the guard's nose with the hard butt of my gun when he tried to grab me. Demi tied her shirt just as More McClouds came running out the door. Arielle threw smoke bombs, and Ivan came barreling toward them from the woods with the shout of a giant. He knocked one man out with one punch and mowed the others down with a stream of bullets from his automatic rifle.

"Oh, no you don't!" Richard shouted, firing at a man whose bullets had narrowly missed Ivan.

Another man took aim at Richard, but before he could get another shot off, his shoulder snapped back and he fell to the ground. My bullet was lodged deeply, and he clutched his shoulder in agony.

"Thanks, boss!" Richard said then got right back to the fight.

I heard a blood-curdling scream to the far right of me. It came from Arielle. One of the McClouds had given her a winding blow to the stomach and before I could get to her, he followed through with one to the face. She lay helpless on the ground with the huge man standing over her.

"Arielle!" I ran toward her, until a strong hand caught me by the neck and pulled me back.

The McCloud who held me in his grip was staring into my eyes, flexing his fist like he was preparing for a deadly blow to my temple. His red hair hung in his sweaty face, and to me, he looked like an older version of Clem. As I was thinking this, he was also noticing a family resemblance in my face. His eyes lit up with satisfaction.

"You're the Duncan boy," he said with a sinister grin. "Here to save Daddy, are we? My father is in there having a ton of fun with him. Maybe we'll keep him alive long enough to see your body."

His raised his weapon and pointed it at my head, but he didn't get the chance to apply pressure to the trigger. Ivan's fist seemed to come from thin air and cracked him so hard in the jaw that I heard it break.

I was happy to see most of the McCloud brothers down, but Arielle was still in trouble. I got up and ran toward her. The man standing over her had pulled his gun from its holster and was toying with her, running the gun up and down her inner thighs as she lay there, terrified.

The distance between us was too great. As he lifted the gun and aimed it at her, I knew I couldn't make it to her in time. He was going to kill her. But then, the back of his head exploded, and he dropped like a sack of potatoes. I looked behind me and saw Natasha stepping from the woods with a smoking gun. I gave her a thumbs up.

"Go, Nevada! Go!" Natasha pointed at the door.

The path had been cleared. I rushed inside the building, and my squad followed behind me. There were a few different ways we could go, so we split up. Ivan and Demi went one way; Arielle, Richard, and Natasha took another; and Ms. Marie came with me.

Ms. Marie and I heard the cries of my father in the distance, and we moved quietly in that direction. My heart pounded in my chest. Dad sounded like he was in pain, but I was grateful to hear his voice and know that my worst fears had not come true. He was alive, thank God.

The long hallway led to what looked like an old wine cellar. We stopped just outside the doorway, and there he was. My dad. His face was bloody and his breathing was labored, but he was alive and conscious. Around him were three more redheaded men. Two of them were Clem's brothers, no doubt about it, and the third was Patrick McCloud, Clem's daddy.

"Dad!"

The younger McCloud's turned at the sound of my voice.

Pfft! Pfft! Marie's gun busted quickly, catching the brothers square. One of them was moving on the ground, but the other was clearly dead.

"Bastards! Don't fucking move!" she shouted with her gun still raised.

Patrick ignored her warning. He hurried to lift my dad up and raised a knife to his throat. I watched the recognition find its way to my dad's eyes when he saw Marie and me standing there. He blinked a few times.

"I should have killed you in New York, you whoring wench," Patrick growled.

"We won't make that mistake," Ms. Marie replied, but as she pulled the trigger to finish him off, we heard nothing but the clicking of an empty gun.

Patrick laughed as he pressed the tip of his knife into my father's throat.

"Shoot him, son! Kill him!" Dad ordered.

"I can't!" I said. Patrick moved himself behind my father. "I'll hit you. I don't have a clear shot."

"Shoot him!"

"I can't take the chance, Dad."

"Put the gun down, boy." Patrick gave a crazed laughed. "You don't want to kill Daddy, do you? Well, I'll do it for you then! Just like I did those girls. Right, Marie? You liked that, didn't you?"

A sob escaped from Ms. Marie's lips.

"Drop your guns!" Patrick yelled. "Drop them or he's a dead man!"

Ms. Marie dropped hers instantly, but not me. I knew if I did, he would kill Dad anyway as soon as I put down my weapon. Dad was his shield, so he couldn't kill him unless I was disarmed. Otherwise, he'd be left wide open when the body dropped. He knew he would be a dead man too.

"Take the shot, son," my dad encouraged weakly. "Take it."

I heard footsteps coming from the hallway behind him.

"My sons are coming to kill you now," Patrick said, then looked at my dad. "But he's mine!"

"Dad!" I screamed as Patrick raised the knife high in the air, preparing to plunge it into my father's neck.

BOOM!

Patrick's eyes grew wide, and his arm froze, suspended in the air for a second. A gurgling sound escaped his mouth, and he swayed slightly. The hand holding the knife fell, and my dad was released. He moved out of the way right before Patrick McCloud hit the ground, face forward, with a bullet hole in his back. Breathing heavily behind him, holding a smoking gun, was Clem McCloud.

Marie

58

I tried to stop the love cries from escaping my lips, but Vegas kept forcing them out. He was hitting all the right spots, and he knew how badly I needed it. We were in pure harmony, all the way up until we shared a beautiful climax together. When he rolled off of me, we were both breathing heavily. I was more than satisfied, but if he could get it up again, I would gladly let him take me on another ride.

I reached over and caressed his face. The bruises were still visible, but he was healing well. It had been almost two weeks since the showdown with the McClouds. All but two of them had been killed, and the two survivors quickly gave up their dead brothers and father as the culprits. They confessed to the murder of my girls, as well as Headmaster Starks. The surviving McClouds also implicated Security Chief Picard and one of the school's board members as co-conspirators. It turned out they had been squad mates with Devin McCloud, Patrick's oldest son. Neither of them had participated in the murders, but they gave the McClouds information and access to campus that allowed them to get to Starks easily. When Vegas and Demetri brought the tape of Starks' murder to Minister Farrah, Picard went into action behind the scenes to stop the minister from calling a meeting of the board. With Minister Farrah and Brother Elijah behind bars, Picard and the McClouds thought they were in the clear. As soon as Minister Farrah and Brother Elijah were released from police custody, Picard and the board member were expelled from the order and stripped of their pins.

"I really needed that," I told Vegas when my breathing steadied. I propped up on my elbow to admire the man lying in the bed next to me. "You always know how to make me feel good."

"Yeah, well, I never thought I'd be making love to Kojak," he joked, rubbing my bald head. I swatted him playfully, and he kissed my forehead. "I like it, though. It makes me appreciate every part of your face. You are beautiful."

I felt warm comfort spread throughout my body as we lay together in a hotel room in Paris. I loved him more than I could ever put into words, though I didn't think I had to. From the way he was staring deeply at me, I could tell he knew.

"You are amazing, Vegas Duncan. I hope you know that."

"Amazing enough for you to come back to New York with me?" he asked.

There it was. The question I knew he was going to ask. I had hoped we would be able to bask in that moment for a little bit longer, but Vegas was Vegas, and I should have known better. I sat up and held the cover to my chest to give him the answer I didn't want to give.

"Not quite that amazing. I think I'm gonna stay here a while longer."

"I kind of figured you would say that."

"How so?" He always had been a know-it-all.

"Isn't it enough for me to tell you that I knew you'd say it?"

"No, it isn't. You wouldn't say something like that without a reason behind it."

"True." He put his hands behind his head. "We know now that the McClouds killed your girls. But that's not the reason you're staying. You're staying because of something else you've been hiding."

Dammit. He knew something. I'd gotten so good at hiding things from him that I didn't know which secret he was talking about. *Stupid, Marie. Just stupid!* The man had just made love to me minutes ago; now he was going to hate me.

"What?" I asked, praying he would drop it.

"You know I'm not stupid. This took me a while to figure out, but I did. The McCloud brothers targeted you because they were after something. They had no interest in you or your girls. They killed your girls because you wouldn't give them what they wanted."

Play dumb, Marie. Act like you don't know what the hell he's talking about! He couldn't know. There's no way he could.

"Vegas, I don't know what you're talking about."

"Sure you do," he said. "You almost told me in the hospital after I beat that McCloud brother's ass."

"Vegas, I don't know—"

"So, you don't know anything about the computer drive they were looking for?"

I stared at him blankly, hoping he would believe that I didn't understand what he was saying.

"I don't know how you got a hold of it, but they wanted it, they wanted it bad, and old man McCloud was willing to do whatever it took to get it. Too bad for him that Bobby Two Fingers had already broken into your safe at The Hellfire Club and stolen it before they showed up."

I felt a stab of pain at the mention of The Hellfire Club and the memory of that awful day when the McClouds tore apart my world.

"You and Bobby had that little rivalry thing going on. He was trying to shake you down, but instead of getting me involved, you tried to outfox him—which pissed him off. So he cleaned out your safe to teach you a lesson, and he found the drive."

"Vegas, I—how do you know all of this?"

"Bobby is no more than a two-bit thief, so his dumb ass didn't even know what he had." He leaned over the side of the bed and opened the drawer of the nightstand, pulling out a small drive.

"Where did you get that?" I asked.

"Like I said, Bobby didn't really know what he was holding. He probably thought it was just some embarrassing photos of me." He pointed at the misleading label on the drive that read: VEGAS XXX. I wondered if he recognized it as my handwriting. I had labeled it that way because most people were smart enough to fear Vegas Duncan and wouldn't have dared to touch that drive if they thought it pertained to him. Bobby Two Fingers was dead now because he was a dumb ass.

But I was also a dumb ass, because putting Vegas's name on that drive had sent the McClouds in his direction and put him and Nevada in danger. Chi's might have trained a lot of students over the years, but somewhere along the line, they had failed to weed out the ones who would grow up to bring chaos right back to the school grounds.

"Everyone in New York knows how Consuela feels about me and Nevada," Vegas continued. "So, he brought it to her, figuring she would pay him for it, which she did. Probably paid him a lot, too, although now she won't admit how much it was. She also won't say shit about why she wanted it. I'm sure she just figured she would save it until she needed leverage against me for whatever. Nevada is growing up, so she can't use him like she used to."

"That still doesn't tell me how you have it," I said.

"It was by accident. I had to consider Consuela a possible suspect for what happened to your girls. Her jealousy of you was out of control. I broke into her office to look for evidence, and I found this in her safe."

I opened my mouth to speak, but nothing came out. I didn't even know where to start. I still didn't know if Vegas had looked at the contents of the drive. If I had been smarter, I would have told him about all of this as soon as it came into my possession.

"But you know the funniest thing about all of this?" he said.

"What?"

"I don't take naked photos, and if there were any of me on this drive like it said, you took them while I was 'sleep. Consuela got taken by a low-life hustler. She probably spent a shitload of money on it, and then she threw it in her safe. You should have seen her face when I told her that it didn't even contain pictures of me."

"So, that means you know what's on it?" I finally asked. "You looked at it?"

"Not right away. Didn't seem important to deal with some naked photos with everything else going on. But when I opened it and realized it was encrypted, I figured it might not be what your label said it was."

So he did know that it was my handwriting.

"I had one of my guys look into it. I have to admit, seeing Patrick McCloud in full-out drag with a dick in his mouth was not pleasing to the eyes. I could see why a man like him would want that drive bad. Or do the things he did to get them back."

He laid the drive back on the nightstand, then turned back to me.

"What I don't understand is how you got the drive."

I released a deep sigh. It was time to tell Vegas the truth I should have shared with him a long time ago. Maybe my girls and our old squad mate would still be alive if I had.

"Jason Starks gave it to me."

Vegas was surprised. "Starks? Why would he have pictures like that?"

"He took them."

"Jason Starks and old man McCloud?" Vegas looked like he was going to fall out of the bed. "Get the fuck outta here. I've known Jason since I was seventeen. I'm one of the people who pushed for him to be headmaster. He's not gay."

"How would you know? Have you been peeking in his bedroom? And for the record, he was not gay. He was genderqueer."

"What the fuck is that?"

"I love you, but you're ignorant, which is why Jason opted not to tell you. You live and work in a macho-man society, Vegas. You may want to pretend that you're accepting, but you're not, at least not right away. Think about how long it took you to accept that your own brother was gay."

His expression told me I was correct, and he didn't try to deny what I'd said.

"How long have you known?" he asked.

"Since the beginning. He used to come to my dorm room and hide his dresses and shoes. We used to put on my makeup and have girl talk. I stopped him from committing suicide at least twice. It was the first secret I ever kept from you."

"It seems like you've kept a lot of secrets from me that are coming to light." This was the first hint that he could be mad at me. I tried to stay grounded in the passionate love that we'd just shared.

"You've had your share of secrets, including a relationship with a certain Mexican woman in the desert," I said.

"Touché," he said. "Why did he send the drive to you?"

"He was in an on-again, off-again relationship with McCloud for years, but because of all the LGBT students coming into the school, he thought it was time for him to come out. He told McCloud and a group of well-respected but closeted pinned members about it. They thought he was going to expose them as well, especially Patrick, who knew he had the pictures.

"When Patrick started threatening Jason, he sent them to me as insurance, but somehow Patrick found out. The rest you pretty much know. My girls are dead, and it's all because of that drive. I put you in danger by writing your name on that thing, and I took away Nevada's first love. I am so sorry, Vegas, and I understand if you hate me."

Vegas pulled me closer as tears fell from my eyes. I feared this would be the last time I felt his embrace, but then he kissed the top of my head and said, "No, babe. I could never hate you." He reached over and picked up the drive, snapping it in half.

Epilogue

I walked across the bridge to the moat, where I found the squad sitting around Ivan's fishing spot. It had become our outdoor hangout now that life had gone somewhat back to normal, and we could be students again with no need to run around campus with automatic weapons. We'd certainly earned the right to relax a little after everything we'd been through.

Natasha was over at the picnic table, setting up some type of lunch, while Richard was giving Arielle a pedicure. Closer to the water, Ivan was trying to teach Demi how to fish. I greeted them all with fist bumps and hugs. I'd just returned from Paris, where I'd seen my family off. They had arrived not long after the showdown with the McClouds, and my grandparents were not about to leave again until they hung around to make sure they could trust Chi's with my safety. Minister Farrah was finally able to convince them the fox had indeed been rooted out of the henhouse and their grandson would be safe at the school.

"Is he back?" I asked. Arielle and Richard gestured about a hundred yards away, where I saw Clem throwing my stars at a tree. Minister Farrah, Brother Elijah, and a couple of well-respected Irish pinned members had accompanied Clem home to retrieve his things. He'd just returned.

I walked over as he was pulling the stars out of the tree.

"You're getting pretty good at that," I said.

"Still not as good as you."

"I've been doing this longer." I pulled the last star out. "How'd everything go?'

"They hate me," he said, turning around and throwing a star dead center. "When we pulled up, they had a nice fire going, about six meters tall, with all of my things—bed, dresser, PlayStation, clothes, everything. So, pretty much a wasted trip."

"I can talk to my dad about getting you some clothes and a new PlayStation."

"It's okay. I've decided to dedicate my life to training. No more video games for me."

"So they're not talking to you?"

"Nope, none of them."

"Even your mom?"

"Especially mum. She hates me, but I knew she would when I pulled the trigger."

I certainly understood mother issues. It turned out my own mother had been paying Picard to keep an eye on me on campus and report everything back to her, and she was still trying to repair our relationship now that I knew about it. It would take me a while, but eventually I would forgive her. Clem had made a choice that he knew would sever his relationship with his mom forever. That was pure bravery.

Clem had made a huge sacrifice that day that he shot his own father, but I had wanted to give him some time to deal with it before I asked him why. It seemed like he was ready to talk now.

"Then why'd you do it? Why did you kill your father to save mine?"

"You know, I've been asking myself that over and over."

"And?"

"And I guess I did it because it was the right thing to do," he said simply, like there wasn't more to it. "Your dad's a special man, Nevada, just like you. My dad was a piece shit that beat me every day I can remember. He used to put me in dresses to humiliate me for the slightest thing—all in his grand plan of making me a man." Clem took a shaky breath. I doubt he had ever admitted that to anyone before.

"But I was able to see what it was to be a man from just watching you and your da. So, killing him was just doing the right thing."

"Then . . . I should say thank you and apologize to you for everything. I love you, man. And don't worry about those folks in Ireland. They may be your family by blood, but I will always be your family." I put a hand on his shoulder.

"Thanks, mate." Clem threw the last star and turned to me. "Does this make us best friends again?"

"This makes us brothers."

We heard footsteps coming toward us. It was the rest of the squad coming to join us. Ivan and Richard gave Clem a pound, and the girls gave him hugs.

"We couldn't take it any longer," Arielle said. "We've been watching you guys ever since Nevada walked over."

"Yeah, we wanted in on the sentimental moment," Demi said. "Are you okay?"

Clem shrugged. "I will be."

"Good. Because you're a freaking hero!" Richard shouted.

"I've heard it once or twice," Clem said with a small smile. He looked around and noticed their bags near the picnic table. "Are you all leaving?"

"Yeah, aren't yo—oh . . ." Richard caught himself, and his voice trailed off.

I cleared my throat. "Clem, why don't you come home with me for the holiday? We celebrate Thanksgiving back at home, and I know you would love my grandma's cooking."

"Are you sure?" he asked.

"Of course! You're part of the family now."

"Then yeah, I'd like that."

"Matter of fact," I said, looking at my squad, "why don't you all come?"

"All of us?" Natasha asked with some uncertainty in her voice. Now that we were no longer pretending to be a couple, she was trying to adjust to whatever our new normal would be.

"All of you. We have more than enough room."

"Well, I'm already used to being around you clowns, so why not?" Richard said.

"I'm down," Arielle said.

"I will have to check and make sure my father is well, and if so, I will come too," Ivan told me.

"My dad has this big thing that he wants me to come to, but I should be able to fly in after," Demi told me.

"Then it's settled. The best squad to ever set foot on Chi's campus is going to New York!"

31901066689193